THE DARK FOUNTAIN

Books by Jay Robert Nash

FICTION

ON ALL FRONTS
A CRIME STORY

NONFICTION

DILLINGER: DEAD OR ALIVE?
CITIZEN HOOVER: A Critical Study of the Life and Times of J. Edgar
Hoover and His F.B.I.
BLOODLETTERS AND BADMEN: A Narrative Encyclopedia of American
Criminals from the Pilgrims to the Present
HUSTLERS AND CON MEN: An Anecdotal History of the Confidence Man
and His Games
DARKEST HOURS: A Narrative Encyclopedia of Worldwide Disasters
from Ancient Times to the Present
AMONG THE MISSING: An Anecdotal History of Missing Persons from
1800 to the Present
MURDER, AMERICA: Homicide in the United States from the Revolution
to the Present
ALMANAC OF WORLD CRIME
LOOK FOR THE WOMEN: A Narrative Encyclopedia of Female Poisoners,
Kidnappers, Thieves, Extortionists, Terrorists, Swindlers and Spies
from Elizabethan Times to the Present
PEOPLE TO SEE: An Anecdotal History of Chicago's Makers and
Breakers
THE TRUE CRIME QUIZ BOOK

POETRY

LOST NATIVES & EXPATRIATES

THEATER

THE WAY BACK
OUTSIDE THE GATES
1947 (LAST RITES FOR THE BOYS)

THE DARK FOUNTAIN

Jay Robert Nash

A NOVEL OF HORROR

A & W PUBLISHERS, INC. • NEW YORK

Published by A & W Publishers, Inc.
95 Madison Avenue
New York, NY 10016

Manufactured in the United States of America
Designed by Regine de Toledo

1 2 3 4 5 6 7 8 9 10

Library of Congress Cataloging in Publication Data
Nash, Jay Robert.
    The dark fountain.

    1. Nelson, Earle Leonard—Fiction.   I. Title.
PS3564.A823D3   813'.54   81-70464
                                     AACR2
            ISBN 0-89479-102-8

This book is for my Chicago friends
Mary and Tom McComas, John
McHugh, Michaela Touhy, and for Jerry
Goldberg of Long Beach, California,
who has his own nightmares.

To evil habit's earliest wile
Lend neither ear, nor glance, nor smile—
Choke the dark fountain ere it flows,
Nor e'en admit the camel's nose.

Lydia Sigourney

Earle Leonard Nelson really lived.
He loved the Bible ... and women.

ONE

In the summer of 1919 Earle Nelson met Gloria Stearn. He was wearing a shabby doughboy's uniform and sitting at a little table across from her in a small San Francisco tea shop. She had taken the chair because there was no room in the crowded restaurant and she had only a half hour for lunch before returning to classes. She nibbled at a sandwich without looking at him but could sense his eyes upon her. He sipped black coffee, large hands curled around the cup, staring at her. She hid beneath a large, flouncing sun hat, which covered long blonde tresses, upswept and pinned tight to the skull.

"My name is Roger Wilson," Earle suddenly blurted. He studied the young woman, noting her turned-up

1

nose, clean oval face, thin, almost imperceptible smile lines closing in on a small mouth, the lower lip firm, not the bee-stung lips of those movie sirens, Theda Bara and Pola Negri, but the lips of a farm girl. Her eyebrows arched high over wide-set hazel eyes. Everything about her, he concluded, was delicate, soft. He glanced beneath the table to see small feet encased in highly polished slippers, and beyond that, trim ankles. Her form was slender, and the fact that she was a small woman pleased him, for he could not tolerate tall women, females he had to look up at.

Earle looked at his own image in the huge restaurant mirror. He did not perceive an exact vision of himself, but an image created in his own mind. He did not really see the short, heavy-shouldered man staring back at him, his own massive forehead, thin brown hair parted in the middle, his deep-set eyes looking as if they had been chiseled sharply from granite, the powerful, jutting, almost pugnacious jaw and full, near-puffy cheeks. He did not see a pouting thin mouth belonging more to a boy than a man, nor the bull's neck and thick stocky body, the too-broad chest that strained against his shirt; in fact his entire body seemed to barely fit inside his uniform, his thick, powerful legs appear to burst the cloth at the seams. And his feet were large, too large for his squat frame. This he knew, and usually slipped his feet beneath chairs when sitting. No, Earle Nelson did not see himself as he was, but as he thought himself to be, lean with shrewdness, tall with guile, and handsome, always handsome with an imagination that allowed him to take any form, be any kind of person. Instinctively he knew what kind of person he

2

should be for this attractive slender woman on the other side of the table.

"Oh." In her nervousness, she dropped her sandwich to the plate. "Wilson, like the President." She looked into his piercing blue eyes.

"He's an old man in the White House—I just got out of the Army," he said in a deep voice. "I was in Germany, Army of Occupation."

"Yes, a lot of our boys are still coming back from there." It wouldn't hurt to be polite. He was a soldier. He had fought for our country. "It's a pity, the war over for a year and you boys having to go on to Germany and stand guard all this time. A pity."

"The Hun can't be trusted."

She was hurrying now with her lunch, almost gulping her lemonade. "I suppose not. But it's good to know the world is at peace."

"There is no peace," he said slowly. "There will never be any peace. Not now, not ever. It's the killing. A lot of people got to like the killing."

The words frightened Gloria, but his uniform was reassuring. Those poor boys in those awful trenches, living like animals, hurting and being hurt. What could one expect but some bitterness?

"You work in San Francisco?" He sipped his coffee and looked about; it was apparent he had no interest in the munching, chewing humanity surrounding him.

"I'm a teacher. I teach music at a small conservatory. Professor Horan's Conservatory of Music on Market Street."

When he smiled his little smile she noticed only one

3

corner of his mouth turned upward. "I like music," he told her in a flat voice. "Bach, Schumann, it's like drinking wine, warm and rosy."

His words touched her, reached into her. How poignant that this veteran of war could still love music. Gloria smiled back at him. "The good things in life can never be destroyed." She glanced at the large clock on the restaurant wall beyond his shoulder. Finishing her lemonade, she stood up, snapping open her small chain purse. "I must be going," she told him in an anxious voice while she rummaged for her money.

"I have it," he said, snapping up the check from beneath her plate.

"Oh, no—"

Earle withdrew a wad of bills from his breast pocket. He held it up. "Let me. I've got plenty of money and nothing to do with it. . . . Mustering-out pay. It's okay."

There was only time for terse gratitude: "Thank you, and good luck to you." She pivoted on her heel and made her way through the crowded tables, going through the door of the restaurant and into the sun-filled street. Before Gloria reached the corner, a hand with a powerful grip clasped her elbow. Startled, she turned to see him.

"You didn't tell me your name. I told you mine." He was a little boy with a deep voice, seeming lost and pathetic in that uniform, a uniform no one cared to see anymore. "Gloria Stearn," she told him. "I'm late for my classes." She glanced at his hand, which he withdrew from her arm. He nodded and she went on, crossed the cobblestones to a waiting trolley, hopped on the lower step, and handed her fare to the conductor. She held onto the steel pole enjoying the soft summer breeze sailing into her and through her cotton dress as the trolley clacked forward. Turning her head slightly, she saw him again, at the end of the trolley, standing on the step, clinging to a handgrip, staring at her. She turned away.

Anxious, jumping off the trolley, Gloria almost ran the block to the Conservatory, turning every now and then. She did not see his face but thought for a moment that inside the moving sea of bodies about her, she saw a khaki uniform, blurred and moving quickly behind her. Poor man, she thought, as she turned at the Conservatory's entrance, poor, lonely soldier.

It was 5:30 PM when Gloria stepped back into Market Street, her classes finished. The fog, fresh from the Bay, rolled in thick, coating the city, cooling it. She could smell the ocean inside the fog. She should stop by the grocer's, she reminded herself, but she was tired. What there was in the icebox in her little apartment halfway up Telegraph Hill would do. She took one step and recoiled; he came at her out of a billowing patch of fog. He had waited.

"How long have you been there?" she asked, annoyed.

"Since lunchtime." He spread his large hands out and then thrust his arms into the swirling fog. "I watched this soup come up from the Bay. It came right up the street making the buildings disappear and the people vanish. That's something for me. I'm from the East. We don't have anything like this."

"I've got to get home." Her tone was taut; she wanted

5

it ended right then. Soldier or not, enough was enough.

He stood close to her. "Are you married? A husband? A boyfriend?"

"You don't ask strangers things like that!" she huffed.

"I've been away a long time," he said as a way of apology.

"I have no one," she was shocked to hear herself say. "No, not a husband, not a boyfriend. My parents died in the fire and quake of 1906. I was raised by the Sisters of Mercy here in the city. I teach music. I live alone. Now you have it all." She found herself unable to move, drawn closer to this forlorn-looking soldier. Instead of repelling her, his abrupt manner was somehow appealing.

"I'm hungry," he said. "I had only coffee for lunch. Let's go somewhere and have dinner."

She remembered the roll of bills he had shown her. "I think you ought to save your money," she told him. "I could make us something at home." She had never been that forward with any man, never, but it all seemed harmless.

"I'd like that," he said. He was at her side, clutching her arm, leading her down the street.

That night, and all the nights he was to spend with Gloria, Earle called himself Roger Wilson. He sat in Gloria's small apartment while she told him of her job, her parents gone in the great earthquake, an unreal shuddering of earth he never knew. He ate her pork chops and mashed potatoes and green beans without comment. He listened and stared through her while she talked and talked. He wanted to stay with her but he sensed her

6

propriety would be offended. It would take time, he concluded. He needed her because they were looking for him. They would not be looking for someone married, someone linked to another's solid, provable identity.

He walked about her small apartment, into the narrow kitchen with the high cupboards, around the living room, back and forth in front of the windows that gave him a niggardly view of the street angling down Telegraph Hill, a jumble of wood-framed three-story buildings, one drearily like the next. Earle brushed the leaves of the many plants resting on the windowsill and those hanging from hooks in the ceiling. Annoying things, he thought, greedy for carbon dioxide. He remembered with gratification how as a boy he had held his breath in front of his aunt's plants, delighted to deny them the contents of his lungs.

Gloria fiddled with the Gramophone, trying to crank it into motion. Earle quietly opened the door to her bedroom while she was placing a record on the turntable. What he expected—lace and chintz, everything so neat, so clean, the hand-crocheted quilt folded neatly at the end of the bed. The plumped-up pillows, the little make-up table and mirror, with brushes, combs in order, even the childhood keepsake, the fragile doll dressed in white lace, sitting in a green velvet chair next to her bed. He took it all in with one long, sweeping glance, and it disgusted him, such predictability. Yes, disgust, he felt it, gagged on it.

He looked at her bending over the machine, a slim body, almost thin, her long narrow fingers toying with the arm of the Gramophone.

7

"It'll only take a minute," she explained. "This tired old machine is temperamental." She laughed a short high laugh. "Like old Professor Horan."

Suddenly Earle found himself walking unsteadily toward her, eyeing the entrance door but moving toward her. He fought to veer away from her and approached the door, mumbling, "I have to leave."

"But I'm putting on the Bach, your favorite—"

His hand was on the doorknob when he shouted, "I have to leave...now!"

Gloria followed him into the hallway, a frown on her pretty face. "But, Roger, I thought we could talk."

"We'll talk some other time."

She reached out and snapped a brass button on his uniform, closing the breast pocket. "Are you staying at a hotel?"

"I'll see you again." There was no emotion in his voice, no expression on his face. He walked swiftly down the hall. She noticed how oddly he kept his arms stiff at his sides. "Good night, Roger," she called out after him. He did not answer, or turn, but went out as would any stranger calling at the wrong address.

A week went by before Gloria saw Earle again. She emerged Friday evening from the entrance of the Conservatory to find him leaning against the building, arms folded, that curious smile signaling to her. He wore a blue suit that appeared to be new. His shoes were new and highly glossed. He cradled flowers in his arms. He held them out to her wordlessly. At first she was angry, having thought about him in the quiet hours of each day, thinking

8

that she would never see him again. But in that moment she forgot her anger. He had returned with flowers, carnations pink and yellow.

"How's the music business?"

"You look like a different man without the uniform."

"I got tired of wearing that old thing." He wiggled the flowers in front of her.

"Thank you, Roger," she said, taking the carnations. "They're beautiful. It's thoughtful of you."

"I'd like to take you to dinner."

She sniffed the flowers without a reply.

"We could go to the St. Francis, a fancy dinner, wine and all."

She thought about it, silently looking at him. He seemed to be pleading.

"Champagne if you like. I'm celebrating."

"What are you celebrating, Roger?"

"The war being over. It's over for me."

"I'm glad of that. It's very nice, the flowers, I'm sure, but—"

"You didn't get married, did you, or find a boyfriend since I saw you last?"

She laughed at that. "In a week?"

"A beautiful girl like you could go any second. They always do. Married, gone. They get married and vanish, like the people in the fog, disappear into little houses." He reached out and firmly took her arm, drawing her closer to him. Suddenly she was walking with him, obedient to his pace, gratefully listening as his deep voice engulfed her. "You see them now and then, these pretties, but only a glimpse do you get. They are in carriages and cars, or

9

behind a screen door. They vanish into love, and the kitchens of the earth. I have walked past their houses at night, grand, towering places. They're upstairs in the bedrooms, disappearing, all the beauties disappearing inside marriage beds."

"That kind of talk doesn't excite me, Roger."

"Yes it does. Wine or Champagne with your dinner?"

"I get drunk on Champagne, silly and forgetful. I make mistakes."

"Champagne it will be. Then it's time to disappear. We will vanish together."

Earle loved to take Gloria shopping and, in the following days, they selected different parts of San Francisco to visit, seeking out all manner of shops, from curios to clothes. Earle would pick up Gloria outside the Conservatory, a bunch of fresh flowers gripped in his huge hand. She came to think about him patiently waiting for her each day, and always with flowers. She had never known such attention. Through the days she found herself hurrying at the end of classes, walking faster, even rushing down the creaking stairs of the old Conservatory building to get to the street to see him. He never missed a day, her Roger, he was always there, offering up the flowers as would a child, that distant grin clinging to his face, pushing his cheeks wide and full.

One day she raced to the street and did not see him. Panic jolted her, clutching her throat. "I'm here," came Earle's voice. He was leaning from the window of a cab, waving her to him. "I thought we'd ride in style." He opened the door and gently pulled her into the back seat, placing his customary bouquet of flowers on her lap.

"These autos are so expensive, Roger."

"Go on—drive around," he told the driver, then turned to her with his grin. "Gloria—the automobile is here to stay. I saw this fellow driving around and I said to myself, there's one of those new Jewett cabs. Well, the rich ride around in them, so why not us?" He patted his vest pocket. "If you've got the money, why not?"

"Have you made up your mind?" the driver said to Earle.

"Sure, take us over to those fancy stores on Grant Avenue." He thought for a moment, feeling the velvet interior of the cab. "You know, Gloria, I could afford to buy a car, maybe a Peerless or a Bay State or a Grant Six."

"Give me a reliable horse and carriage," Gloria said, sliding closer to him on the seat. "Speed frightens me."

Earle leaned close to her, putting his heavy arm about her small shoulders. "No, no, Gloria. Speed is the future. I was reading in the paper this morning that there's only three million autos on the roads and twenty million horses and they say that in twenty years that will be turned around."

"Twenty million automobiles?" She found the thought disturbing. "I wouldn't want to see the horses go."

He pulled her tighter to his side. "Aww, don't be sad about the horses. They'll be on the farms, at the race-tracks, they'll always find a way to use horses." Earle spotted a shop with windows full of dresses. "Stop here, driver, right here." He dug into the vest pocket of his suit,

11

drawing forth a dollar which he threw into the front seat. He had the door of the cab open before the car came to a stop, pulling Gloria onto the sidewalk.

She stood before the shop gazing at the expensive gowns in the windows. He stood behind her, his hands on her shoulders.

"What do you like?"

"The dresses are all so beautiful," Gloria said.

"No more beautiful than you are," Earle told her.

She looked at his reflection in the window and smiled. "Those dresses are almost midcalf."

"You should show your pretty legs," Earle whispered in her ear.

"You're making me blush."

"Come on." He took her by the hand and led her into the shop.

Gloria watched him, amused, as she stood at the hosiery counter. Earle hung back, looking everywhere except at the hosiery Gloria examined as the counter girl brought out box after box. "What colors do you like," Gloria teased him, holding up some of the hose, "Beige? Airedale? Peach? Rose?"

Earle glanced nervously at the stockings in Gloria's hands. "I don't know about such things."

"We have the Holeproof from Milwaukee and the Onyx brand from New York," the salesgirl said. "I prefer Onyx myself."

"Wrap up six pair of each for her," Earle ordered.

"Roger—I don't *need* that much hosiery."

He walked close to the counter, bunching up the

12

stockings. "Sure you do." Then to the counter girl: "Six pair of each, mix up the colors."

"You're an astounding man," Gloria told him. "I shouldn't let you buy things for me. It's shameful of me, really."

"Applesauce," said the counter girl under her breath.

"What?"

"Nothing, miss—only if the gentleman wants to buy you this lovely hosiery, well, kiddo, if it were me...."

"C'mon, Gloria." Earle turned her toward another department. "Let's get a bunch of dresses to go with those stockings, and hats to go with the dresses and—"

"Roger, now you *must* stop." There was little authority in Gloria's voice.

"Wrap up those stockings, miss," Earle told the salesgirl. "We'll be back for that stuff." He ushered Gloria toward the dress department. "And shoes to go with the stockings. I noticed that you wore the same dress twice in a row this week." He slipped his arm about her narrow waist. "Nobody as pretty as you should ever wear the same dress twice in a row."

Gloria shook her head slightly, amazed at his generosity, but enjoying the gifts he lavished upon her. She gave herself to the idea; it had been years since she had bought a dress she really didn't need, a pair of shoes before the old ones had worn out, a hat or a purse beyond everyday use. It was a grand feeling and Roger had given her that feeling, a sense of freedom she had longed for as deeply as the Suffragettes desired the vote.

They went to her apartment that night weighed down

JAY ROBERT NASH

with boxes of clothes. "Christmas in August," Gloria
bubbled as she unlocked her apartment door. Earle stood
at the threshold, putting packages inside the apartment
but not entering. "Please, come in, I can make some
coffee."

He drew her forward, kissed her softly, then held her.
Gloria's arms tightened about him as they embraced. She
buried her face in his wide shoulder and felt grateful
knowing him, this strange and impetuous man.

Then he backed away, telling her, "I have a room at
the St. Francis Hotel."

She held out her hands to him. "Stay for a few
minutes, Roger."

"I'll see you tomorrow." He was already going down
the hallway.

The following Saturday morning, Earle arrived at
Gloria's apartment with a large picnic basket filled with
food that had been prepared at his hotel. Gloria met him
at the door in her bathrobe, apologizing for her appearance. Earle laughed, closed the door behind him, and
placed the basket on a chair. "We're going on a picnic," he
announced. In a second he was next to her, his hands
caressing her body, from waist to hips. "I thought about
you last night in my hotel room," he told her in a choking
voice.

She returned his embrace. "What did you think?"

"What you look like under all those new clothes we
bought."

"Like a woman."

He seemed to be trembling as he held her. His hands

14

parted her robe for a moment, slipping inside, his fingers brushing her stomach, then withdrawing quickly. Gloria did not protest, in fact she felt alarm that he had pulled back.

It was all flooding over her head, all the years of loneliness forgotten in an instant, her life suddenly, happily, being filled by this unpredictable, generous man, whose impulses thrilled her, brought forth desires she could not condemn, creating in her for the first time wonderful new yearnings.

"I don't think I can go picnicking, Roger," she told him.

He stepped back, hurt.

"Professor Horan expects me to work on Saturday mornings, preparing classes for the next week. He insists."

"He can't do that. He can't take a beautiful day like today away from us."

Gloria bit her lip pensively. "I could call him."

"Do that."

They went to the wall phone in the hall. Earle stood close to the phone box, watching Gloria make the call, the receiver held flat against her head. She had to stand on her toes to talk to the operator when placing the call since the mouthpiece was placed high.

"Professor Horan? This is Gloria—Gloria Stearn, yes. I know this is irregular, Professor, but I hoped it would be all right if I didn't come in this morning. What? No, I'm not ill. I—I have something I must do. What?" Gloria went flat on her feet, covering the mouthpiece, and telling Earle, "He won't hear of it...says if I want to keep my job I must be there this morning."

Earle nodded, leaned over, and, to Gloria's amazement, removed her hand from the mouthpiece and with his other hand gently took the phone receiver. He talked deliberately into the mouthpiece: "Gloria doesn't want your old job anymore." Gloria shook her head in shock as Earle continued to speak, but she made no effort to stop him. "She wants to enjoy life and live in the sun." He hung up the receiver.

"Why did you do that?"

"I told him the truth, didn't I?"

Gloria stared at Earle, the man she had allowed to disrupt her orderly life, her predictable world. But she felt no anger, only a strange but pleasurable feeling of freedom. He leaned forward, kissing her, then took her by the arm, leading her back to her rooms. "Can we go on our picnic now?" he asked like a little boy late for a circus.

They spread a blanket on a hillside near the Presidio, so that they could look down on San Francisco Bay as they munched on sandwiches. Earle studied Gloria, who gazed at the watery vista, the brown hills of Sausalito rolling beyond the Bay and the Bay itself stretching inland to points of land barely outlined in the haze of the hot day.

"There's no city in the country like this," Gloria said.

"Have you seen other cities?"

"Only a few in California. And I have seen Portland, Oregon, where a distant relative used to live, but·I have read about all the American cities.... Here in San Francisco we have something different. It's a Mediterranean city—that's it—completely different from anything else in America."

16

Earle moved next to Gloria, holding her about the shoulders as they sat, knees drawn up, watching the ships entering the Bay, their foamy white wakes captivating them for the moment.

"They want to build a big bridge there some day," Earle told her.

"Where?"

"About from here to that point of land out there."

"Can they build a bridge that far? It doesn't seem possible."

"The world's changing fast," Earle told her with conviction. "Machines are doing the work." He scooped up some dirt and threw it down the hill. "Steel instead of land, big buildings, not farms."

"That almost sounds like poetry, Roger."

He didn't hear her, but was lost in his own impenetrable thoughts. "I don't think God wanted it that way," he said slowly.

He was suddenly aware of her attention to his words. Earle gave her his practiced smile. "They want to call the bridge 'The Golden Gate.' I read about the plans in the paper but it will take years, I guess, years and years to build it. Now we have to go across by boat...or swim. Can you swim, Gloria?"

"Like a fish. I like the sound of the name, 'The Golden Gate.' It has promise in it." She faced him squarely. "Now, you know I'm going to have to apologize to Professor Horan, don't you—to get my job back."

Earle ran his massive hand lightly down her cheek. "No you don't. That job is all gone. It's time to be happy, Gloria. No going back to that old broken-down Conservatory and that cranky old Professor telling you what to do." He eased close to her so that his face was only inches away. "Time to enjoy your life." He kissed her quickly.

"But I've got to live, to support myself."

"You will—with me—as my wife."

She expected it, this proposal, and had waited with ready excuses, reasons why marriage was not right for her now—that she wasn't prepared, but she knew him well enough, or thought she did, to know that a rejection would mean his utter disappearance. He was a deliberate man and there would only be one chance with Roger Wilson.

"We'll travel all over the country," Earle told her. "Maybe buy a farm or an orange grove down south, near Oxnard maybe—I used to live down that way. It'll be a good life, you'll see."

"Yes," Gloria said, envisioning the orange grove, "it could be a good life."

"Then we'll get married," Earle said. It was definite in his mind. The matter was settled. He had managed to be the person she wanted.

Here was the opportunity to escape her loneliness, Gloria thought, her humdrum life, the terrible routine of her tightly organized existence. Here was a future with someone who understood the future and here—she was at that moment convinced—was love. "Yes," she said in a weak voice, startled at the sound of the word but going forward helplessly, loving Roger's strength and loving his desire to have her. She also saw him as the image of a rescuing knight, riding from the pages of the Gothic novels of the past, books she had consumed as a child by the score, books read by a love-hungry orphan girl who had sustained herself for years with the thought that one day the gallant man in shining armor would appear. She nodded. "Yes, we will marry."

"Right away." He held her tightly, twisting, so that a small black book slipped from his pocket.

Over his shoulder Gloria saw that it was embossed with the words "Holy Bible." At the sight of the book she clutched him even tighter. "You *are* a good man, Roger."

A week later, on August 12, 1919, Gloria Stearn married the man she knew as Roger Wilson.

TWO

Earle moved into Gloria's apartment. On their wedding day he bought her more clothes. He bought a sofa and two stuffed chairs. Her diamond wedding ring was larger than what she expected. Earle had money, a lot of it, more than she thought so young a man would have. It was an inheritance, he told her. His saintly maiden aunt had died in Philadelphia, and left him several thousand dollars. "Such a good woman, one with God," he was fond of saying whenever he mentioned her.

Gloria was happy to be with him, a cultured human being, whose kindness and sudden bursts of romantic talk had survived the carnage of the Western Front. "Snatched from the eternal fires, I was," he told her. "I held death at

21

gunpoint, I jabbed him with my bayonet. The bugle sounded peace at the last moment. I walked through the mud of death but it did not enter me. I am whole."

That first night together Earle sat on the new sofa with Gloria, holding her, kissing her. There were unintelligible words inside his sighs. She put her arms about his neck, sliding forward. Quickly his muscles tensed, his body stiffened as he stood up, pulling away from her.

"What is it?"

"I need something," he said softly, almost to himself. He went to the hall closet and groped through the pockets of his three coats. He found a book and walked into the kitchen. He sat down, thumbing the pages, then stopped to read, moving his lips as he read the words underscored by his moving finger.

Gloria now stood looking down on him, perplexed. "What book is that?"

"The only book," he said in a cold voice. "The Bible, my very own Bible." His head did not move but his eyes rolled up to her, shadowed by his heavy brow.

She reached out to touch his hand. In a lightning movement, a flick of his hand, he slapped her hand away.

"It's all right, Roger," she said knowingly. "I'll wait in the bedroom."

He spoke to her without looking up from the page. "Yes, you undress in the bedroom. I'll undress out here."

Gloria went into the bedroom. He is shy, she told herself. Carefully, she removed her clothes, hanging them neatly in the closet, then slipping beneath the cool sheets, which outlined her naked body. She smiled in her anticipation as she look toward the crack of light streaming through the open bedroom door. She waited for minutes, longer it seemed, hearing nothing from the other rooms.

"Roger?"

He didn't answer.

"Roger, darling," she cooed, "I'm waiting.... Come and disappear with me."

Minutes evaporated. Gloria began to realize a creeping fear. She bolted upright, threw back the sheet, and slipped on her nightgown. Stepping into the living room, she found it vacant. The kitchen, too, was empty. Earle was gone. So was his Bible.

When she awoke the next morning, he was in the kitchen. He had made breakfast: eggs and toast and strong black coffee. Gloria said nothing about his disappearance. She was a patient woman; the nuns had taught her patience.

The next five days they spent shopping. Earle loved to buy things, especially clothes, ties he didn't need, hats Gloria would never wear. They dined in San Francisco's best restaurants. Roger tipped with the extravagance of a Riviera prince. It struck her as curious that he almost gave his money away, saying repeatedly, "Well, it's not mine anyway. I didn't work for it." He never spoke about his work, if he had any profession to claim. And Gloria found that disturbing. Patience, she told herself. He's finding his way back.

Each night she made herself as alluring as her propriety would allow, wearing a low-cut nightgown, scenting her body with cologne, but each time she fondled him, he drew away to thumb through that worn-out Bible. Each night he left her alone, only to reappear in the morning.

On the seventh day, hell opened its mouth and swallowed Gloria Stearn Wilson.

As before, Gloria had gone into the bedroom, waiting for him, tired and depressed at the thought of waiting, closing her eyes to beg sleep. But the routine had changed. She heard her Roger in the kitchen, reading his Bible, his voice growing louder and louder, his words incoherent, rising from a grumble to a roar. His outburst frightened her. Then she heard him running.

He burst into the bedroom, the door slamming against the wall with such force that the plaster chipped behind the knob and fell in shards to the floor.

"Roger, what is it?"

He stood for a moment, his face hidden by the shadows, the light at his back silhouetting his thick frame. Gloria instinctively drew back against the pillows, pulling her legs up so that her knees almost touched her breasts beneath the nightgown she wore. She focused upon his face. His eyes were wide, his mouth gaped, and spittle drooled from his lower lip. Inside of his fast breathing was an angry gibberish rooted deeply in some strange rage. He stalked forward.

"Are you ill?"

He grabbed the brass railing at the end of the bed, gripping it with such ferocity that his knuckles whitened. He worked his way across the railing, his legs moving as if encased in concrete. Then he was at her side, peering down on her with a twisted maniacal look.

24

"Oh, my God—"

With one hand he covered her mouth, his hand flat and curling about her face while the other reached to the top of her gown, pulling downward and out, ripping the flimsy fabric away to expose her small breasts.

Gloria twisted her head violently, wrenching free. "Roger," she screamed, "for God's sake, we're married—it doesn't have to be this way!"

He babbled, a froth of near-words bubbling on his lips, as he forced her head close to him with his massive hands on either side of her head, a powerful grip that told her that he could easily, should he desire, crush her skull.

"Please remove your clothes," she whimpered, miserable, "not this way—carnal, dirty—I can hear the obscene words under your breath, Roger—I can hear them!"

Earle was a man apart now, timelessly floating on a river of the past, with other women, reaching, clutching, slapping, pinching, drawing ancient flesh around his being. Without removing his clothes, he assaulted Gloria, penetrating her in every possible way in several hours. Her pain was excruciating, without joy, pain that lovelessly spilled her virginal blood.

Out of exhaustion, a fatigue of muscle and rage, he finally found release, but he did not relent.

"Dirty—" she moaned as he staggered from the room. She wept out the words: "....a carnal—animal— from the lowest—of gutters—a beast let loose—"

Earle said nothing as he locked the bedroom door. For two days, allowing Gloria only a few minutes to eat and visit the bathroom, he held her prisoner, sexually abusing her every half hour or so until her thin body, her small breasts, flat stomach, thighs and legs and arms were a mass of bruises and welts, for he whipped her, too, with his thick belt. She begged him, pleaded desperately for him to stop, but he dragged out her agony, always returning briefly to his perch in the kitchen, where he would grunt and groan over the same passages in the Bible, reading the same pages, turning back, reading them again and again.

During this time Earle discarded all pretense of civilized behavior. Half guarding her, he slept in his clothes, propped against the bedroom door. She begged him to wash, but he only smiled his half smile, once breaking the ominous silence with the shout: "You should learn to love the smell of your own reality!" He prepared food for them, providing a common bowl from which he ate with his hands. His fingers became permanently coated with the grease from the barely fried meat. He habitually combed his hair, wiry hair that stood up in directionless licks. As Gloria watched, he would stand in front of her little bedroom mirror, pounding the hair down hard to his skull with a stiff brush, coating it with pomade, humming all the while.

Gloria saw it all without hate; she could not hate him, deceived and beaten as she was. He could not be naturally cruel, she was convinced. The war had worked these horrors upon him, the brutality of those awful trenches had caused terrible ghosts to enter his body, controlling his mind. No, she loved Roger, her Roger, a lover of music, a giver of flowers. There was a way out of all of this. She drew on all her strength and spoke in a firm voice, words of authority: "I can put this aside, Roger," she said, watching him from the bed, forgetting the pain of her body. "Now you stop it, all the rage and the threats, and the hurting. I won't permit it anymore."

He put down the hairbrush carefully on her make-up table. "You won't permit?" He turned, staring blankly at her. "Permit?" He walked slowly to her. She did not cringe, but faced him with a determined look. Thrusting out his arms, he grabbed her wrists, held them so tight Gloria felt the flow of her blood stop. "*You*, a whore? A slut of the night, won't *permit*? This way?" He yanked her forward, naked, on her feet, dragging her into the kitchen, spinning her about, and throwing her into a chair. "You will listen to what God has to say about *you*, about what *He* will permit!" He sat down across from her, opening his Bible, reading with such speed that his words meshed into an incomprehensible jumble of sounds, hurled at her like stinging pebbles. Gloria stared just over his hunched shoulder at the little clock on the kitchen wall, timing the fit. It lasted for three hours. Then he collapsed, all energy drained, into silence.

Four months of such agony Gloria endured with Earle constantly at her side, leaving her only to slip out at night, when she fell trembling and thankful into sleep, but always returning before she could awaken and escape. Opportunities to escape presented themselves, but Gloria did not, or could not, make the attempt. She was waiting out his terrible anger, refusing to label it insanity, though that reality occurred to her in countless moments. He would calm, he would gentle, she was sure of it; the rage *had* to subside.

In early December, it ended. She was on the street

with Earle. He was going to take her to lunch, he said. He suddenly stood rock still, squinting at a streetcar, or one of its occupants. He shoved her forward, climbing after her. She stood near the conductor, who held out his hand to Earle for the fares.

Earle glared wide-eyed at the man.

"Two nickels," said the conductor.

"What did you say?"

"Look, fella. It's a nickel a fare, you and the lady."

"I'm not going to give you any nickels," Earle growled. He clenched his fists.

"C'mon fella, I ain't got all day. Two nickels, that's the fare if you want to ride."

"I know who you are. Get away from me!"

"Roger," Gloria said with a tired, thin voice. "Give the man the money."

"You shut up! I know all about you and this man."

The conductor looked closely at Earle, at the strange light in his eyes, and moved backward a few steps in the aisle of the already moving car. "I don't want no trouble—"

"You thought she was alone, didn't you?" Earle shouted at the top of his voice, a shriek, really, that electrified and silenced all in the car.

The conductor was moving backward, Earle stalking him down the aisle, frenetically jerking his neck around to glance back at Gloria, who was petrified.

"The two of you," Earle shouted at the conductor, "fornicating, you and my wife."

"You're crazy, mister—"

Lunging, Earle grabbed the conductor by the throat,

28

arching the man's body backward, causing the silver in his
coin changer to scatter, clinking onto the iron floor of
the car. Gloria rushed forward, attempting to pull him off,
yelling, "He's a stranger, Roger, this man is a stranger!"

Throttling the man, Earle sneered in her direction,
"Your lover is going to die!"

The shock registered. Gloria saw it all in one terrible
moment. It was she, not the conductor, nor any man in the
world who jeopardized her husband. Gloria quickly
turned, ran down the aisle, and jumped from the rear
entrance just as the motorman, seeing the struggle, braked
the streetcar and began to cautiously make his way back
toward Earle and his victim.

"You there, you!" cried the bewildered motorman.

Earle did not hear the motorman's yell; his eyes and
mind were riveted upon the fleeing Gloria. He dropped
the conductor to the floor, and, with a wild scream, gave
chase, leaping from the car and racing up the street. He
caught up with Gloria inside of two blocks. Before she
could utter a word he dove to the cement on his knees.
Oblivious to the stares of dozens of passersby, he began to
weep. "Forgive me, my beloved," he wailed. "Forgive
your troubled Roger. I beg you—" His quaking hands
fumbled at the hem of her dress, bringing it to his lips. He
kissed the fabric, peering up over it with watery blue eyes,
tears coursing down his full cheeks. "I beg you, I beg you,
I beg you!"

She pulled away, repelled more by this display than
all the beatings and sexual assaults she had endured. She
pulled back, her long fingers clutching her dress, dragging
it with her, disgust and resignation filling her.

"Ahhgggggg!" he groaned. She wrenched free and began to run again. Earle crumpled to the sidewalk in a quivering knot, pounding his fists and forehead against the cement with a force that caused his blood to flow, blotching the sidewalk, staining his clothes, as he screamed in a voice not his own, "You *will* do that, will you? Will you?"

In a nerve-tingling, semi-conscious state, Gloria reached the apartment, her lungs aching from her long run. She locked the front door and ran to the bedroom, where she began throwing the clothes from her closet onto the bed in a frenzy. She would take only what she needed. There was no time. He was coming, she knew it, he was up on his feet by now, his face full of blood, and coming as fast as those heavy legs would carry him, running, as she had run, panting, aching. Quickly, Gloria reached to the shelf high in the closet and pulled down her suitcase. Coming away with it, sliding over the suitcase and momentarily covering her face was Earle's folded uniform. She dropped the suitcase, tearing away the uniform with a shriek.

She knelt, opened the case, and stuffed her clothes inside. She stopped, peering at the uniform spread before her. A pocket in the lining gaped, a newspaper clipping jutted forth. She pulled it out, and read the headline with a jump in her heart: ARMY PAYROLL CLERK MURDERED. The dateline was Los Angeles, July 24, 1919. She read the brief account aloud, stumbling over the words:

Private Roger Wilson, an armed payroll clerk messenger, en route to Camp Matthews, was attacked near

30

the Poindexter Bridge, this city, last night, apparently strangled to death by his assailant. Taken from Trooper Wilson was a locked pouch containing $12,576, part of the camp's weekly payroll. Private Wilson's naked body was found stuffed into a culvert next to the bridge. His uniform, undergarments, shoes, and identification were missing, apparently taken by the murderer. Federal agents and Los Angeles police have formed an intensive search for the killer.

Don't collapse, Gloria told herself, don't, if you want to live. He wasn't Roger Wilson. Who was he? Roger Wilson was a dead man. Who then was her husband? Who? No time for that. He's coming. Hurry, girl, hurry.

Snapping the lid of the case, Gloria stood up, and started for the door. She thought for a moment, remembering the uniform. He'll know it all then. It won't be beatings and love and whippings and love after that. It will be death.

Gloria gathered up the uniform, returning the newsclip, bundled it together, and tossed it onto the high closet shelf. She grabbed her bag and took two steps toward the front door. The knob moved slowly, then rattled faster and faster. From the hallway she heard him scream, "You bitch! Unlock the door! I'll break it, you diseased whore! I'll break it in." The old wood of the door began to creak and groan as he repeatedly slammed his thick body against it.

Get out, get out any way, Gloria's brain pounded. The fire escape. She went to the bedroom window, threw it open, and clambered over the sill, pushing the suitcase onto the rickety iron fire escape in front of her. She began her descent, her shoes banging against the iron gratings as she fled downward one flight, then two. She was on the street, running, with the case banging against one leg, running and weeping to the corner. She looked back once to the open window of the bedroom and did not see him. She turned the corner, the muscles of her legs quivering with strain as she ran.

Then she heard him at the open window, his voice a terrifying, wordless slashing screech like that of an injured animal. Gloria fled down the hill, running so fast that she thought her heart would burst.

THREE

Nothing plagued Gloria's body. It was her nerves, tension, she told the doctors, when she entered St. Mary's Memorial Hospital. She could not sleep. A month following her escape from Roger Wilson she began a restless odyssey through the rolling hills of San Francisco that took her from one apartment, one small cranny, to another. She changed her address several times. She took different jobs. She worked as a seamstress for a week until she glimpsed a man entering the shop, a man who looked like Roger. Next she chaperoned three wealthy Nob Hill children, but was fired when she inexplicably refused to escort the youngsters to public events. There was even one stint as a cook's assistant in a waterfront restaurant. But

33

late one night, leaving the place by the rear door—
entering and leaving by the rear doors had become her
ritual—she sensed someone or something was lurking in
the shadows of the alley. She turned and saw nothing, but
heard a scraping sound, as if feet were shuffling in the
darkness. A man's silhouette, a sudden noise, then she was
off running. No building afforded her safety from fear.
Everywhere loomed the image of Roger Wilson, a nightmare figure whose shadow seemed to darken her every
path, one that engulfed her and robbed her of sleep, of
peace and hope.

She had thought long of going to the police, but what
could she tell them? That she had married a disturbed
man? And why had she stayed so long with such a
creature? Was she herself disturbed? She had continued to
live with him as he slid in and out of madness. Why did
you stay? They would ask her that. They would suspect
her sanity. The story of the Army messenger killed in Los
Angeles wouldn't help. That proved what? It was all a
mistake, she was certain. Mistakes happen every second
after a war in an army, the world of confusion, everyone
mixed up, changed, lost, the way it was in San Francisco
when she was a child, wandering through the ruins of the
city, her head bleeding, her clothes torn, walking on hot
cobblestones, bare feet on burning stones, her parents
somewhere back there in the fires, lost.

Roger had been a mistake, a poor troubled soul in so
much fear that he brought fear to others, to her, but she
knew he loved her. He had never said the words but she
knew it, or, the thought gnawed at her, she needed to
know it. She would move to another city, north perhaps to

34

Portland, even Seattle, move and change and live without fear and guilt. She was young, and there was in her a surviving ambition for happiness. First, she needed rest, the security of the hospital for a week. When she was fit she would take the train north.

It was close to midnight during Gloria's third night in the hospital when she heard the door to her room open. In her half-sleep she thought the night nurse was making her usual rounds. The door opened and closed quickly, a yellow shaft of light from the hall globe blinking for a few seconds. Gloria rolled over slowly in the bed, smelling the starched sheets covering her before drifting downward into blessed slumber. Far off, like that of a cat purring, she heard a low hum, rising in volume until it became the distinct deep voice she had not heard in weeks. "You can't hide from me," the voice softly called. "You can't ever get rid of me." She forced her eyes open to slits. The dull light curling around the window blinds outlined a form sitting close by in a chair. It wasn't possible; it was the sedative she had taken, the fear again struggling to become a reality. She looked about the room, trying to penetrate the darkness, averting her eyes from the chair. She kept her head perfectly still. She *could* hear breathing. One glimpse toward that chair sent her spine tingling. He was there, sitting in the dark.

"Oh, God, no," she moaned in a voice so weak it was hardly a whisper.

"A wife's got responsibilities," the deep voice said in a monotone.

"Is that you...Roger?"

He breathed heavily for some moments before responding, "You know who it really is." She could not see him clearly, but she was certain he was smiling with that triumphant, hateful smile she had seen before.

"Please, Roger... I'm sick... I'm tired and sick and—"

"It's your beloved Roger," he said quickly. Then in a wild staccato: "It's Roger, Roger, Roger, Roger, your lover Roger, the husband Roger." The voice did not belong to the body, she thought in her half-conscious state.

Gloria's nerves felt as though they were pushing through her flesh. "Please leave... me... Roger.... I promise... I'll see you... tomorrow.... Please—"

"I love you," he shot out dully. "You must return the love. That's the way it works. You give and you get—you get and you give—nice, ehh—give, get—get, give—it's all figured out—it's in the good book—even for sluts like you!" His words were running together again, his voice rising, and the emotion with it. "Christ forgave the Magdalene, didn't he—a diseased animal? Wellllll, I forgive you, Gloria."

"Roger—"

"I forgive you!" His words came like a hailstorm: "I forgive you! I love you! Now say you love me—hurry up, say it, 'I love you, Roger, I love you, Roger, I love you, Roger!' Hurry up, up, up, say it three times, like the Trinity, three times." He laughed, a series of convulsive catches in his throat. He slowed, seeming to be patient as she cowered in dark terror. "I *knooow*, my sweetness, I can hear you thinking it. I know what you're really thinking about."

He stood up carefully in the dark, working his way toward the bed. One large hand grasped the edge of the sheet. He drew it down and away from her body. His other hand went to her throat and hovered. She moaned weakly. She had no strength to yell out. His fingers twitched and toyed with the tiestrings of her nightgown, which he suddenly threw open.

"Nooo...I'm sick, please..."

"Time to love your darling Roger, Mrs. Wilson!" Without removing his clothes, he slipped his heavy form over her thin frame, with only his trousers lowered, painfully entering her, his words chanted in rhythm with his lunging movements: "Time—to be—Mrs. Wilson—the respectful—time—to be—Mrs. Wilson—the dutiful—time—to be—Mrs. Wilson—the obedient—time—"

Hate and disgust finally forced from her one great burst of strength, one defiant shriek: "For God's sake, help me!"

He went on as before, laughing, a choking laugh.

There was nothing left of her, Gloria thought. Everything was going out of her, energy, feeling, under the razor pain of his attack.

"Lord above!" she heard a man's voice shout. The door flew open and a man in white rushed forward. The sound of running feet and shouts filled the hospital corridor. The weight upon her was being lifted, dragged away.

"You bastard!" The doctor was half-pulling him out of the room as he struggled to hitch his trousers. Others arrived and pinioned his arms, dragging him backward into the hallway, his heels scuffing the floor. They were shouting at him. Gloria turned her head weakly to see his face in the hallway light. He smiled that terrible smile.

Earle twisted to face the doctor, an amazed gray-haired man: "You've been sleeping with my wife!" he spat at the doctor. "You and the slut making love in there!"

"What?"

"I just caught you at it. You're the hospital pimp, she's the hospital whore, a fine racket."

"He's a lunatic," one of the attendants holding him said.

"Take this beast out of here."

"I think we ought to call the coppers."

"You can't do a thing to me—that bitch in there is my wife. I can prove it."

"Throw him out!"

They were closing the door behind them, a nurse already covering Gloria's shivering form with blankets. In her shock and horror she could not take her eyes from him as he screamed and ranted at the doctors. He leered at her once and offered a dreadful promise: "I'll see you soon my dear, very soon." The closing door shut off the sight of his distorted face, red with rushing blood.

Two days later, hospital guards at her side, Gloria Stearn Wilson boarded the northbound train for Portland. As she stared with vacant eyes at the city from the moving train she was comforted with the thought that she no longer cared what happened to the man she knew as Roger Wilson. She saw him as in the rubble of that burned-out city of her youth, back there in the shambles of San Francisco, a dead city, searching for her in the ruins, stumbling cretinously over the ashes of her parents.

Five years would go by before she concerned herself again with the nightmare. She would read of his exploits and identify him. She would know his deeds, she would know his work.

FOUR

Earle could feel the return of the visions, the hot sensation of their arrival, beginning with a throb at the back of his head. There was no pain, there never was any kind of real pain, only the heat—swelling, spreading toward his eyes. He sat on the park bench in the square alone, without expression, his features ambiguous, like many of the lonely figures on park benches about him. As the cold morning wind nipped up from the Bay he turned the collar of his suitcoat so that it rode high on his neck. He glanced down at large, gnarled hands clasped before him.

He never moved when the visions began. He trembled slightly at the thought of disturbing them, and then he imagined the familiar panorama about to engulf him, like a hot red liquid oozing inside his head toward blue

39

eyes with unblinking granulated lids—pale eyes that revealed only the usual stare of the unemployed to the outward world of 1926.

In blissful seconds he no longer saw the seagulls and pigeons pecking at the crumbs dropped by the mottled hands of the old in the park. The visions veiled his sight with pleasant, memorable forms, beautiful women, flesh-swaying women rocking on bare feet in ancient rhythms. They danced for him alone, danced and crouched and crawled and danced again, the famed dead—Bathsheba of large brown breasts, Salome with tremulous long sleek legs, the open red mouth of Jezebel—glistening bodies rippling flesh inside the dance—twisting slowly at first, then turning tightly, spreading, yawning naked limbs before him.

There was torment for Earle, joy-pain, he termed it—the shimmering, quivering flesh blanket over his eyes, the vision burning down the length of his arms and through his massive hands. Again he heard that mysterious music, wild and foreign, bleating drums flatly thumped by the hands of spangled slaves, strange horns and stringed instruments, tooting, plucking sensual melodies. But always the drums, beating, beating as the women danced for him.

Earle smiled on the park bench, a creeping smile, a glimmer of the dark expression he felt when possessing the sight of his lovelies dancing, muscles pumping from ankle to shoulder inside the dance ground, no longer a square in San Francisco, its cold, raw day beaten back from him by his wonderful visions.

He perspired, oblivious to the chilling wind that

swirled about his lonely, bench-kept figure. It was joy, yes, as he peered into the wet, dark maws of the women forced before his sight by that hot thing working in frenzied tempo with the drums at the back of his head.

Abruptly, the beat of the drums grew weaker, the floodtide of visions in his head contracting, withdrawing. He was once again alone, hating the feeling, friendless, with the uninviting park spread before him. All of the air went rattling through his throat and it startled him. He groped with both hands toward the pockets of his frayed suitcoat. His fingers traced the sharp outline of the book at his side, his Bible. No, he did not want that. The other hand had already drawn forth the newspaper, carefully folded at the rooms-to-let want ads. Swiftly, Earle held up the paper, studying the ads with intense blue eyes. His index finger ran nervously down the little blocks of type and stopped.

"Rooms," he said to himself, dumbly reading, "clean, inexpensive." His deep voice drew out the words. "Twenty-six-ten Chestnut Hill. Ask for Mrs. Clara Spencer."

Earle's long, dirty fingernail began to trace the advertisement, making an indentation in the paper. He stood up on his short, stocky frame, his suit a mass of creases. He straightened his coat and, with the newspaper tucked beneath his arm, adjusted a faded, permanently knotted tie, a green tie with white polka dots turned gray with dirt.

He headed for Chestnut Hill with steady strides. As he moved, his voice grated lowly so that only he could hear, repeating with each determined step, "Ask for Mrs.

Clara Spencer...Ask for Mrs. Clara Spencer...Ask for
Mrs. Clara Spencer."

She sat in the parlor waiting. Clara Spencer was
nervous. This was the worst part, the new boarders. You
couldn't know. There was no way of knowing what they
would be like. Somebody respectable who paid the rent
on time and didn't make trouble, that's all she asked. She
had made her concession in life, her compromise with
survival since her husband had died in that locomotive
accident, a sacrifice to the railroad, an ache of the past that
would not leave the middle of Clara Spencer's throat. So
she had thrown open the family house, divided the rooms
on the second floor and in the attic, and took in boarders,
good boarders, widowers, bachelors, but churchgoers all
whose table manners were polite in her large dining room.

The men had been leaving in the last few months;
jobs were falling off in San Francisco, another depression.
Her boarders had taken trains east, to Salt Lake City, to
Denver, in search of work. Their empty rooms made
Clara Spencer lonely, bringing back to her those deep
images of her dead Joe.

Clara scanned the newspaper advertisement she had
placed and noticed the date, February 20. "I'll have no
trouble today," she sighed confidently to herself. She had
been married on the twentieth. It had always been a lucky
date for her.

When Clara stood up, dropping the newspaper on a
thickly waxed parlor table, her matronly black dress
rustled, a crisp sound, as her full, well-rounded body
moved against it. She was an attractive woman approach-

ing middle age, with large, dark eyes that fluttered in the company of men, a suggestion of shy, rose-blossoming womanhood from a gentler era.

She walked through her heavily furnished parlor—a maze of Turkish and Oriental furniture, tables, drapes, bric-a-brac in vogue before the First World War—pinching pillows and straightening doilies. Clara fondled the rope of pearls that hung about her neck, Joe's pearls, the finest jewelry she owned.

In the hall, she primped her hair before a mirror with a wrought-iron frame, thick black bands of hair now bobbed in fashion which gave her smooth face the look of a pixie. Once her hair had fallen waist-long but the styles had changed after the war. Everything had changed after the war.

She had bobbed her hair, another concession, she felt, but her dresses remained three-quarter length, and dark and matronly in the tassel-mad and faded style of Paul Poiret. She didn't hold with the slinky sacks and leg-revealing skirts inspired by that French lunatic and most immoral Gabrielle Chanel. After all, she wasn't a girl anymore, Clara reminded herself. Yes, women her age and older played the vamp, the flapper. Let them. She was an adult who accepted her years as should a sophisticated, mature woman, a woman of some means—she had a cook, one maid—and stature, being a property holder, a taxpayer. And the old era of gracious restraint, of mannered decorum was not that far gone or one bit forgotten by Clara Spencer.

Footfalls. There was someone coming up the front porchway. Clara hurried into the parlor.

He stood on the front porch. She watched him through the lace curtains of the side window, which angled in the direction of the porch, the street, and the hill slicing downward. The first thing she noticed was that his short-cropped hair was combed backward and coated with what looked like some kind of grease.

A young man, Clara realized, with boyish, hairless skin. She noted that his suit needed pressing, wrinkled there at the back and the knees, pockets of flabby fabric bulging at the knees. She could see that he carried the paper in his left hand. His right hand lightly caressed a book in his pocket. It protruded and Clara Spencer read the large, gold letters imprinted on its black cover, read in a reverential whisper, "Holy Bible."

She smiled then. A devout young man. She was pleased, and went with a confident stride to the hallway. She waited as the caller rang the doorbell twice and then opened the front door, showing her most gracious smile.

He was short, shorter than she was, standing a bit hunched and forward. "Are you Mrs. Clara Spencer?" His voice was deep; he spoke almost in a murmur and his words seemed to run together.

"Yes."

Earle looked her over while glancing several times at the folded newspaper in his hand, jutting out like a passport to be shown to an inspector. His pale, blue eyes darted over her body—the trim, long legs, what he could see of them, the widening hips, a startling tapered waist, the large breasts behind the black lace at the top of her dress heaving and supporting the pearl necklace encircling her throat, then curving downward and disappearing in

44

the crevice of her bosom. Earle saw it all in one brilliant glance. The hot thing in the back of his head jerked awake.

"Are you the lady who advertised a room for rent?" He held out the newspaper in a pathetic thrust, the crinkled reason for his presence.

He looked all right to her, a quiet, little fellow. Such tender blue eyes. Her Joe had blue eyes. "I have three rooms vacant at the moment," her voice fluttered. "There are two very nice rooms, large rooms, on the second floor."

He edged forward under the small porch roof and out of the wind.

"They rent for six dollars a week," Clara continued.

Earle worked his lips slowly together and Clara Spencer noticed his hesitation, thinking quickly—good, clean lodgers were hard to come by these days, disgusting days with snarling gangsters and red-painted hussies in the streets.

"I also have a small room on the top floor. It's a nice, little room that I could let you have for three dollars. Is three dollars too much?" As she looked for a response, she saw his eyes change somehow, infiltrated by an odd glow.

An anemic smile animated only one side of Earle's face. "Could I please see the room on the top floor?" He tugged forth the holy book, showing it to her, seeming to offer it. "I'm a divinity student. I do like a nice quiet place for my Bible studies. I dislike being interrupted when I'm at my meditations."

Clara beamed at that. "Yes, meditations. Oh, you'll be perfectly alone on the top floor. No one will bother you there. I'll see to that."

Earle stuck out his full, heavy chin even more. "One more thing, Mrs. Spencer."

"Yes?"

"Are there any churches nearby, Presbyterian churches that is?"

For an instant Clara nervously scraped her full lower lip with white, even teeth. "About four blocks away, but I'm sure—"

"It will be all right," he said and moved forward with his head bent down, his step surer now. She yielded to his quick movement and backed away. Once he was inside, she closed the door and started up the hallway stairs.

For a moment Earle's attention was captured by the dull glow made by Clara Spencer's pearl necklace when the yellow light of the hall chandelier sprinkled across it. She turned her back to him and his eyes fixed upon the soft, gentle folds of flesh around her long and graceful neck.

"It's really not such a bad climb," her voice trailed back to him. He barely heard her words as he watched greedily her full woman's body move in front of him, excited at the swing of her hips, the flare of legs encased in black stockings, her small, shiny, thick-heeled shoes lifting, her waist, her back, her dark, bobbed hair trailing a sweet scent down to him as he meekly followed.

The knot of delicious pain was enlarging at the back of his head, he was sure. Not now, he told himself, drive it back. He kept his white-knuckled hands clenched and his arms stiff at his sides as he moved stoically upward. Suddenly, he heard fast-moving feet coming down the stairs.

46

A tall, young man came loping past them, hardly looking. He wore a sweater with a college emblem on it and his long legs took the stairs down two at a time. "I've got to make a class, Aunt Clara," he said in a breaking voice.

"Don't be late for dinner, Harold," she called after him. He did not answer. The front door banged as he went out. She continued her climb. "My nephew, Harold," she told Earle, her head held high, looking upward. "He's a student, too...dentistry at Berkeley. His people, my brother, live in Portland...wonderful young man...so well-mannered."

They turned on the second floor. Although he moved steadily, Earle felt dizzy, as if at any moment he would stagger; he clutched the rail with his huge powerful hands and followed the landlady.

Entering the small atticlike room on the third floor, Earle stared without interest at the small bed with its brass posts, the overstuffed chair beneath the slanting roof, the heavy wooden bureau, a table nearby with porcelain wash pitcher and basin. He stood inside the room, Clara in the hallway.

"Is three dollars a week too much?" Clara said timidly to his back.

He did not turn but mechanically slipped his hand into his pocket, taking forth currency. He looked at it, separated six dollars, spun about, and handed it to Clara.

"Two weeks in advance?" she said through a smile.

"Thank you," he muttered and then began to close the door.

"I'll bring you some towels. The maid is out shopping

47

with our cook. It's the least I can do." She had to hurry her words; he was closing the door in her face.

"Appreciate it," he said so low she could hardly make out the words before he closed the door.

Clara stood before the closed door, startled. His mind is occupied with his studies, she concluded. Of course, it was the same with Harold. He doesn't mean to be rude. He is a nice young man, the kind of boarder any landlady would be happy to have.

She went to the stairs and began her walk for the towels that were piled high and folded neat and clean in the first-floor linen closet.

Earle's legs wobbled as he moved to the bed. He sat down on it, feeling the hard mattress and then quickly turned and stretched full-length, lying on the floral-printed bedspread, face up, staring at the slanted ceiling. She's not fooling me with all that talk, dainty talk, he told himself firmly. They all got that dainty talk in front of what they are. *Mrs.* Clara Spencer! I'm no fool. I know her, yes I do.

He was feeling better, stronger, almost good and warm with his thoughts in this new loneliness. His thoughts were powerful against the loneliness. He was no stranger to this place. He knew the real Clara Spencer, all the Clara Spencers, and he smiled one-sidedly with his knowledge. Gloria tried to hide beneath that talk, too, he remembered. "And I walked through Gloria," he said in a whisper, "just like a ghost through a wall." He pressed his eyes shut, remembering Gloria, his odd smile clinging as the pictures of her came rushing back to him, pictures he had designed, he had painted into reality. She was hiding

48

from him now, he knew, she had been hiding for more than five years, somewhere...but he could see her helpless before him.

A light knock on the door roused him from his dozing reveries.

"It's Mrs. Spencer. I have your towels. May I enter?"

He swung upward and around so that his feet dangled over the bed. "Yes."

When she entered Earle was looking up at her, his intense gaze capturing her large and outlined breasts heaving fast as she walked quickly to the room's only window. She set the towels down on the small bedside table. He stood up behind her, facing her back, suddenly dizzy, as if at any moment he felt he might fall. He clutched the bed rail.

"Sometimes it gets a bit stuffy in here, but you can always have fresh air." She parted the wispy curtains and leaned over, hitching buttocks high, higher in the air under Earle's blazing stare. She tugged at the sash. "All you have to do is open the window, Mr....Mr...." She pulled at the obstinate sash. "You know, I don't even know your—"

He was on her.

Earle squeezed his eyes shut very hard, so hard that the flesh around his lids bunched into ugly bumpy mounds. Both of his arms went tightly around Clara Spencer—the left thrown across her ample breasts, mashing them, the right up high, his hand in a fist clutching and twisting the pearl necklace like a noose into her throat, severing her short scream.

His head, he thought, was full of a sluggish jelly,

49

unleashed by the knot of pain. It ran thickly through his being, coursing to his legs, which quivered in his strange ecstacy.

Clara Spencer's rosy mouth was an open, wordless gash, struggling, straining for sound and breath, but neither came to her ever again. Her large expressive eyes bulged and the lids disappeared completely.

Her terror-stiffened body gradually relaxed, limb by limb, as Earle tightened the string of pearls until the little, golden links that locked the soft jewels together buckled in tiny barbs and made small, jagged holes in Mrs. Spencer's neck, a dozen trickles of bright red blood running and joining down to her bosom.

Earle's voice came then, a gutteral sound hissed through gritted teeth. "Harlot! Whore! Slut!" He felt her body sagging now against his and he allowed her to slip to the floor, dead.

Methodically, he positioned her flat on the small rug, spreading wide her legs. He knelt between them and reached with a steady, determined hand to the top of her dress. He clutched its lace.

He remained immobile, a dark form bending over her as the gray light of the fading day lazed through the window, blemishing the wall with his shadow. His great thoughts now came to him, forming words that tumbled from his sensitive mouth, rapidly, a staccato drone of words, running like spittle from his gaping mouth.

"Is not this Bathsheba, the daughter of Eliam, the wife of Uriah the Hittite? And David...took her...and lay with her...and the woman conceived..." Then, in a low growl as he tore away the top of Clara Spencer's dress, exposing her large breasts, "Samuel, Eleven..."

Dead eyes, dark, large, the pupils dilated, stared up at him. He did not look at them. He was busy tearing away Mrs. Spencer's underclothes and spreading her legs further outward with his knees. Quickly, with one hand, he felt the inside of her thighs in a semi-circle, swinging back until he clutched her with stubby fingers.

She was still warm. Earle's great thoughts flooded from his mouth. "If a man be found lying with a woman married," he shrieked the words, "to an husband, then they shall both of them die, *both* the man that lay with the woman, and the woman!"

Pulling himself low over her limp unresponsive body, Earle separated her and entered her with a lunge toward her breasts, which he cupped with both hands and pressed against his burning temples.

With each thrust of his body, he attributed, with gasps, his last quote—"Deu...ter...on...o...my... Twen...ty...two...Twen...ty...two!"

All of the thick, demanding substance that had flowed from the back of his head now emptied itself into her and Earle felt an ebbing and utterly saddening release of the pressure.

Abruptly, he was on his feet, still not looking at the open eyes of the dead woman. He wiped himself on the floral bedspread wrinkled on the iron bed. As he buttoned his trousers and smoothed down his clothes, he looked down at Clara Spencer. "You look ridiculous," he said, matter-of-factly.

Earle walked to the window, opened it easily, and sucked in the cool air. He filled his lungs deeply and it gave him pleasure. He noticed wisps of fog curling close to the old cobblestones in the street and watched for a moment as it inched upward around a new 1926 black Packard parked at the curb. He saw the car as a sleek, dead animal.

Now his voice was calm and serious and not a strain of passion in it, an observer's voice, distant from its owner. "Babylon is fallen, is fallen, that great city, because she made all nations drink of the wine of the wrath of her fornication. Revelation, Fourteen, Eight."

With a thud, the sash came down under the weight of his arms. Tucking away the folded newspaper, he hauntingly touched the outline of his Bible still in his suitcoat pocket. Earle stooped quickly in second thought, snatching the necklace away from the throat of the dead woman, then stepped gingerly over Clara Spencer's body and went softly down the stairs.

FIVE

"I dunno, I dunno, God, how would I know?" Harold Spencer ran his hands through his hair, fidgeting, his speech about to break into a stutter as they milled around him in Clara Spencer's tidy parlor. "It was only a second," Spencer said. "I only saw him for a second."

Lieutenant Art Lowell had seen it all before, twenty-five years of it. He stood looking down at the Spencer boy, deadpan. "Gimme the description again, Harold," the heavy-set detective ordered. "Everything you can remember. Everything and anything you can remember about this man."

"I dunno, it was only a sec——" Spencer's eyebrows arched in shock as he caught sight of two attendants in white moving with agile steps from the stairs through the outer hall, carrying the body of his aunt, the sheet over her face drifting at the sides of the stretcher, white blurry figures gliding by. Harold Spencer started to rise but Lowell's firm hand pressed him back into the overstuffed chair.

"Oh, Jesus, Aunt Clara," implored Spencer toward the hallway.

"It don't matter now, Harold. She's gone." Then Lowell said hesitantly and unconvincingly, "Your aunt is with God now, boy."

Harold's lower lip blubbered in grief. "That man—why kill Aunt Clara? And what did he do to her..." His young face jerked upward. "Did you see that? God Almighty, did you see what he did to her? What kind—"

Lowell didn't have any time for grief and cut him off with a "yes, yes, but she's with God now and none of that matters anymore, the way she looked." Lowell's drooping eyes glanced to a corner where a tall man in a dark suit sat on an armrest listening. Policemen shuffled in and out of the parlor, searching, sniffing, clue-lusting behind furniture, drapes, cushions.

The lieutenant of detectives had no belief for his own words, which he delivered in a monotone. "Harold, you've got to give me that description again. Harold?"

The boy cradled his head with slender, bony arms. "Harold?"

Spencer was crying.

"Listen, boy—"

"Art?," the tall man said from the corner in a way pleading him to leave off the questioning.

54

Feebly, Lowell waved him off. "Harold. We've got to know what this man looked like. It's the only way we're ever going to get him. You saw him, you were the only one."

"It was only for a second," Spencer sobbed through his folded arms and then looked up, his eyes drifting toward the hallway. "I was going out...out..."

The large pocket watch nestling in Lowell's mammoth hand told him they had been at it for over an hour.

"Yeah," the detective grunted, changing his approach, "you were going out. Then what?"

Spencer suddenly sat upright, pushing himself back into the chair. He was ready. "I was on my way out and I passed Aunt Clara going up the stairs. He was right behind her, walking upward, a little guy. I'm not sure, but maybe five foot four or five inches tall."

"How old was he would you say, Harold?" Lowell was writing in his notebook.

"I dunno." He shook his head as if trying to clear it and trying to recapture that momentary image of the man on the stairs. "Maybe thirty, or more. He had light hair. Some of it was comin out—"

"Receding hairline," Lowell grumbled and wrote in his book.

"Yes, receding. It was combed funny. Sort of pressed down flat against his head."

"Was it thin hair?"

"Sort of thin. It had bunches."

"Bunches."

"You could call him dark-complexioned, that's it."

"Okay."

Harold wrinkled his brow. "He didn't look at me. He kept staring ahead."

"At your Aunt Clara?"

"Yes. She was standing a couple of steps higher than he was. I guess he was staring at..." Harold's lips turned down in disgust.

"Staring at what, Harold?"

"At her behind," he shot out quickly. "I didn't pay too much attention to it. Aunt Clara was nice to look at, you know. Attractive."

"Ummm-hmm," Lowell hummed knowingly and stepped backward slightly, not taking his eyes off Spencer. He looked down into his book and then spoke deliberately: "Did you ever stare at your Aunt Clara's behind, Harold?"

Spencer bolted forward and upright. "Wait a minute, Lieutenant. What do you think I am? You know where I was. I told you, and you can call the girl, too. She'll tell you. You can't say things like that."

Lowell shrugged. "I guess you're right, but we gotta check everyone, Harold. I'm sure you know that and understand how we gotta be careful and sometimes we say things like that. It don't mean nothin'."

"I didn't kill Aunt Clara. I loved her. She was kind and sweet, a sweet woman."

"Okay, I'm sorry I said that, Harold. It's my profession talking, not me." His voice was flat.

"I didn't like that."

"The profession, only the profession."

Spencer relaxed and walked to the window. He peered out into the darkness and the fog. "He had blue eyes."

"Huh?"

"They were very large, blue eyes. Kinda strange."

"Large, blue eyes," Lowell mumbled and went back to writing in his book. "How about a bag. Did he carry a bag, Harold?"

"No, only the newspaper."

"Newspaper? You didn't mention any newspaper before."

"I didn't remember it. It was folded the long way, you know the way some people read the paper by folding it the long way." Spencer paused for a moment. "It must have been the ad. Aunt Clara placed the ad in the newspaper."

One of the detectives held up a newspaper folded the long way. "There's a copy over here on the table."

"That's my Aunt Clara's copy. She got one to check the ad. We don't take the *Sentinel* every day. She got it special to check the ad."

"How about the shoes?" Lowell went on.

"I didn't see them."

"Suit?"

Kind of baggy, not a bad suit, light, but kind of baggy."

"Tie?"

"Yes, but I don't remember the color."

"Anything else?"

"On his hair. He might have used some pomade on it. I told you it was smacked down against his head, parted toward the side, thin. A lot of guys use that pomade stuff, I guess."

"That it, Harold?"

"No, that's not all. I'm trying to remember what it was

57

he had in his pocket. It stuck out a way. I saw it when I rounded the landing on the second floor, through the spokes of the bannister. I could only see part of his suit where the pocket was from there, as they were coming up...a book." Spencer faced Lowell and blinked. "I think it was a Bible."

"A Bible!"

"I think so."

"How do you know that?"

" 'Cause the book was sticking out on top and it was black with a rough cover just like those pocket Bibles you can buy at the five-and-tens, and there was gold, old-fashioned lettering on it—the pocket cut through the middle of the words—but the gold lettering was like the ones in the stores, sort of pressed in on the cover, you know what I mean?"

"Embossed," the tall man in the dark suit said clearly from across the room.

"Sergeant Davis, I'll handle it," Lowell carped.

Detective Sergeant John Davis crossed his long legs.

Unlike any of the unkempt, beefy detectives in the room, Davis' appearance was singularly neat and fresh, his three-piece suit more like that of a young businessman of the day. Everything about him was lean, including a thin but handsome face with a straight nose, a prominent V-shaped jaw, freshly shaved but dark. His thick black hair was meticulously combed with a sharp part to one side. Dark eyebrows shaded his coal-black eyes; he had a straight mouth with thin lips that gave him the image of a man verging on a grin. He had an altogether pleasant face but a serious one, a middle-European face, while the faces of his peers were decidedly the florid faces of the Irish or the Italian that portrayed the easy-living, self-indulgent cops of the era. Davis had little use for Lieutenant Lowell, a cop without a conscience to him, a man whose paper reports and politics had brought him his rank, along with the colorful flatfoot quotes Lowell theatrically offered the press. Davis was a different breed of cop, one who held science high, and the understanding of human character as the greatest weapon against the criminal mind. A quiet reader, intellectual by most standards, Davis was shunned by his fellows, which was the way he liked it. He preferred to work alone, depending upon himself and his own wits. "Embossed," Davis repeated defiantly.

"Yeah, embossed," Spencer nodded emphatically, he was positive. "It was embossed right on the front of the cover with gold letters. It stood out."

"Embossed letters," Lowell wrote down with an angry glance toward Davis. He put up his book. "All right, Harold, you better get some rest now."

"Not here. I can't stay here anymore."

"Why not."

"I couldn't stay here anymore, sleeping in the same house with that room up there where he did all those things to Aunt Clara. That room." He shook his head in final decision. "I just couldn't stay anywhere near that room."

"Where will you go?"

"I'll stay with a friend."

"Gimme the address." Lowell held out the black notebook open to a blank page and offered his pencil. Harold Spencer wrote out the address. Then he ran his

59

hand through his hair and turned toward the hallway.

"Do you want a patrolman to walk with you, Harold?"

"No, I don't need that," Spencer replied, and walked out.

The coroner's assistant, Jake Taylor, ambled into the parlor through the dining room, after noisily sliding oak doors into the wall. He veered toward Lowell. Wearing his bowler hat low on the forehead, he carried his bag in one hand and a tall glass of milk in the other. He placed the bag on a chair and then drank from the glass.

"Where'd you get that, Jake?"

Taylor smacked his lips. "Kitchen."

"You're not supposed to be doing things like that." Lowell shook his head. "You're always doing things like that, helping yourself."

Gulping, Taylor finished the milk. "Death by strangulation." His voice was high and unemotional. "The pearl necklace the boy said she was wearing. That did it. Pearls are gone. He must have taken them."

Lowell looked at one of his detectives. "Gone," the man echoed. "No necklace, anything, Lieutenant. We've sifted every piece of lint in this house. No pearls."

"He take anything else?"

"Not that we know of, nothing. Just the pearls."

'What about the other thing, Jake?"

"You saw the way she was, Lieutenant. He killed her and raped her."

Lowell took the empty glass gently out of Taylor's hand. "You mean he raped her and then killed her, Jake."

"No."

"What?" Davis stood up.

"I mean," Taylor said, drawing out his words carefully, professionally, talking directly into Lowell's blank face, "the man first strangled her to death and then he raped her."

Davis approached the center of the room for the first time. "You sure of that?"

Taylor glanced at him and then back to Lowell. "Absolutely, all the signs. He's a necrophiliac, they call 'em."

"Who calls them that—necro—whatever?" Lowell asked with a glare.

"Psychiatrists—alienists to you, Lieutenant, it's their term."

Lowell jammed a cigar in his mouth and fished out a kitchen match from his vest, which bulged away from his paunch. He lit the match under his thumbnail. "A sex nut," he said with a grunt. "A goddamn sex nut. Those guys are hard to get a hold of. No motivation, not related, they don't fence things, no records most of the time. Hard." He puffed rapidly on the cigar, getting up the flame at the end so that it flared red. "A rapist," he snorted.

Taylor cocked his head wisely. "This man is no rapist."

"Whaddya mean?"

"He's disturbed."

"Jesus Christ, is he ever disturbed! I know he's disturbed, Mr. Taylor. Sane people don't do things like that, even sane thieves."

"He's still no rapist, Lieutenant. Look at the room,

look for yourself." Taylor bobbed his head and pushed out his jaw. "He took too much time up there. He wiped himself on the bedspread. And the way her clothes were. He arranged her just that way to look like that."

"For us?"

"For himself.... And the clothes wouldn't be arranged like that if there had been a natural struggle. No, he killed her so that he *could* rape her. She had to be dead first before he could have sexual intercourse with her."

The detectives stood motionless as Taylor spoke in his high, measured tone. Lowell sat down and slid his notebook into an inside coat pocket. "You mean he just didn't want to lay her?"

Taylor's wince was noticeable. "No, Lieutenant. I don't think so. This man isn't normal. He's mentally deranged, sick, what certain doctors call a psy—"

"A sex maniac," Lowell said.

"Maniac. Yes, he is that all right. A necrophiliac, like I said."

"What's that again?" Lowell's dull, watery eyes focused on Taylor's bowler.

As if addressing a small child or a deaf, uncomprehending elder, Taylor pronounced every syllable of his words sharply: "A person who makes love to the dead, Lieutenant."

Lowell's eyes opened. He set his jaw grimly. "He gonna do that again, Mr. Taylor?"

"It's his need, I think."

San Francisco newspapers bannered the Spencer slaying, liberally sprinkling the boasts and cracks of

Lieutenant Art Lowell through their speculative stories. Ten days later, on March 2, 1926, Mrs. Laura Harding opened the front door of her rooming house on Russian Hill to a short, stocky man with blue eyes.

"You the lady who advertised a room for rent?" he asked in a low voice.

"Right this way," said Mrs. Harding, affably ushering him inside.

<u>SIX</u>

Detective John Davis stood uneasily before the desk of Captain Guido Vertali, as his superior shuffled several file folders. Vertali was a line policeman who had been with the force for twenty-eight years and would die inside his uniform. He was old-fashioned, suspicious of change, but a fair-minded man who liked the quiet Davis even though he was wary of the younger man's notions of police procedures. Davis had new twists to the work, "inventions," Vertali called them, that said, in effect, that he, Vertali, and men like him, were old-fashioned, perhaps obsolete.

"Sit down, Davis," Vertali told his detective. "Over there." He motioned to a hard-backed chair that was a respectful distance from the desk.

Davis walked to the chair and sat down, stretching out his long legs, studying Vertali.

"You're a good cop, Davis."

"Thanks."

"But you don't always go along with the boys, do you?"

"I don't rubber-hose suspects, if that's what you mean, Captain."

Vertali's broad, florid face pinched in a brief frown, his lips coming together before he formed his words: "I got a complaint here against you." He held up one of the folders in front of him, ceremoniously pulling forth a sheet, a police report marked CONFIDENTIAL.

"What's the trouble?" Davis remained calm. He knew what the trouble was, Lieutenant Art Lowell.

"One of your superiors," Vertali intoned without the slightest trace of emotion, "says you're—well—uncooperative—that you made him look bad with the press the other day."

Davis nodded knowingly. "Lowell. Right?"

"*Lieutenant* Lowell says here—" He held up the report and read slowly, trying to get the handwritten words on the sheet correct. "That you interrupted him several times when he was talkin' to the boys with the *Examiner* and some other papers, that you *corrected* him on some police matters. Did you do that? Did you *correct* your superior?"

"Yes, on the strangler case."

Vertali dropped the report from his hand, letting it fall gently to his desk. He clasped his hands while staring straight ahead at his office wall, a movement to gather in patience that Davis had seen before. Abruptly, Vertali swung only his head in Davis' direction. "Now, you know you can't do things like that, Davis. *Correctin'* superiors." The captain then eased his heavy frame around to follow the line of his head, his swivel chair squealing at the wheels. He opened his hands, spreading his palms in a plea. "My boy, don't we in the department have a hard enough time without making ourselves look bad to those guys on the papers?"

Davis pulled himself up in the chair. He leaned forward, bony arms resting on his knees, hunching toward Vertali. "Lowell talks too much to the press about whatever we find, especially in the strangler jobs. That maniac reads the papers, too, Captain. I was trying to stop Lowell from giving the news guys what we know about this character, which isn't much. If the strangler knows what we know, he might change his *modus operandi—*"

"What?"

"He'll change the style of his killing."

"I *know* what *modus operandi* means, Sergeant."

Davis decided to pour it out, give Vertali what he thought about the strangler. Vertali was a fair man; he would listen and think. "This man is sane most of the time, I think, but he goes crazy at times and when he does he's in a dream, a nightmare maybe. Then he kills. And when the dream is over and somebody new has been strangled by his own hands, well, he's had his dream—it was only a dream, you see, and he hasn't killed anyone. We can get close to this character if we don't remind him of what he's done in the press. If we don't give out any news stories about him he won't be frightened off by his own nightmare."

"You sound like you're protecting this lunatic."

"I don't want him to skip town. I want him to stay in San Francisco."

"Where do you get ideas like that, Davis, that nightmare stuff?" Vertali blinked his eyes in disbelief.

"In books, criminologists like Lombroso and Orfila."

Vertali waved a hand in disgust. "Aw, those guys were professors tellin' college kids bogeyman stories."

"I also talked to my friend, Professor Heinrich over in Berkeley."

"Heinrich? That test-tube guy?"

"He's a great criminologist, a scientist."

"He's a crackpot!"

"Whatever you and the department may think of Edward Oscar Heinrich," Davis told Captain Vertali patiently, "he's proved his ability to determine the identity of wanted criminals. With a sliver of wood under his microscope, he got the d'Autremont boys for that train holdup back in twenty-three."

"Yeah—I heard about that," Vertali conceded. Then he jabbed an accusatory finger in Davis' direction. "But he also found a postal receipt in them overalls the Oregon cops gave him to examine, and that's what really led to the arrest of them d'Autremonts." Vertali smiled a broad, flashy smile. "Now who's kiddin' who, huh, Sergeant?"

Davis was adamant. "When it comes to forensic science, you can't beat Heinrich."

Vertali waved him off, yanking another file from beneath the small mound of folders on his desk. "None of that matters anyway, Sergeant. Not right now." He held up another report between a thick thumb and forefinger, waving it like fresh laundry. "Came in this morning from Santa Barbara over the wire."

Davis jumped forward, leaning on Vertali's desk. "Goddamn—he's out of the city! Is that right?"

With a short movement, Vertali dropped the report in front of Davis. "A Mrs. George Russell down in Santa Barbara. She was strangled only a few hours ago—then raped, the coroner down there says."

"Santa Barbara," Davis hissed angrily at himself. "If Lowell had kept his mouth shut—"

"That *don't* matter any more!" Vertali snatched back the report, placed it in front of his large body, and stared down at it, continuing to stare as he talked. "We got three strangulations in San Francisco since the Spencer woman in February. Mrs. Laura Harding in March. Mrs. Lillian St. Mary sixteen days ago." He looked up at Davis, who was still peering down at him, his face taut. "Now this Russell woman in Santa Barbara ... Well, don't hang over me that way, Davis, goddamnit! Sit down over there!" Vertali pointed to the chair.

Davis didn't move. "Well?"

Vertali reluctantly handed Davis the report. Davis stood up, reading it word for word.

"They got a small force down there, Davis," Vertali said in a lifeless voice. "They could use some help. Right now, we got three dead ones, looks like by the same crazy, and now they got one, and the feeling here is that since it started in San Francisco, we got a responsibility to follow this last one up."

Turning his head from the report, Davis looked down at Captain Vertali with a hint of a smile at his lips. "And I get the job, is that right?"

In one swift move, Vertali had swiveled about and was on his feet, his large frame equal in height to Davis'.

"I'm sendin' you down there, Davis, to do what you can, to help those people out. They know all about our dead ones up here. As far as they're concerned, the killer is our maniac, and they're awfully sore, our garbage spillin' over into their town like this. Anyway, you go down there for a few days and see what you can do."

Davis was pocketing the report before Vertali finished speaking. He headed for the door, then stopped in the middle of the small office. "What about Lowell?"

Vertali plopped down in his swivel chair. "He's off of it." The captain then gave Davis a look of anger. "I'll tell you the real truth, smart guy. The reason why I'm sendin' you down there is to get you out of here—none of the boys want you around, don't want to work with you. You're a smart aleck, Davis. The boys hate it, the way you talk, the way you think. So I ain't doin' you no favors, see? Right now, it works out good. You just stay on the case, wherever it goes, for now. You got that?"

Davis smiled. "And I've been waiting a long time to get it."

"Send in your daily reports to me, and your expense vouchers—don't forget those expense vouchers."

"Thanks, Captain."

Vertali held up two beefy arms, shaking his large hands in the air at Davis. "I ain't doin' you no favors, Sergeant—God forbid, if we had enough stranglers, like this one, we could keep you out of town for a year!"

Comfortably, John Davis moved slowly around the cluttered counters in the laboratory of his friend, Professor Edward Oscar Heinrich, talking, as he moved, to the intense little man with glasses perched at the end of his nose.

"What are you working on now, Professor Heinrich?" Davis asked the small man politely.

"Ballistics, mostly." Heinrich answered him in the usual matter-of-fact voice, his words flat and broad and betraying his Wisconsin heritage. The chemist was perched on a stool, placing slides into a microscope and periodically staring down into it, meticulously adjusting the lens, edging the glass slide beneath his gaze like a man gently tapping the balance of a delicate scale. He looked up at Davis. "Don't touch anything, John. There are several harmful acids in containers on that counter."

Davis slipped his hands into his trouser pockets. "I'm going on a job for the department, Professor Heinrich— down to Santa Barbara."

"What a lovely little town that is," Heinrich said, back to staring into the microscope. "The waters of the Pacific always seem warmer there. I was bathing in Santa Barbara last year and it was like being in my own bathtub. Must be the islands blocking the Santa Barbara Channel, breaking up those cold currents."

"I'm not going to Santa Barbara to go swimming. I'm looking for a strangler."

Heinrich sat upright on the high stool, pushing away the microscope. "The one we've had around here for some months, yes." He scratched the back of his head, then adjusted the white smock at his front. "Has he done something down there?"

"Another woman, another landlady."

"The same methods I suspect?"

"The same, strangled, then raped after death."

Heinrich rested his hands on the counter before him. "Peculiar, that sort of killer. The police over in San Francisco never asked for my help." He was hurt, not being asked for his advice on the strangler; the tone of his voice said it, quavering for an instant. "There was a fellow in Chicago, if I remember correctly, who operated like this man you're dealing with now." Heinrich removed his glasses, and, taking an immaculate handkerchief from a vest pocket beneath his smock, began to wipe the lenses. "Hoch was this man's name, Johann Otto Hoch."

"A strangler?"

"No, he poisoned his victims, all women he married. He was in the insurance business—their life insurance. Fifty women, maybe more, all met death at his hands. Of course, this is over a number of years, mind you, perhaps two decades."

Davis moved around the counter, so that he faced Heinrich. "How does this fellow tie in with the strangler?"

Heinrich pointed to Davis' hand. "Careful, young fellow. That steaming little vial in the holder there contains enough vitriol to eat away your fingers in seconds."

Davis put his hands back into his pockets.

"Well, no direct tie-in, mind you. But the same kind of—shall we call it dedication? Your strangler had killed three times since the first one in San Francisco—in February—and now you say in Santa Barbara, four times then, and all in the same fashion, and all the same type of women—landladies. Hoch's victims were also mostly landladies he first boarded with, then pitched woo to and married. An industrious fellow, really. He would take two

72

or three months usually to poison his victims, but toward the end, when he needed money, he rushed it, and took only a few days to give the women arsenic." Heinrich shook his head and replaced his glasses. "Crude poison, arsenic. Then Hoch wasn't a very bright person." Head down, he thought for a moment, telling himself, "Strychnine would have been better, yes, less detectable."

"How are they similar, these two men, Professor Heinrich?" Though Davis respected the man, he knew Heinrich's penchant for lengthy academic monologues and he was impatient; he would have to catch a train for Santa Barbara in four hours.

"Well, these types of killers are methodical and repetitious. They usually have a quirk, a trait, a habit that is predictable." Heinrich stood up, gently shoving the stool away from him with his foot. "Come along with me, young man, into the trophy room."

Davis followed Heinrich from the laboratory into a large dark chamber. Heinrich paused inside the doorway, flicking on the wall switch. Before Davis were high walls adorned with the oddest collection of "trophies" one could imagine a chemist assembling.

"You haven't seen this room, have you, John?"

"No," Davis replied, as he took in the wild sight of scythes, axes, knives, pistols, automatics, rifles of all makes, even a musket, affixed to the high walls. All of these items were labeled with a number and some letters. Several large tables in the room were laden with innumerable weapons and homicidal bric-a-brac.

"I call this my—murder room." A slight smile played about Heinrich's thin lips. "Self-indulgent, I know, but these artifacts of killing remind me of the inventiveness of man in his most lethal state. And they can teach."

Davis took in the room with curious amusement. He folded his arms and leaned against the wall, but he pulled away abruptly when his head struck a sharp instrument. He turned about to see a long-handled shovel quivering in a wall socket.

"That's Hightower's shovel," Heinrich said, pulling a pipe from a baggy pocket of his smock.

"Hightower?"

"Nineteen twenty-one. I don't think you were on the force then."

"I joined in twenty-three, just before you worked on the d'Autremont case."

"This fellow Hightower—" Heinrich spoke between deep puffs on his pipe, "murdered a priest that year, a Father Heslin, and tried to collect some ransom for him. William A. Hightower's his name—he's up in San Quentin now doing life. Well, when the ransom wasn't paid, Hightower thought he'd do the next best thing and lead the cops to the grave on the beach where he buried the priest for a reward of some sort—he told the police that he had spotted some bootleggers burying something strange in the sand." Heinrich gestured toward the shovel as if it were the embodiment of William A. Hightower. "He led Police Chief O'Brien and others to a deserted spot on the beach and they all began to dig, including Hightower." Heinrich laughed a short laugh. "Crazy little fellow was digging so fast that Chief O'Brien told him to slow down, that he might mutilate the corpse digging so wildly. And Hightower looked up at O'Brien and said"—Heinrich

74

laughed again, a brief knowing laugh—"and Hightower said—'Don't worry, I'm digging at the feet.'"

"I remember him now, that slip of the tongue."

"It got him convicted, that little comment while digging, along with a lot of other evidence—ransom notes, a typewriter—I've got the typewriter in another room, would you like to see it?"

"No—we were talking about a man named Hoch, and similarities, maybe, between him and the strangler."

Heinrich nodded and moved with Davis to a table next to the wall. "You see this?" The chemist held up an old-fashioned fountain pen. "No matter where Johann Otto Hoch, the Chicago poisoner, traveled—and he moved from New York to San Francisco in his years of marrying and poisoning—he never got rid of this pen, kept it with him always. It brought about his capture. He carried this pen to the hangman in Chicago in 1906....It was given to me by a Chicago cop of my acquaintance as—ah—a sort of keepsake." Heinrich unscrewed the top of the pen, showing the long top to Davis. "This is where Hoch carried his poison, in the top of his fountain pen, in a little capsule, arsenic. You can see the top is much too long for the tip of the pen to reach all the way." Heinrich screwed the top back on and carefully replaced the pen on the table. "They always keep something, that type of killer."

"I think our man carries a Bible," confided Davis. "But we've got absolutely nothing else."

"A Bible, hmmm." Heinrich looked about the trophy room, but he spotted nothing that triggered his imagination relating to Bibles. "No, I can't help you on that, Davis, but I'll think about it. Do you have anything of his, some personal belonging he left behind in those rooming houses I could look at?"

Davis shook his head sadly. "He doesn't stay long enough. He takes a room, and within an hour or so he's killed the landlady and attacked her."

Heavy clouds of smoke emanated from Heinrich's pipe. Through the haze Heinrich said, "Necrophilia. I don't profess to understand that kind of mind. I don't know if any scientist or alienist can determine the actions of such a creature. But, as you know, he will follow his habits and his habits won't change." Heinrich fished out a large, gold pocket watch. "You don't have a good deal of time to catch your train to Santa Barbara, John." They began walking from the trophy room. Heinrich patted Davis on the back. "You'll find him, my boy, if anyone will, but if you can, get something of his, a shoe, a fingernail, a glass he has used, anything."

"I'll try."

Working the straps around his one bag, Davis finished his packing. He wheeled about in the upstairs bedroom to the sound of the angry wheezing honk of a car horn outside. He went to the open window, and brushed back the lace curtains, looking down to see the taxi he had phoned for waiting outside. "I'll be right down, cabbie!" he shouted to the driver.

Davis snatched up his bag and walked from the bedroom, and down the stairs of the small house, his house, where he now lived alone. He paused before the living-room entrance to see if he had remembered to pull the shades. He had.

He lingered, sadly looking into the living room, his dead wife's living room. Davis had changed nothing inside that room since Nellie had died of influenza during the epidemic of 1924. He looked at the large, yellowed portrait of both of them, their wedding picture, which hung over the fireplace, her dark beauty unchanged, and he thought how she would remain inside of that moment for all time. He would age. But her long, black hair would never know gray, her wholesome face never wrinkle, her blazing, dark brown eyes never grow dull.

The sofa and easy chairs were in the same positions as when she had died, as were the little antique rosewood tables she had delighted in finding in dusty shops on Powell Street, and the crazy upright lamps he had never liked, and the intimidating break-front bureaus with glass doors against the wall and inside of these all of Nellie's family photos and mementoes going back a half century, the faces of her long dead family staring back at him, shopkeepers and their wives from Waukegan, Illinois, and farmers from Ohio and Pennsylvania.

They had married in Waukegan when Davis had graduated college and he had taken her as far west as the continent could go, to build a life in the most beautiful city in America, he thought then. But he was convinced now in his melancholy way that he had taken her away to die, and the guilt he felt every time he stared into that room was overpowering; for him the air in that room was so thick he could barely breathe.

Nellie had liked his being on the force, she was proud of his being a policeman and he would never forget the wonderful surprise party she had given him when he was promoted to detective, a party full of laughing, back-slapping neighbors and friends inside that very living room. He couldn't stand to more than glance at the room. It hurt him physically—in the throat, behind the eyes.

The insistent cab horn beckoned again. Davis picked up his bag and went out the door, locking it, and turning toward the street.

At that moment he saw Anne Simmons coming through his gate with a package in her arms, a pretty blonde, tall, full-lipped, with extraordinarily high cheek-bones, and clear blue eyes. She walked with a firm, self-assured stride, a woman confident of background and place. She had been to college in the East, earning a liberal arts degree and in this, Davis knew, she was an exception. The women of the day did not attend college unless their families possessed wealth. They either married or went to work in their teens. There was no in-between time for self-improvement, that was a man's luxury.

Anne Simmons never flaunted her wealth, her degree —she was a woman of taste and compassion. Her affection for Davis was deep. His integrity and dedication to duty drew her to him and his always-curious mind fascinated her. Davis was like her, Anne was convinced, a man outside of his time, beyond his field—two secret social pariahs in love.

As she walked toward him, Davis admired her full body outlined by the short dress she wore, a dress that amply showed the long curves of her legs. Her dress, her page-boy bob, the cloche hat pressed down on her golden hair were all the trappings of the nineteen-twenties flapper, but somehow she avoided that image. She was in the fashion but not of it. Her dress fluttered upward in the mild breeze and she swept a creamy arm downward to hold the hem in place.

"I thought I'd surprise you with dinner," she said, through a wide smile, holding up the package. "Spaghetti."

Davis had been going with Anne for several months, and was in love with her, he thought. But Anne's background worried him; her father was a wealthy importer of foreign goods. Joshua Simmons had spent years in the Orient and controlled most of San Francisco's import of delicate lace and silk from those dreamlands of India and China. He disapproved of Davis, a cop, as a potential son-in-law. To Simmons, Davis was a man without a future, a man who would never rise to the opulent heights of Nob Hill, where the Simmons mansion stood cheek to jowl with those other mansions of the super rich, all of them rebuilt and more glorious than their predecessors taken to ruin by the fire and earthquake of 1906.

Davis looked at Anne Simmons and asked himself why he had been lucky enough to have met her at a charity bazaar, and then reminded himself that luck had nothing to do with it. He never believed in luck, or chance, or fate, or whatever name the truly optimistic gave to their blessings.

"I could kick myself," Davis told her. "I forgot about our dinner." He held up his bag. "I've got to go to Santa Barbara."

The hurt was visible on her pretty face. Anne

Simmons looked down at the package in her arms. "I feel a little ridiculous."

"It's my fault for not calling you. I was over at Berkeley talking to Heinrich and I got tied up—" He knew excuses only made it worse. He dropped his bag and put his hands on her arms, pulling her towards him. He kissed her softly. "I'm terribly sorry. I'll be back in a few days and we'll have a fine dinner."

The cabbie, a thick-set man wearing a soft cap pulled low over his forehead and chewing a stub of a cigar jammed into the corner of his lips, leaned across the front seat of the taxi, shouting through the open window, "Hey, buddy, I ain't got all day if you're goin' over to Oakland to catch the train."

"It's all right, John," Anne told him softly, looking into his eyes and asking questions without words.

"I'll call you, Anne, dearest, from Santa Barbara when I get down there."

She nodded.

"Hey, buddy, damnit all!"

Davis slipped his wallet from his inside suitcoat pocket, flipping it open in the direction of the cab. "I'm a police officer." The driver drew back stiff behind the wheel, staring straight ahead.

"How's your mother and your kid brother?" Davis asked stupidly as he worried about the time.

Anne laughed. "Go along." She kissed him on the cheek. "Catch your train. Go along now, I mean it, and no small talk."

Davis picked up his bag and moved with Anne through the gate and to the cab, pulling open the rear door and tossing the bag inside. "I'll call tonight, sweetheart." He kissed her once more and got into the cab, which began to slowly struggle up the steep hill. Davis looked back out the small rear oval window to see Anne Simmons walk slowly to the corner, dump the package into a city wastecan, and cross the street.

SEVEN

The Coast Line express of the Southern Pacific Railway steamed down through the Santa Ynez Mountains and onto the coastal plain that sloped southward toward beautiful Santa Barbara. Davis sat in a rattling coach next to an open window. The night breezes brought him the exhilarating smells of the walnut, lemon, olive, and orange groves populating the gentle countryside. It was, Davis thought, as if he were descending into an embracing paradise, and he was glad to leave behind him the harsh winds and nipping fog-bound air of San Francisco and the north country.

Davis had enjoyed the long ride; he had plenty of time to think about the strangler, *his* strangler now;

Captain Vertali had willed the killer to him. He was no ordinary man, this violator of the dead. Perhaps he would obtain something, anything, the killer might have left behind in Santa Barbara. Davis laughed quietly to himself, remembering Heinrich's words—"even a fingernail." Now what the hell would the chemist turn up with a fingernail? Well, it's human fiber. His microscope whispered secrets in his ear when sliding a fingernail beneath the lens.

The steady pumping of oil wells in the darkness could be heard as the train slipped through a field. To Davis, this rhythmic thrumping sounded like huge generators beginning to turn.

"The big fields are south of the city." Davis turned away from the window to see a conductor leaning over him, peering into the night. "The Santa Maria field is a whopper, young fella."

"I heard about that field," Davis said. "Thousands of barrels a day come out of there, don't, they?"

The conductor straightened in his blue uniform, brass buttons gleaming, his aged face all smiles. "Twenty-five thousand barrels a day, young fella. Now there's a future for a fella like you—the oil business, yes, sir."

"I'm a policeman," Davis told him.

"That's a good trade, too," the conductor said with little enthusiasm. "On vacation?"

"Sort of."

"You'll like Santa Barbara. One of the most peaceful little towns along the whole California coast. I've lived in the town since the Southern Pacific put the line in—that was 1887, my boy. Yes, a great town if you want to raise a family. Weather's good, business is good. Very little

84

trouble in Santa Barbara, very little." He looked at his large silver embossed railroad pocket watch. "Heard from the stationmaster in Lompoc up the line that some poor woman was attacked yesterday, a landlady."

"Murdered," volunteered Davis.

"That why you're coming down here, young fella?"

"Uh-huh."

"Well, don't you believe for a minute that that sort of thing goes on in Santa Barbara, no, sir. We don't have things like that happen in our town—well, not much, hardly ever. A dark thing like that—don't belong in Santa Barbara." The conductor suddenly grasped the handrails on the seats next to the aisle as the train slowed. "We should be in soon, about ten minutes. Hope you enjoyed your trip, officer."

Davis nodded, stood up, his long frame extending so that his head almost bumped the overhead rack. He reached above for his bag, then began to make his way down the aisle toward the exit.

A short, squat man met Davis on the platform of the Santa Barbara station. "You the detective from San Francisco?" The short man popped a piece of hard candy into his mouth and began sucking loudly.

"Detective Sergeant Davis."

"Okay, Davis. I got a cab over here to take you to your hotel. Let's go." He began to move around the station building.

"Wait a minute. Let's see your identification."

The short man came back at him out of the shadows, still nonchalantly sucking on the candy. "Formal, ain't we?" He brushed aside his coat to reveal a star on his vest.

"I'm a sergeant, too. Wolinski. C'mon, now. Your train was two hours late, it's the middle of the night and I'm bushed. We'll show you what we got in the morning, *late* morning."

Inside the moving cab, Davis turned to Wolinski, who had propped his head up on one arm and was dozing. Davis pushed Wolinski's arm, dislodging his head from its uncomfortable perch.

"Whaddya doing?"

"Who's in charge of the Russell murder?"

"Captain Shuttler."

"Where's he?"

"In bed...where I should be."

"Okay, let's go over to his place."

Wolinski sat up, looking Davis over with new interest. "You gotta be a little crazy, fella. Shuttler don't like nobody disturbing his sleep." He leaned against the padded wall of the cab and closed his eyes.

"I don't care whether he's sleeping or not. I want to see Shuttler now, right now."

Wolinski was staring again, this time at his watch. "You realize it's almost three in the morning, fella?"

"Right now."

"Okay," Wolinski told Davis in a resigned voice, "but I ain't knocking on that man's door—you are."

Captain Ben Shuttler lived in a large, white house set back on a residential street, an imposing three-storied Victorian wooden structure topped with gables and cupolas. Davis studied the house for a minute from the cab.

"I told you, Davis," Wolinski's voice said behind him, "I ain't gonna wake up that Shuttler for no reason."

"Go back to sleep, then." Davis got out of the cab, walked across the street, and up to the front door, and rang the bell. After several rings the downstairs lights went on and he could see someone moving toward him through the lace curtains covering the half windows of the front door. The door flew open and a gaunt, bald man wearing a flowing nightshirt confronted him.

"Who the hell are you?" growled the bald man.

"Davis, from San Francisco. My train just got in—"

The bald-headed man slammed the door in Davis' face. Davis rang the bell again. Once more the bald-headed man threw open the door, glaring, scowling.

"You are Captain Shuttler?"

"I'm Shuttler, and you're an idiot."

Davis ignored the remark. "You've got a strangler in town."

"He'll keep. The Russell woman is dead and nobody's bringing her back." Shuttler put a bony hand to the edge of the door, about to close it once more.

"I know it's late, Captain Shuttler, but you're dealing with a fellow who could be murdering another woman—another landlady—right now. He's killed three in San Francisco already. The second one was only ten days after the first."

Shuttler smirked, which made his horseface look even longer. "All right, with that kind of time schedule, none of us need lose any sleep. The Russell woman has been dead for twenty-four hours. That means we got another nine days. Good night."

"He doesn't kill on schedule. He could wait three months or three hours." A bit of apology crept into Davis' voice: "I know it's late, but if you could just tell me what you know."

Shuttler glanced to his rear, then slipped outside to the porch, closing the door. "I don't want to wake up my family. Come with me." He padded along the L-shaped porchway in his long, bare feet, stopping to lean on the low railing, looking to the waiting cab across the street. "Is that you, Wolinski?" Shuttler shouted.

Wolinski leaned out of the cab window. "It's me, Captain." His voice was low and full of fright.

"You stay right there until I finish talking to this fellow." Shuttler pointed to a porch swing. "Sit down, Davis." Davis sat down in the swing, Shuttler next to him. The police captain pushed the swing a bit with his bare feet and the two men began to sway.

"I hate to admit it, but we got nothing but that poor woman's body." He shook his head. "And what that fellow did to it. Damn! Never seen anything like it." He turned to Davis with a look of disgust. "You know them beaters?"

"Beaters?"

"Rug beaters—what you use to beat the dust out of rugs, they're made of iron." Shuttler continued to push the swing with his bare feet. "He used one of those things on her, after he strangled her. First himself, according to the pathologist, then he sticks the end of that beater inside her. What kind of person does a thing like that—and to an old woman?"

"Old—how old?"

"Mrs. Russell? Maybe sixty, maybe more."

"That's the first time he's attacked an older woman. The landladies in San Francisco were mostly middle-aged or younger. Did he leave anything, personal effects, behind?"

"No calling card ... only poor old Mrs. Russell's body. We figure he rented the room from her and in about a couple of hours he went after her—trapped her in the pantry. I guess the rug beater was hanging on the wall. A neighbor saw him go in and out. Not much of a description—short, stocky, his clothes all wrinkled, wearing a workman's cap. He was carrying a little book. That's it."

"A Bible," Davis said, smelling the deep scent of roses growing near Shuttler's porch.

Shuttler threw out his feet, stopping the swing, his night shirt fluttering up to his bony knees. "A Bible? You mean to tell me a killer like that is carrying a Bible around with him? In God's name, why?"

"It's a device, I think, to disarm suspicions. He tells the landlady that he's a divinity student or something like that."

Shuttler looked ahead at the shrubbery inching over the porch railing and said in a sleepy voice, "The Devil can quote scripture better than anybody."

Davis dug into his suitcoat pocket and brought out a wrinkled piece of paper. "I wrote this on the train down here, Captain." He handed it to Shuttler. "I think it would be good to print up copies of this and distribute it to every rooming house in Santa Barbara."

Holding up the paper in the dim light, Shuttler squinted and read:

Be on the alert for a dangerous criminal—short of stature, about five-foot-six, blue eyes, stocky build, brown hair. Polite manners, quiet nature, carries a Bible. May state that he is a divinity student. Should he apply for a room, detain him as best you can and summon the police immediately. This man is wanted for questioning in a number of murders involving landladies.

Shuttler handed the notice back to Davis. "I send something like that around it'll cause a panic in town. You know how many rooming houses we got in Santa Barbara, Davis?"

"I wouldn't even guess."

"Lord's sake, there must be hundreds, five hundred maybe."

"You'll have to contact them all."

Standing up, Shuttler walked slowly around the porchway toward the front door. "I haven't got the men for that sort of thing." His voice trailed over his shoulder to Davis who followed him.

"I'll do it myself...if you'll give me a little help."

Shuttler turned at the door to Davis, his face flushed with anger. "You ought to, damnit—this killer is from San Francisco anyway—your responsibility."

"I can't make the rooming houses alone."

Shuttler looked over Davis' shoulder to the cab across the street. He waved in that direction. "Use Wolinski. He'll tell you where the notices should get printed up."

"Wolinski—that's it?"

"You're lucky to get him." Shuttler gave Davis a thoughtful look. "I should send the funeral bill for poor old Mrs. Russell up to your chief. She didn't have anyone, no insurance, nothing, just that broken-down boarding house her father left her. It's a goddamn, crying shame, that's what it is, Davis!" He was silent for a moment. "So this little bastard is walking around with a Bible, doing what he does, huh? ... That's a new one on me."

Davis and Wolinski stood in the hallway of the rooming house. They could smell corned beef and cabbage steaming in the kitchen and Wolinski hungrily eyed the serving girl setting the large table in the dining room. Mrs. Sheridan, the landlady, finished reading the description on Davis' wanted poster. Suddenly, her thin white hand went to her mouth.

"What is it?" Davis asked her.

"My young man, Mr. Stevens, he's just moved in, why—he—"

"He, what?"

"He looks like what your poster says here."

Davis' eyes widened. He rubbed the stubble of dark beard on his haggard face. "What room is this Stevens fellow in?"

Mrs. Sheridan moved instinctively so that she blocked the stairs—her boarders were a sacred trust. "But it's absurd, Mr. Stevens is such a nice young man, so religious—"

"I asked you, what room?" Davis advanced toward her. Wolinski grabbed his arm but he shook loose. "We don't have a lot of time, lady. You just read about what kind of man we're looking for. What room?"

Craning her neck about to look up the stairs, Mrs. Sheridan answered nervously, "There's no need to disturb that young man, Detective. We're just about to eat dinner.

We were just about to call him and the rest of our guests. He'll be right down to—"

Clutching her wrist, the wanted poster crumpling in her hand, the detective's question was more like an order. "I want that room number."

"Room two-oh-two," Mrs. Sheridan said with quivering lips.

"Just a minute, Davis," Wolinski said, going after him.

"To hell with it," Davis said and bounded up the stairs. He stopped at the top of the landing, looking about. Room 202 was at the head of the stairs. He banged on the door. "Come on out of there!"

"Who's there?" replied a soft voice.

"Police. Open the door."

"I haven't done anything."

"Just open the door—now!"

"I have nothing to talk to the police about." The voice was fading, as if moving further away from the other side of the door.

Davis leaned against the door, then began to move his body against the door in jerks. "You'd better open this door!"

"Davis!" Wolinski shouted up to him from the bottom of the staircase. "Davis—you can't do that!"

"Open this door, or I'll break it in!"

Mrs. Sheridan screamed.

"Davis—stop it!" shouted Wolinski, but he didn't move from the bottom of the staircase.

"I have nothing to do with the police," said the voice on the other side of the door, so softly it was almost a whisper.

92

Davis slammed his shoulder hard against the door, repeatedly hitting it. Mrs. Sheridan ran screaming into her kitchen. Doors on the second and third floors of the rooming house snapped open, guests cautiously sticking out their heads in wonder and shock.

The door began to give, splintering at the lock.

"You're breaking the door."

"I know," puffed Davis, "open it—so I—won't have to."

"All right, please," the voice begged, now close to the door. "All right, back away so I can open it."

Davis kept banging at the door. "Open the damned door—then—"

"You're still hitting it!"

"Unlock it, damn you!"

"For Chrissakes, stop, Davis, stop," shouted Wolinski.

"I'm opening it, I'm opening it," yelled the voice inside the room, frantically working the lock.

"Open it!" yelled Davis.

The lock sprang back just as Davis was putting his shoulder once more to the cracking wood. The door flew back, slamming against a mirror on the wall, shattering it. Before the panting Davis stood a short blond-haired young man wearing glasses, his face sheet-white. Beyond him Davis saw a large desk piled with books and stacks of foolscap covered with handwritten notes. The terrified youth calmly removed his glasses, carefully placing them on a table next to the door, and speechlessly opened the palms of his hands. He fainted, falling forward into the hall. Davis caught him only a second before he struck the floor.

Davis and Wolinski wearily walked down the porch stairs of Mrs. Sheridan's boarding house. Twilight settled about them and lights in the houses along the quiet block clicked on. They were near the waterfront and could hear the boat horns of the ships coming to dock.

"Let's try a couple more," Davis urged the squat man walking next to him.

"I ain't had my dinner," complained Wolinski. "We did more than fifty boarding houses today—ain't that enough?"

"Forty-three. We should try some more."

"Nope." Wolinski popped a hard candy into his mouth. "I'm gonna get dinner and then to bed. We done enough for the day."

Davis stopped and looked down at Wolinski, showing his disgust for the man. "Look, we've only gotten to about one hundred and thirty places in the last three days—"

"*And* nights."

"That maniac could still be in town."

Wolinski shrugged. "Maybe he is. We got thirty thousand people here. What do you want? The captain had the warning announced over the radio stations. We got out the posters. You can't inspect every boarding house in town. It ain't possible, just the two of us. I'm sick of it, a waste of time."

"Would you rather wait until another woman shows up dead?"

Wolinski wagged a pudgy finger at Davis. "You're getting us in bad with everyone, Davis. You hear an old lady tell you that she's got a young fella who she thinks answers your description of the strangler and you almost knock her down running up the stairs to the fella's room, and almost break down the door when he doesn't answer fast enough. He turns out to be a student at the Franciscan College by the Mission."

"I'm sorry that happened, but I don't like to take chances."

Wolinski nodded knowingly. "Sure, you don't, but the kid passed out from fright. You can get into real trouble doing things like that, Davis. I talked to the landlady about that kid—his old man's a big shot over in Fillmore—he's got a chain of hardware stores all over this part of the country, and you scaring his kid half to death!" He clucked his tongue disapprovingly. "Can't go on like that. People in Santa Barbara won't stand for it—Christ, Shuttler won't stand for it." Wolinski's shoulders sagged as he heaved a great sigh. "My feet are burning, my head is woozy, and my stomach's empty. Going home." He began to walk ahead of Davis, crossing the street. "I'll see you in the morning—maybe."

Two men ambled before Davis in the night, talking expressively as they moved down the street, both of them, the detective thought, a little tight. He half-listened to their conversation as it drifted back to him in the cool night air. He was in the waterfront district of Santa Barbara and had a long walk back to his hotel; it had been three hours since Wolinski had gone home, three hours and four rooming houses later.

"If a fella can't take a drink without gettin' a lecture, well, it's a sorry state of affairs, Harold."

Harold agreed and stumbled into his companion,

bumping him at the shoulder. "Why—I would like to ask why—if you ain't gonna have a drink—go into a speak and bother decent citizens with Sunday school lectures. Why?"

"I dunno. The guy was one of them—what do you call 'em?"

"Eccentrics?" guessed the other.

"No, that ain't it."

They stopped when the shorter man came to a halt, grabbing the lapel of his friend's coat. "I got it—fanatic, ain't that the word?"

"That's the word." The tall man slapped the shorter one's shoulder.

Davis was about to turn the corner, leaving the pair to wander off.

"Only a fanatic goes into a speak to bother decent citizens with all that talk of God," slurred the taller man in disgust. "And shoving that Bible in my face—"

Davis stopped in his tracks and spun around, listening.

"Terrible, misusin' the Bible that way." His voice rose in pitch with his indignation. "Did you see that old thing— beat up old Bible, raggedy edges, the cover all chewed up?"

"I certainly did—told him it was disgraceful to treat the good book that way, didn't I tell him?"

"Fanatic, that's what he was, and—"

Davis had come up behind the men and suddenly confronted the taller one. The man straightened so quickly at the sight of Davis' badge that he almost fell backward, his straw boater slipping back on his head.

"I ain't done nothin' wrong, officer," he told Davis.

"I know. All I want is some information. You were talking to your friend here about—"

"Shorty," the taller one said with affection and put his arm around the shorter man, pulling him to his side, "my friend, Shorty."

"—about some fellow in a speakeasy with a Bible."

"He was quoting scripture," volunteered Shorty.

"Says we're all goin' to hell," snorted the taller man. "Goin' to hell anyway, I suppose. Don't need that pip-squeak pointin' the way!"

"Where's that speakeasy?"

The taller man hesitated, the smile disappeared from his face. "I don't want to get Dutch in trouble." he said.

"I don't care about the speak. I'm looking for the man with the Bible, that's all."

"What did he do, officer—steal the parson's Bible?" He giggled.

"Or plank the parson's missus?" added the shorter man. He, too, found his comment hilarious.

"Where's the speak?" Davis leaned close to the taller man, telling him in his look that he was in no mood for drunken jokes. "C'mon, I haven't got all night. Where is it?"

"Back down this block, by the harbor. The old covered barge. There's a big, yellow light outside."

"Harold—you're gonna get in bad with Dutch," said Shorty. "Ohhhh, is Dutch gonna get sore at you, Harold."

"Thanks," murmured Davis, and he was off down the street, walking fast and finding it hard to believe that he still had such energy.

The barge was lashed to a dock by thick ropes. Above its flat hull rose a large, wooden houselike structure, the wood stained and rotting. Tiny windows were curtained with canvas, and behind these Davis could see dull lights.

He walked across a short gangplank to a heavy door and knocked. The door swung open, a burly man holding the handle from inside. "Whaddya want?" said the man at the door.

"Never mind that," Davis replied, and walked inside to see a large bar with several patrons, mostly men, leaning forward over their drinks. There was a sitting area, battered tables and chairs, where men and some overly made-up women sat, drunkenly fondling each other. A player piano tinkled in the corner. Cigar and cigarette smoke billowed in the air like a San Francisco fog.

Davis went to the bar. He looked up to see a large portrait of President Calvin Coolidge on the wall. The burly doorman and the bartender converged on him.

"I asked him who you were, mister," threatened the doorman.

Davis showed his badge.

"This a pinch?" frowned the bartender, wiping his hands nervously on a soiled apron.

"No, get me a beer and go back to work."

The bartender waved off the doorman. "Always glad to oblige an officer of the law," beamed the bartender. He brought Davis a large stein of beer, never taking his eyes from the detective. "You ain't a local cop."

Davis put a quarter on the bar. The bartender shoved it back to him, spreading his hands for an instant to wordlessly tell Davis that the beer was "on the house."

"San Francisco," Davis admitted and looked around the bar. It was difficult to see through the smoke. The people inside the speakeasy were gray in the smoke. The acrid smell of spilled beer was everywhere.

"I'll bet there's a lot of swell speaks up in San Francisco," said the bartender, nervously attempting conversation with Davis. "I don't suppose much of the old Barbary Coast guys are still around up there?"

Davis ignored him. He turned around, trying to focus upon a young man sitting with a young woman on the other side of the bar, where the bar hooked around a large wooden pillar. He craned his head to listen to their conversation.

"I know, honey," the woman purred. "But it ain't no sin to make a livin'." Her dark bobbed hair sported a comb with sequins that hung precariously by only a few strands of hair at the side. The woman's face was a smear of rouge, her lips and cheeks blotched with make-up. The young man studied her. A workman's cap was pulled low over his full face so that Davis found it hard to see him clearly.

The woman tilted her head and her arms moved quickly downward, out of sight.

"Put your dress down," sneered the man in the cap as he stared downward.

Davis sipped his beer and edged down the bar toward the couple.

"Don't you like what you see, honey?" persisted the bleary-eyed woman. "It's sweet and it don't cost much."

The young man's words then came in a rush, rising in volume: "You blasphemous harlot of hell ... Almighty God has damned you.... The eternal flames await!" He thrust up his hand only inches from her terrified face, shrinking from him, holding a small, black book in his hand.

"You!" Davis shouted across the bar.

99

The young man jerked his head in the direction of the detective. His wide-eyed gaze revealed piercing blue eyes. He pulled back his outstretched hand, the one that held the book, and spun off his chair. He bolted for a side door of the barge, Davis in pursuit.

When Davis reached the door, he saw the man running alongside the barge on a small deck toward the dock. The detective raced after him, the sounds of their running feet upon the rickety wooden deck causing clumping sounds that reverberated above the sloshing water.

"You—stop!" Davis shouted. "I'm a policeman—I want to talk to you!"

The man kept going, moving his stubby legs in chopping motions. He was on shore now, running across a dimly lit street; Davis saw him cut into an alley as he followed on the run. There was a row of shops on the street and in front of an all-night diner, Davis saw a taxi.

"Who owns the cab outside?" Davis stood breathlessly in the doorway of the diner. "I'm a police officer."

"I'm parked legally," complained a swarthy-looking fellow.

"Put down that cup of coffee and come with me. That's an order."

The driver jumped from his stool at the lunch counter and dashed to his cab. Davis was already sitting in the front passenger seat when the cabbie started the engine. "What do you want me to do?" the driver asked him nervously.

"Go up to the corner, turn right, then go slowly for a few blocks. I'm after a guy."

100

"Okay." The cab pulled away toward the corner, then turned.

"And turn out your lights."

"What? How am I gonna see to drive?"

Davis was looking along the block, peering into the spacious yards between the houses. "By streetlamp, by moonlight," Davis grumbled.

The cab churned down the block, then another, the driver nervously glancing at the street and at Davis who was leaning out of the window, looking, looking.

"Turn at the corner, start to circle back," Davis ordered the driver.

Just as the cab turned the next corner, Davis thought he saw a man dart across the street far down the block in front of the cab. "Did you see him?"

"Who?" The driver's hands were trembling at the wheel.

"The fellow who ran across the street, I think he ran across the street."

"How can I see anything? I got the damned lights off."

"Stop the car." Davis thought for a moment. He nodded to the side of the cab where the driver was sitting. "What's up that way?"

"There's a park on the other side of this block. Then there's a ravine. On the other side of that are the train yards."

"That son-of-a-bitch," Davis said in a whisper. "Is there a train leaving about now?"

The driver fumbled with his pockets. "I don't have the schedule but I think so." He looked at his watch. "I took some people down to the depot about a half hour ago. The flyer for Oakland is leaving pretty soon, yes, maybe ten minutes or so."

"Get me over to the depot fast."

It was all wrong, Davis thought. He should report to Shuttler, explain what happened and do it in an orderly fashion. Running to the depot like this—and he wasn't sure about the man. But he fit the description. That little black book in his hand was a Bible, wasn't it? Wasn't it? The way he acted in the speak with that whore. That was the man, he was sure of it. Could he be that lucky? Luck had nothing to do with it. He had followed up a lead, that's all, and it had worked out.

They were crossing a bridge over the sprawling train yard. "That's the depot over there," the driver told Davis. The detective looked down to see a small crowd of people boarding a waiting train, the yellow lights from the depot playing upon the steam gushing from the engine. He was at a great distance, but for one fleeting moment Davis thought he saw the tiny form of a man running across the train yards, moving from one silent freight car to another, making for the passenger train. He pulled out a notebook and wrote as the cab turned off the bridge and sailed down a hill toward the depot. He tore off the page from the notebook, stuffing this into the driver's pocket. "I want you to call Police Captain Shuttler with that message, you understand."

"Right," said the driver, glancing anxiously at his pocket.

"You tell him that I got on that train—that the man we're after is probably on it."

"What else?"

"Just read him the note in your pocket."

"Christ!" The driver pointed to the station only a half block away. "She's pulling out!"

"Don't turn in at the station—go to the train crossing." Davis opened the door a crack, ready to leap out. "I want you to tell the stationmaster to wire the next stop—what is it?"

"Listen, pal—I don't work for the railroad, Santa Maria or Guadalupe, I dunno."

"Whichever one—have them wire the police in the next stop and have some officers waiting for me there. You got that?"

They were approaching the railroad crossing. The train had left the station and was getting up steam, the engine already rumbling over the crossing, its wheels grinding on the rails, the ties beneath heaving under its great weight.

"You ain't even showed me your badge, fella," the driver said.

Davis opened the car door as the cab began to screech to a stop in front of the wooden guard rail across the road. He showed his identification. "My name's Davis, San Francisco." He was out of the car, ducking beneath the rail and running awkwardly alongside the slowly moving train, trying not to fall between the ties, the gravel beneath his feet grinding into his ankles and sending pebbles into his shoes. The first passenger car went by, then the second. Davis dropped behind, then sped up as he caught the handrail of the third car, swinging his feet up in one motion to the metal steps of the platform. A startled black porter stood in the gangway, his white jacket flapping in the wind. Winded, Davis leaned with relief against the wall of the jiggling car.

"This is a sleeper, mister," the porter finally said. "I hope you got a reservation."

"Get the conductor," Davis said, showing his badge. He moved painfully to the other side of the platform, braced himself against the locked door and removed his shoes, dumping out the pebbles.

The conductor was standing before Davis in minutes, arguing: "This is the Oakland Flyer of the Southern Pacific, officer, and I can't go waking up every passenger because you *think* a wanted man got on this train." Two porters nodded in agreement. "The police will be waiting at Guadalupe, anyway, isn't that what you said?"

"I'm not looking for a purse snatcher, conductor. This man is a killer. He's insane and he's already murdered four women, strangling them. Maybe you'd just as soon wait until one of your female passengers gets choked to death?"

Taking off his hat, the conductor wiped down the gray hairs far back on his head, matted in sweat. "I guess we better search if it's a killer."

Davis slipped his hand inside his suitcoat pocket, withdrawing his police special from its arm holster. He checked the weapon to see that it was fully loaded.

One of the porters stepped back and stared at the pistol. "You gonna use that, mister?"

Davis returned the pistol to the holster. "C'mon. We'll start with the first car and work backward to the sleepers."

They went through the coaches slowly, eyeing the

passengers, most of whom were curled up sleeping in their seats. Davis impartially lifted hats, caps, and blankets, as he moved down the aisle to inspect faces. The conductor and porters followed.

When the group reached the sleeping cars, Davis turned to the porters. "You go ahead and check the washrooms on either end of these two cars. Knock on the doors. If a door is locked and there is no answer, call me." The porters pushed past him into the first sleeping car. The detective turned to the wizened conductor. "Have you got your flashlight?"

"Yes, but I don't want to shine it on their faces. That's a terrible thing to do to a sleeping person."

Davis shook his head at the fierce propriety of the man. They began working their way down the aisle of the old-fashioned sleeping car with its double berths covered by curtains that swayed with the movement of the train. Davis slowly pulled back the curtain of each berth, holding his hand next to his revolver. The conductor trained a quick beam of light from his flashlight onto the face of each sleeping passenger. Midway down the aisle, one of the porters raced up to them.

"Officer," the porter said breathlessly, "we got a locked washroom, the woman's washroom, at the head of the next car. I knocked, but nobody answered."

Before Davis could move, the conductor gripped his arm. "That don't mean your man is inside that washroom. Could be a passenger fell asleep in there—sometimes happens."

Davis pulled away, stepped around the porter, and moved quickly down the aisle. The conductor was right behind him, cautioning, "Just don't do anything rash, young man."

"Like what?" Davis said over his shoulder, irritated.

"Like shooting through the washroom door, that's what."

He turned for a moment to face the conductor. "I'm a cop—not William S. Hart!"

"I just don't want to see any innocent people get hurt, that's all."

"Neither do I."

When they got to the door of the washroom, Davis tried the handle slowly. To his surprise, the handle, just as slowly, began to turn upward against his downward grip, as if someone were moving it from the inside. Davis jerked down hard but the door was locked. He pushed the conductor and porter back. Then he spoke to the closed door: "Come out of there...Conductor."

He waited a few seconds, then said again, "Come out, please. It's the conductor. I want to check your ticket." He glanced at the conductor to see the old man nod his approval.

"I *know* who you are," came a husky voice from the other side of the door. A moment later Davis heard the smashing of glass and felt a rush of cold wind escape from beneath the bottom of the door.

The detective pulled the conductor to his side. "Use your key, quick!"

Nervously, the conductor slipped his key into the lock and the second Davis heard the bolt slip back he kicked open the door, his revolver in hand, aiming. The washroom was empty. The small window had been shattered.

"My God, he's jumped," gasped the conductor.

Davis leaned out of the window, the cold wind lashing at his face. In the moonlight he could make out the open fields rising toward the Santa Ynez Mountains and little else. He peered down the tracks and saw no movement along the embankment.

"Was it him do you think?" The conductor stood blinking inside the washroom.

Holstering his revolver, Davis leaned over the basin, running some cold water in his hands and splashing his face. He looked at himself in the mirror. His white shirt was streaked with dirt, his suit was dusty, his tie pulled down. He had somehow lost two buttons on his vest, probably when he had run for the train, Davis thought. His thin face was dark with grit and beard and his dark brown eyes stared back at him bloodshot, the lids drooping. The porter handed him a towel and Davis wiped his face as he turned to the conductor. "Sure it was him."

The second porter was suddenly at the washroom door. He pointed upward with a quaking finger. "There's —there's somebody on top—runnin'."

"What? Now, Jimmy, you sure?" the conductor said in disbelief.

Davis went to the window and looked to the side of the car, seeing that handrails led to the roof. He put one foot on the window sill, kicking out some jagged pieces of glass, then reached with his left hand and grabbed a rail, swinging over a foot. He was outside, climbing the handrails to the roof. At the top he inched his body over to the center duckboard that ran along the roof of each car. He moved in a crouch, holding onto handrails. He saw nothing in front or behind but he crawled along, choking on the smoke from the engine, his suitcoat flapping in the gusting wind.

At the end of the fourth passenger car, Davis looked down into the tender, which was brimming with coal. Beyond that was the open cab of the engine with the engineer at the throttle and the fireman busily shoveling coal into the roaring furnace of the ancient engine. Davis crawled down the ladder to the platform. The conductor and the porters were there to meet him.

"Not a thing up there," he told them.

"But I heard them footsteps banging along up top," the porter insisted. "Lotsa people in the coach here heard them steps. Ask 'em, go on ask 'em, officer."

Davis was exhausted. For a moment, as he clutched the ladder on the platform, he thought he might pass out. "If he was up there, he jumped." Davis walked past them and into the coach, saying, "I'll be sitting in the coach. If you hear any more footsteps, call me." He sank down into an empty seat. The conductor sat down across from him.

"What will you do now?" the old man asked Davis.

The detective closed his eyes, then opened them, glancing out the window. "Wake me when we get to Guadalupe. I'll have the local police search this area. It'll be dawn soon. That should give them an edge." His head slipped backward and rolled sideways against the seat cushion.

The conductor watched Davis fall asleep. His coat was open and pulled to one side so that the revolver in the holster showed. The conductor reached over and pulled the flap of Davis' suitcoat over his vest so that the weapon was hidden, then went up the aisle after the porters.

The Oakland Flyer made good time through the mountains, coming close to the town of Guadalupe near dawn. Cassidy, the engineer, smoked his pipe, hand on the throttle, settled back against the iron wall of the engine's cab and adjusted his weight on the iron fold-up seat. This was the best part of the run for him, the wall of mountains to his right, the wide, blue Pacific on the left, the rich scent of the mountaintop pine forests swelling about him.

Russo, the fireman, stood by the tender, knocking small chunks of coal from the bottoms of his shoes, using his shovel to bang the coal free. Cassidy looked over at him, then at his pressure gauges. "Gotta keep the steam up, Frankie," he shouted above the thundering engine. "We're dropping a little—better feed her!"

Using the end of the shovel, Russo knocked back the bolt holding the sluice gate to the coal in the tender. Chunks of coal spilled forward at his feet and onto the floor of the cab. Russo turned, kicked open the furnace door, and began to shovel, tossing several loads of coal into the furnace as the flames licked back at him. He stepped away toward Cassidy, wiping his grimy brow, and a ribbon of sweat came away with his sleeve. He was looking upward at the coal reserve in the tender when he saw, in awe, the coal move, a few large chunks falling away at the top, then more spilling backward as a human hand emerged, large thick fingers curled about a book that smashed upward, followed by an arm and the head of

109

a man with a cap pushed so low it covered his ears. Transfixed by the incredible sight, Russo stood staring wordlessly, pointing to the emerging body in the coal tender. Cassidy was preoccupied by the vision of the ocean waves lapping at the golden shores beyond the ridge on which the train rumbled.

The man, his skin and clothes black with coal dust, wriggled free, and was soon standing unsteadily on the mound of coal in the tender, his thick-set frame jostled by the veering train. He pocketed his book and wiped the coal dust from his eyes with a ragged handkerchief.

Russo found his voice: "Get the hell off of there, you tramp!" He picked up some large chunks of coal and began to pelt the man with them. "Get the hell off!"

The man kicked chunks of coal back at Russo. One sharp-edged lump of coal struck the fireman, gashing his forehead. The man kept kicking coal into the cab, moving forward in the tender, cursing Russo, but his words were unintelligible against the roar and hiss of the train. A chunk of coal flew past Cassidy's face, striking a pressure gauge, breaking the glass. The engineer turned, startled, to see Russo lift his shovel, swing it wildly in the air, and hurl it at the man in the tender. The man twisted sideways and took the flat of the shovel on the back as it struck him. Angrily, he picked up the shovel and threw it back at Russo; it clanged to the cab floor.

"He's a madman!" Russo screamed to Cassidy.

"Get him off of there," ordered the engineer, but Russo only backed further into the cab next to Cassidy, as the man moved shakily forward, coming to the edge of the tender, grabbing the pin at the top corner of the tender, yanking it free, then scrambling to the other corner and grabbing that pin.

"He's gonna let that wall down on us," Cassidy said, his pipe dropping from his mouth and clattering to the iron floor.

"Get your hand off that pin!" Russo tried to find safety inside the little corner of the cab. "You stupid bastard—you'll wreck us!"

The man was lying flat now on top of the coal, both hands on the remaining pin, his huge head stuck over the edge of the front wall of the tender so that he looked down upon the two terrified men in the cab. He smiled wide, white teeth gleaming inside a coal-smeared face. "You're damned, you scum of the earth—damned!" He grunted as he pulled at the pin holding the wall, slipping his body over the side of the tender as he pulled with his fantastic strength. The pin jerked free with a squeal of metal. The wall collapsed forward under the weight of the coal which slammed into the cab, smashing Russo into the furnace, burying him to his armpits. Cassidy was crushed by the cascading coal, his body sent across the controls so that he was bent over the brake, forcing the stick downward.

Inside the first coach Davis felt his body being lifted by the momentum of the train as it braked; he was sent headfirst into the opposite seat. Screams and yells of passengers in panic erupted. Davis rolled off the seat and stayed on the floor as the train came to a stop, bags, clothing, and pillows sailing past him like a wild sheet of rain down the aisle toward the front of the train. He shook his head and felt his chin. It was bloody. He had cut it on an uprooted floor bolt. He stood up, staggering toward the door, throwing it open, then jumping onto the walkway of the tender. He made his way along the side working around toward the cab of the engine. He could see coal spilling out of the side of the cab. He had to climb the side of the tender to see into the cab. Russo was deep in coal, a look of horror on his face. The engineer was nowhere to be seen.

"Mister! A lunatic dumped the tender on us—the engineer's underneath."

"Where's the guy who did it?" Davis looked about frantically.

"He jumped before we stopped—help me dig old Cassidy out will you? He's underneath somewhere—God, Almighty, he might be dead. Help me, mister!"

Steam gushed from the sides of the engine, sending up enormous clouds. A wooded slope rose to the right, and beyond the hissing of the steam and the muffled cries of the injured passengers back in the cars, Davis thought he heard someone running through the underbrush, going up the slope through the pines. He jumped from the tender and felt a sharp pain in his left ankle. His leg gave way. He stood up again, hobbling upward so that he was clear of the steam from the engine and had a good view of the slope.

He could see a man moving upward, running in a crouch. Davis cupped his hand and shouted, "Stop or I'll shoot! This is the police!" The man stopped for a moment, then continued his goatlike ascent. Davis whipped out the revolver and aimed, squeezing off a shot that rang through the trees and smacked into a towering redwood, the

112

splinters falling where the man had been only a second earlier. He fired again and again, kicking up red dust at the man's heels, but it was no use. He was out of range.

"Hey, mister!" Russo was yelling. "Will you help me out here?"

Davis watched his quarry reach the top of the slope and turn. The man waved both arms in triumph. The rising sun caught him and outlined his thick figure, shooting his shadow down the slope. Then Davis heard his laughter—hysterical, deep laughter. Taunting words echoed down to him: "Here I am! Here I am!"

Davis lowered his head, feeling utterly defeated. He pocketed the empty revolver. He looked up once more, strangely satisfied to see that the man had vanished over the slope.

Russo was still crying out from the coal-buried cab: "Hey, mister, where'd you go? Are you there? How about giving me a hand, huh?"

Pushing up from his kneeling position, Davis spotted a small piece of paper fluttering toward him, a small piece of tissue-thin paper with ornate printing on it. He snatched it up. It was torn and smudged, but the detective recognized it instantly as a page from a Bible.

"Hey, mister!" whimpered Russo.

"I'm coming!" Davis shouted back. He slipped the page into his pocket and lurched in the direction of the engine.

<u>EIGHT</u>

Nelson stood in the queue of men before the payment shack in the lumberyard. He had worked there for two days, picking up scraps of wood, performing menial chores in the busy yard. As he inched forward, he momentarily lifted his solemn face to the afternoon sun. Sweat streamed across his full cheeks. The thought of his pay, meager though it was, gave him a warm reassurance. He would not have to sleep in the yard again as he had for the past two nights. He could afford to rent a room, to sleep on clean cool sheets. Yes, he would get a room in Oakland in a few hours. He smiled, or the muscles at his mouth twitched satisfaction.

"Somethin' funny, Harris?"

Nelson did not respond to the large man wearing boots and a huge soft felt hat who stood next to him, hands on hips. He only glanced in the man's direction.

"You hear me, Harris?"

"I heard you, Mr. Garfield."

"I asked you what you were smilin' about?"

Nelson peered ahead, staring at the sweat-soaked shirt of the man in front of him, shuffling forward toward the pay shack. "Nothing."

"I've been foreman in this yard for sixteen years, Harris, and I've never seen such a worker. You got nothin' to smile about. I been watchin' you—you move like a snail. You spend half your time starin' at nothin'. And you forget what you're told to do. Collectin' money for punk work ain't no joke to me, Harris."

Nelson jerked his body about so fast that the foreman took a step back. He faced the man with a smile, saying, "I'd like to work with the big saw in the shop—when can I do that?"

The foreman squinted at him, then snorted. "You? Hell, I'd never let you get near that machine. You'd cut off your arm and it would be half an hour before someone told you about it."

"Keep movin', buddy, will you," grumbled the man behind Nelson, giving him a gentle shove. "I wanna get paid today, not next week."

With a sideways look, Nelson told the man, "Don't touch me like that. Wait your turn." Then to the foreman, sweetly, "I'll do better, Mr. Garfield, really. It's just that I've been sick and I must build up my strength." He saw no compassion in the foreman's squint. Nelson next spoke haltingly, his words measured, as he looked first at the veteran's pin the foreman wore on the lapel on his jacket and then down to his own shabby shoes, his trousers, frayed and torn at the cuffs. "It's taken a long time for my health to come back since the war," he said in a low, apologetic voice.

"In the war, were you?" The foreman slipped his hands into his pockets. He looked at the line of men passing the pay shack. "Okay, you better step up and get your pay." He moved closer. "I'll keep you on for another week," he almost whispered, "but that's only 'cause you're a vet—and so am I—a corporal in the old Rainbow Division. But I better see you hustle, fella, or it's out the gate with you. Got me?"

Nelson smiled. "Sure, I'll hustle, Mr. Garfield. I'll show you some real hustling next week."

"Step up and get your pay, fella." The foreman walked off.

The man behind Nelson said, "I'm sorry I shoved ya, Harris. It's just that I gotta get home to—"

"It's okay," Nelson said in a calm voice. "I can take a little shoving."

He took his time, ambling lazily down the residential streets of the city, admiring the trim lawns of the large houses, the white fences surrounding each lot, fences so white that they appeared freshly painted. It was suppertime and children ran before him, hurrying home to kitchens smelling of fried potatoes and porkchops.

As Nelson moved he casually brushed his jacket and pants, wiping away the sawdust and small woodchips

clinging to him. He paused at each large structure he
thought to be a boarding house, straining for the sign in
the first-floor parlor window. But there were no rooms to
let, it seemed, as he continued his aimless search. He
trudged on, heavy-footed but confident that by nightfall
he would stretch out upon crisp sheets.

Thoughts nagged him, vague memories of only a few
days earlier. He remembered being hunted, being shot at
as he left a train. As that cloudy memory returned, he
ached for a sharper vision. It came to him in fragments of
light, showing his own form climbing fast up the steep hill,
crashing into trees, the low pine branches he had clutched
tearing and ripping his hands with sharp needles. He saw
himself at the top of the hill, gloating as he looked down at
a man with an empty revolver. He had laughed then
victoriously and the memory of his taunt gave him deep
pleasure.

He whistled down the Oakland street as he remembered whistling over the hills during his escape, sauntering
down to a road where he had hitched a ride to a small
town, and then another ride and another, until he had
worked his way into San Jose, then San Francisco where
he caught the ferry to Oakland.

The days are passing, he told himself, like before with
those other women, disgusting women. They paid for
their charms, didn't they? Days pass and distances in-
crease and there is safety in distance.

Nelson turned a corner, and spotted a clothesline at
the back of a house. He slipped through a gate and
casually walked down the rope holding the drying clothes
and helped himself to a pair of men's pants, a shirt, a

sweater. He folded these clothes beneath his arm as he went into an alleyway. A small girl stood staring at him, holding a hoop and a stick.

"Those are my daddy's clothes," she said.

Nelson looked down at her and smiled. He patted her on the head. "Your daddy didn't want them anymore, little darling," he cooed, and stepped around her.

With a jump, the little girl dropped her hoop and stick and ran into the yard, shouting after him, "I'm telling my daddy!"

"Go right ahead, little darling," Nelson said but she was beyond earshot and he said it smugly to himself.

It was nearing dusk when Nelson stepped into an unlocked garage. He stripped, putting on the clothes he had taken from the yard. Into the pockets of the clean clothes he jammed his pay, and his Bible. He neatly bundled his old, tattered garments and slipped these into a trash can, careful to bury them deep beneath the garbage. He peered down for an instant in the half light at his shoes. There was nothing he could do about them now. He could find shoes later.

Nelson put his ear to the alley door of the garage. He heard heavy footsteps coming and pressed himself against the wall, waiting. Next he heard the voices of men, angry voices.

"Forget it, Ben," one said. "Christ, it's only a few clothes."

"Goddamn tramps," said another. "They gotta learn you just can't take whatever's on a man's property. He could have hurt Jenny, you know?"

"C'mon, Ben—it's getting dark. Just a bindle stiff. They don't hurt kids. So he took some old clothes. It's only clothes. The Bible tells us to share our capes with the naked."

"To hell with that—he's a thief, and it ain't capes, it's cloaks, and I ain't got no goddamn cloaks. They was my best workclothes, damnit."

"I'm goin' home. I missed my supper and I'm tired and Grace is gonna want to fool around—"

They were working their way to the end of the alley, their voices fading. "All the same, if I caught that guy I'd bash his face for sure."

"Naw, you wouldn't, you ain't the kind."

They were gone.

Nelson relaxed, pushing away from the garage wall, standing in the semi-dark, smelling musty odors. He felt exhilarated, triumphant. "Smash me in the face, huh?" he hissed. "You came close, mister." But there were three of them. Three of *what*? Nothing to fear—they had never killed to cleanse the heart and the soul. They work for women and live and die for women. Stupid and weak. Three would not have been a problem.

Opening the garage door a crack, Nelson stared with one eye into the alley. All was quiet. He stepped outside and walked in the opposite direction of the path the men had taken. At the end of the alley he turned the corner and walked for several blocks, or was it several miles, he did not remember. Nearing a corner, he spotted a sign in the parlor window of a sprawling three-story wooden building: ROOM TO LET.

Nelson looked up and down the block and, seeing no

one near, went through the gate. Slowly, working himself behind the high shrubbery that encircled the house, he peered into each window. Only one person was present on the first floor, an elderly woman washing dishes in the kitchen. He studied the windows of the upper floors. No lights showed. He went to the front porch and rang the bell. At the sound of the sharp clang of the bell a sliver of excruciating pain shot across the forehead of Earle Leonard Nelson, exciting him.

"It's the fifth killing in California, the same as the others," the reporter blurted into John Davis' immobile face. "All of them strangled, all of them attacked, a few trinkets taken, some clothes. Is this the same guy doing all this, Davis?"

The other reporters waited as Davis glanced into the half-opened desk drawer where he kept the slim reports on the strangler. He slowly closed the door with his foot, and looked around the small office he had been given, staring coolly at the newsmen.

"The Oakland woman, Mrs. Beth Coolie, she was a landlady, too, just like the others. It's the same guy, isn't it, Davis?"

Davis studied the big-boned reporter who had led the quiz, studied his bad, yellow teeth and smelled the faint aroma of gin on his breath as he leaned across the desk. Gently, he pushed the reporter back at the shoulder and stood up. "Oakland is not my jurisdiction, as you all know. You should be talking to the Oakland cops."

"C'mon, Davis, Captain Vertali told us you were now in charge of this Dark Strangler case."

"Is that what you're calling it?" Davis had no stomach for the kind of answers they wanted and the thought that Vertali had dumped the entire matter on him, making him alone responsible for the case, angered him. It was a convenient assignment—giving him an apparently unsolvable case and shunting the force's embarrassment on to him exclusively. Now he could handle the press. Now he could be responsible for answers that did not exist.

"What have you got, Davis?"

"Yeah," piped another reporter. "We know you went down to Santa Barbara on the strangulation there. That ain't your jurisdiction either. What gives?"

"Nothing gives," Davis told them all in a flat tone. "You know what you know—five women, all landladies, all strangled and then attacked, small thefts. Only two quick glimpses of the killer, if he is the same killer, and no positive identification."

"You know he's the same killer, Sergeant."

Davis was convinced that the strangler was responsible for all the murders but he remained silent.

"What kind of guy is this? How does he live? Why does he kill like this?"

"Look, fellas," Davis sighed. "If I answered those questions I'd be giving you a lot of theories—"

The heavy-set reporter towering over Davis' desk reddened. "Well—goddamnit—give us something! You got an epidemic here. This guy kills at will or whim it seems, hopping up and down the coast—no rhyme or reason to it. And what are the police departments of three cities doing about it? They all tell us to see you and what

122

do you do? You sit there and evade questions. Every woman over twenty-one in this state is terrified, afraid to answer the front door. Do you know that some anxious wife over in Bakersfield shot her husband in the legs last night when he came home drunk, thinking the guy was the Dark Strangler?"

"I read the story in the *Call*," Davis said.

"If this keeps up, a lot of innocent people are gonna be hurt," another reporter said.

Davis had had enough. "Gentlemen, the force is doing its best to apprehend this man—"

"Like what—you're the only guy workin' on this."

"Looks to us like a dead end." The reporter who said this jerked his thumbs outward. "This office, you, that's it, and a lot of empty statements."

"Thank you," Davis said as he stood up, motioning toward the door. "I think we've concluded the interview. You'll have to excuse me. I've got to get to work."

The reporters began to file out of the small office. The heavy-set reporter with the bad teeth paused in the doorway. He held up an opened notebook into which he scribbled hastily, speaking the words mockingly to Davis: "Police have no clues in strangler case—a dead end."

Davis slowly walked to the door, smiling faintly, and closed it. "Good, print it," he whispered to himself.

Professor Heinrich sat on the park bench holding a thin envelope, tapping this casually against his knee. John Davis sat beside the scientist, eyeing the envelope and munching on a sandwich. Peering straight ahead into the park where children were at play, Heinrich suddenly handed over the envelope to the detective, saying flatly, "So now he visits our pretty little town of Oakland."

"The town doesn't matter to him," Davis said as he put aside the sandwich, carefully placing it on a flattened-out brown bag. He cradled the envelope between his long legs and wiped his fingers with his handkerchief. He slowly opened the envelope, withdrawing the thin, faded piece of paper, the page from the Bible left by the lunatic at the train. Clipped to the page was a photograph showing a thumbprint.

"The smudge at the bottom of the page was enough for a print," Heinrich told the detective. "It's clear enough. I compared it with yours and it belongs to someone else. Hopefully, it will be your man."

Davis was grateful but not optimistic. "Fingerprints," he said, drawing out the word. "There's only a few departments in the state who rely on them, even keep files."

"Hoover in Washington is trying to convert his bureau to complete fingerprint indentification—but that will take years." Then Heinrich added with a bright smile. "It's standard identification at Scotland Yard—has been since 1910."

"I wish the bastard were strangling women in England. I'll send the print on to the Clearing House in Chicago—it's the largest fingerprint collection in the country."

"Don't be discouraged, my boy. What have you done on your end?"

Davis slipped the envelope into his pocket, squeezed the flesh at the bridge of his nose and said, "Going blind looking through files of mug shots. Nothing close to the fellow I saw down in Santa Barbara and on the train. I'm going to try the state mental institution in Sacramento as soon as I finish up the files in Frisco. Unless I get lucky and I can't count on luck."

"No, you can't."

Davis picked up the remains of his sandwich, looked at it, then placed it inside the brown bag and crumpled it. "He's going to go on killing at random, Professor Heinrich. Live off the land, take the bare minimum to survive, and go on moving and killing."

"Correct, but the opportunities for him to remain in the shadows diminish with each new killing. It will become more and more of a risk."

"I don't think he's aware of that—if he is, he doesn't care."

"He cares." Heinrich placed his hands on his knees and pushed forward as he stood up. "Must get back to the lab. I'm busy with a forgery case."

"Thank you," Davis said, offering his hand.

The scientist was gone with a handshake. Davis watched him stroll down the sidewalk through the park, watching the children play, thinking him to be a funny-looking little genius.

Joshua Simmons moved with ease through his expansive parlor, the cigar in his delicate hand streaming smoke. Davis sat with Anne on a red plush couch. Simmons poured a brandy, then held up the decanter for a moment. "One for you, John?"

"No, sir, too early in the day."

Simmons sank into a huge wing-back chair. "I read in the *Chronicle* that you're handling this terrible strangler case on your own."

"Pretty much, sir, yes."

"Terrible," clucked Simmons.

"True—it's an awful thing, Mr. Simmons."

"I meant that you should be involved in such work," Simmons said sternly, sipping his brandy.

Anne slid her hand to Davis'. "I think we should consider the department's decision to give John such responsibility an honor."

"Not at all, my dear." Simmons leaned forward, his glare squarely on the detective. "They're making a fool of you in the press, boy. And that's exactly what the authorities want. You take all the ridicule and the blame for this lunatic running around murdering helpless women. They know it's hopeless."

"Father—"

"Please, Anne, dear—he knows it's hopeless, too." Then back to Davis who was quietly gritting his teeth. "Don't you, John?"

"It's my case." He thought for a moment as he stared back at Joshua Simmons, his burly frame packed into an expensive tailor-made suit, his beet-red, puffy face and thick-white, neatly combed hair, the cigar and brandy, the very image of opulence and power, and, suddenly jolted with anger, shot back: "And I'll get that fellow." He regretted the words instantly.

126

Simmons lifted an ancient bushy eyebrow. "You will, huh?" He laughed softly. He winked knowingly at his daughter. "Young Sherlock Holmes."

Anne ignored the remark, turning to Davis. "If John says he will catch the man, then he will do it."

Davis eased back against the couch. "I don't know, honey. I want to catch the guy so much—that's why I came out with—" He turned to Simmons: "You have a way of making me breathe fire, Mr. Simmons."

"I guess it's because we don't like each other," Simmons said with a thin smile. "I might like you better if you got into some decent sort of work."

"There's nothing wrong with being a policeman."

Simmons waved away the argument. "Cops are low creatures, like the scum they must deal with, everyone knows."

"Father!"

"It's a known fact, Anne. Oh I think John is above the cut of most cops. His error is in trying to make a profession out of a brutal job—and, John, don't hand me that nonsense about science. Cops are what we pay them to be—brutes on the side of the laws we create. How intelligent do you think Praetorian Guards were, huh? Now you *could* think of leaving the force."

"And go to work for you."

Simmons nodded. "Your perception delights me, John. I could use a smart young general manager."

"I don't want to talk about that again, Mr. Simmons. We've gone through that before."

"If you intend to marry my daughter—" Simmons' face hardened, the muscles of his jaw flexing, his eyes narrowing to a menacing squint. "You'll have to do better than chasing lunatics." He puffed on his cigar thoughtfully. "Besides—I will not tolerate the thought of Anne in jeopardy. What if this man decides to kill you, Davis? And my daughter is with you? What about that? Have you thought about that?"

"That's nonsense, Father," Anne laughed. "If you don't like a man's line of work—well, that's one thing. But to conjure the image of an attack on me because of what John does, well, that's nonsense."

"It could happen," Simmons said, mostly to himself.

"I'd never endanger your daughter, Mr. Simmons. You know that."

"I didn't raise my daughter to expose her to killers, thugs, and thieves. Even if you only talk about it with her, you'd be changing her life, her perspective—you'd bring the dirt of the streets into her mind. If her mother were alive today she'd tell you the same thing, John. Anne has a brilliant education, she moves in a very high level of society, and she has obligations to her status in life."

Anne Simmons spoke clearly and deliberately: "Father, I want you to realize that I love John and whatever he does in life is decent and I want to share that life."

"And I suppose all my grandchildren," Simmons said with a growl, "will grow up to be flatfoots, twirling night sticks, stealing apples, and whistling 'Sweet Rosie O'Grady'!" He stood up and walked forward so that he was close to Davis, leaning down. "Young man, if *anything* unpleasant *ever* happens to my daughter because of you—"

"Yes?"

"Well, you can guess your future."

Davis stood up quickly, clenching his fists but holding them stiff at his sides. "I won't be threatened."

Simmons turned abruptly, walking away. With his back to Davis he said, "You're not being threatened. You're merely unwanted."

"I want him, Father," Anne said. She stood up, taking Davis' hand. "Let's get some dinner."

Davis nodded, and began to lead her from the huge parlor, into the reception hall of the mansion.

"I thought you were having dinner here, the both of you," Simmons called after them in a startled voice.

Neither replied.

"What time will you be home, Anne?"

She did not respond.

Simmons watched them leave through the ornate stained-glass doors of the front hall. "Goddamned cop," he said with a grunt as he sat down to finish his brandy.

They stared at the ceiling of the small bedroom as the streetlight played through the lace curtain covering the open window, the curtain dancing in the breeze, filtering the light and moving shadowy patterns across the ceiling. Davis propped his lean frame on an elbow and looked at Anne's naked body before him.

"What are you doing?"

"Admiring you." He ran his bony right hand around her full breasts, encircling them with fingers that squeezed lightly.

"You're going to get me excited again."

His hand lazily drifted down the length of her lithe body, probing.

"John, darling," she said in groans of pleasure, "I'm starting again—oh, God, I'm starting again." She reached out and drew him closer, pulling his long, lean frame over her like a blanket to engulf her.

Davis worked slowly, gently, losing himself inside of her, slowly pacing himself, easing into passion. "Anne— my lovely Anne."

"Oh, God," she panted beneath his moving body, "I love—the—jeopardy—you place—me in—"

Davis glanced for an instant to the window and saw a figure moving across the street, a shadow, really. In that moment his mind turned to another corner of thought. He stopped his downward motion and sighed. He slipped away from her.

"What is it?" Anne said, catching her breath.

"I'm sorry, darling. Guess I'm tired."

She snuggled close. "It's father, isn't it?"

"No," Davis snorted. "The old bear doesn't bother me. I expect his roaring."

"It's that killer then."

"Yes, the dirty pictures of his dead victims, those pathetic bodies shoved beneath beds. He's probably walking around out there somewhere, maybe down my own street. I'm giving him too much, I know, but for me he's evil and he takes great joy in his evil. Oh, I'm giving him too much."

"What will you do when you find him?" Her voice was low, the tone understanding and confident.

130

John Davis thought in silence for some time and then said, "I think I want to kill him."

Not until the third week of October, 1926, did John Davis get his first real clue as to the whereabouts of the Dark Strangler, a slim clue, if that at all. He had ordered circulars sent to all the pawnshops in San Francisco, reasoning that the killer might attempt to pawn the miserable trinkets he had stolen. The circular gave a brief description of the suspect. Davis had received a phone call from one Melvin Ankrim, a pawnbroker on Powell Street, telling him that he might have some information.

The detective stood in front of the old-fashioned iron grillwork that caged the shop owner. Ankrim stared back at him through thick glasses. His lips trembled as he held forth the stub of a pawn ticket. "I read your flyer, mister, and I think the man you're looking for is the man who pawned some old clothes two days ago." He held up a small brooch encrusted with rhinestones. "And this article of jewelry—not worth much. He said it was his aunt's who died and left it to him."

"What did he look like?"

"Like what you said in the flyer," shrugged Ankrim. "Short, stocky, thin hair, kind of light brown hair. A strange customer, I tell you. He gave me the clothes off his back, the young man, and swaps me for an old blue suit. Even changed shoes. With the brooch, he went away with ten dollars."

Davis reached into his coat pocket and withdrew a paper listing the items stolen from the homes of the five known murder victims. His eyes searched hungrily down

131

the list and halted under the name of Mrs. Beth Coolie, the last victim in Oakland, reading aloud: "Small brooch, onyx center, rhinestones encircling."

"Is that onyx?"

"That's onyx, mister—not worth much—it's quartz, just quartz, a gemstone, yes, but quartz nevertheless. The man tells me it's from his aunt in Portland, fine, I don't argue."

"Where?"

"Where what?"

"The aunt, you said Portland."

Ankrim nodded. "Yes, an aunt in Portland dies, he says, so I—"

"Let me take a look at that bundle of clothes."

The pawnbroker pushed the bundle through the cage opening. "I went through everything," he added. "Nothing in the pockets, except a train timetable." He opened a drawer behind the counter and handed the timetable to Davis.

"The train schedule between here and Portland," Davis said.

"And Seattle."

"No, it's Portland all right. Did you notice anything he took from his pockets when he changed?"

Ankrim shrugged. "I should notice such things when the fella is changing in the washroom? I don't pry. He took a little book with a black cover out of his coat pocket and put it into the suit coat I swapped. That's all I saw, mister."

"I have to have the brooch."

"Why is that?"

"Hand it over."

Ankrim handed over the brooch. "Why is that again?"

"It's stolen property. It's got to be returned."

"This is from one of the unfortunate ladies who got killed?"

"It appears so."

The pawnbroker held up the palms of his hands. "Such items are not for me, poor women. So I'm out ten dollars and some old clothes."

"And shoes."

"Ah, the shoes were cardboard. I want nothing to do with such a fellow, mister, believe me. Nothing. So tell me, does this fella go to Portland?"

"Yes," Davis said slowly, his mind churning with anticipation. "I think he does.

NINE

Nelson squeezed through a small hole in the lumber-yard fence, feeling ecstatic, a sensation almost equal to other times he then vividly remembered when he had escaped from prisons and jails. He remembered how he had sneaked as a boy into the attic of his aunt's decrepit boarding house to sit in the dark and the dust reading those first passages in the Bible by moonlight through a cracked window and how the discoveries caused his blood to run hot, his muscles to twitch in anticipation of the illicit. God, he loved the loneliness of the night, and if there was terror in the night it belonged to him. He wielded it as a club and that power sent shivers of delight through him, he thought, making him stronger and stronger.

He inhaled the pleasant smell of the fresh-cut lumber and thought: I will do this thing and then go to Portland. Gloria is in Portland, the record I took from the hospital in San Francisco told me all I needed to know. Nice how they keep such accurate records, that wonderful line: "Patient relocated to Portland, Oregon." I will "relocate" to Portland, Oregon, and Gloria. I will go tonight, on the late flyer. But first I must destroy Mr. Garfield and his brutal kindness, Mr. Garfield the war hero and his veteran's pin. How Nelson hated the man—stuck-up bastard with his lumberyard authority, his seniority, his place in life. Mr. Garfield was going to go to jail, Nelson thought, and almost laughed aloud. Let him wear his veteran's pin in jail, huh? Let him order prisoners around, sure. They'll carve that big body into little pieces. I've seen them carve on men in prison. Yes I have, Mr. Garfield. They'll tell you when *you* can work, foreman. And when you can beg to die behind those walls.

Nelson crept forward to the main shack where the big saw was kept. Using a screwdriver he easily broke the door lock and stepped inside. He passed the huge saw, running his hand lovingly over it. He walked to the wall where heavy equipment was hung from hooks and took a chisel and hammer. Then he stepped into the dressing area in the back of the shop, going to the locker where the foreman kept his work clothes. With a single stroke Nelson smashed the hammer down upon the chisel, which he had placed against the padlock of the locker and broke the lock. He jerked the locker open and withdrew Garfield's

136

jacket with the veteran's pin affixed to it. Holding this over his arm, a great smile spreading over his apple cheeks, he stepped back into the main shop. He walked to a huge box containing sawdust and wood waste. He lit a match, holding it high as he looked about the shop for a minute, uttering, "You're an arsonist, Mr. Garfield!" He dropped the match into the box, watched for a second to see the woodchips and sawdust ignite and then ran from the shop, throwing Garfield's jacket far out into the yard near the front gate.

Good, he commended himself, the jacket will not burn there and they will find it. And they will make up reasons why you did it, Mr. Garfield, no matter what you say or what you do. And you will be guilty because someone always must be guilty. They will rebuild their lumberyard and you will be in prison, Mr. Garfield.

Behind him the shop burst into flames, roaring, crackling fire that fed on the virgin wood, tiny explosions increasing to larger ones as the stacks of waiting lumber ignited. Smoke billowed out into the yard. Nelson stood paralyzed with joy for some moments, transfixed by the sight of the roaring flames, then raced for the hole in the fence and slipped through. He looked back once to see the foreman's jacket lying in the dust near the main gate. He bowed slightly in that direction, hissing in a soft voice, "Isn't that nice, Mr. Garfield? Arson, Mr. Garfield! Hmmm?"

Davis had been in Portland for two days. He had gone to the city police department and alerted a Captain Richard Wranley at homicide that the strangler might

137

make an appearance in the city. He was met with an indifferent shrug and was told that "nobody like that comes to the good city of Portland."

On the night of October 20, 1926, Davis had gone back wearily to his small hotel room after eating a meatloaf dinner in a dreary little cafe. His stomach was upset, and he sprawled heavily on the hotel bed. He got up to close the window; the air was chilly and he regretted not bringing along his overcoat. Davis sat on the edge of the bed wondering if he should order a bicarbonate from room service. He switched on the light next to the bed and lay back, unfolding the evening newspaper he had picked up in the lobby an hour earlier. He began to read item by item from the front page working back in the first section. A brief item buried in the local news jumped from the page:

WOMAN FOUND DEAD IN ATTIC BY SON—MYS-
TERIOUS CIRCUMSTANCES
Mrs. Jane Beale, an attractive thirty-five-year-old di-
vorcee and owner of a boarding house at 415 Glanway
Ave. was found dead yesterday in the attic of her
home. Mrs. Beale's 15-year-old son Harvey discovered
his mother's body while looking for his kite. Police
refused to disclose the nature of Mrs. Beale's death.

Davis lunged for the phone, calling Captain Wranley. As he waited for the officer to come on the line the detective folded the newspaper page with the death item into a small square and slipped this into his breast shirt pocket.

"Wranley, homicide," a tired voice finally grumbled over the line.

"Captain, this is Detective Davis."

There was a long pause and then an audible sigh. "I thought we saw the last of you today, Davis. You've gone through our mug shots. You've worn out our homicide people. Don't you ever sleep?"

"There's an item in tonight's paper about a young woman, a landlady, found dead on Glan——"

"We've already taken care of that, Davis," Wranley said in a dull voice.

Davis sat stiff on the edge of the bed holding the receiver to his ear with one hand, the mouthpiece close to his lean face with the other. "I'd like to come down and look at the report."

"Why?"

"I think it has something to do with my man."

"Why?"

"The woman was a landlady—was she advertising rooms to let?"

"Yes, she was, but that has nothing to do with your strangler."

"I'd like to look at the report, Captain." Davis put some bark into his voice.

Wranley told him, "It's routine, Sergeant. We ruled it a suicide."

"How did the woman die?"

"A suicide, Davis. I'll have to hang up now—I'm late for my Moose Lodge meeting." He hung up.

Slowly, Davis placed the receiver back on the cradle

and eased the phone onto the bedstand. He slipped off his shoes and pressed back against the pillows of the bed. He lit a cigarette and puffed silently, then slipped the folded-up news item from his shirt pocket, reading it again and again. He extinguished his cigarette, then turned off the light and closed his eyes. Why, he asked himself, would a *pretty* thirty-five-year-old woman, a woman who owned property, a woman with a future, kill herself? "He's in Portland," Davis said as he lay in the dark. "It's his work."

Inside of another minute Davis was sitting up, putting on his shoes, straightening his tie, and slipping into his suitcoat, buttoning his vest hurriedly as he headed for the door. He thought about buying another overcoat in the morning; he would be in Portland for a while.

An assistant pathologist named Herkimer fiddled with an envelope that held the reports, standing beneath the glare of an overhead light in the basement of the morgue. Davis was losing his patience. The little man with the bald head and pince-nez slapped the envelope against the front of his morgue smock.

"I didn't get any instructions to let anyone look at the report on the Beale woman."

"Look, Mr. Herkimer," Davis said pleasantly, "I've already shown the sergeant upstairs my credentials. You've seen them, too. The sergeant called down here and asked you to cooperate. Now can I see those reports?"

"Captain Wranley's in charge—he's gotta say it's all right."

Davis thought for a minute and said, "Wranley went to a lodge meeting and can't be disturbed. Call his office and find out. If I weren't working hand-and-glove with

140

him, how would I know where he is from one minute to the next? Call his office."

Herkimer went to a wall phone, slipping the reports into the large pocket of his smock, palming them protectively. He removed the receiver with one hand and dialed awkwardly, staring at Davis and saying, "I dunno about you out-of-town cops coming up here and—" He turned to the phone. "Captain Wranley's office? Yes, this is Mel Herkimer over at the morgue. Where's Captain Wranley? Uh-huh, yeah, uh-huh. Just a minute." With an agile movement, the assistant pathologist covered the mouthpiece of the phone, managing all the while to hold the neck of the receiver between two fingers and keeping the other free hand cupped over the reports in his pocket. He peered at Davis suspiciously. "Okay, Mr. Out-of-Town Cop—what lodge did Captain Wranley attend tonight?"

"Moose," remembered Davis. Then he lied: "I belong to the same lodge in San Francisco. Brother Moose."

Herkimer turned back to the phone with a snort. "Okay, Larry. Just checking." He hung up and then walked with small steps to Davis and whipped out the reports, handing them over. "These are carbon copies. Keep them."

"Thanks, Mr. Herkimer." Davis headed for the stairs.

Upstairs, Davis found an empty desk in the duty sergeant's area and began to study the reports dealing with Mrs. Beale's death. He made small notes in pencil on the official pages, shaking his head. "God help us!" he finally said in an anguished voice.

The duty sergeant squealed about his swivel chair. "Something wrong?"

Davis slapped the report against the palm of his hand. "Everything is wrong."

It was close to nine o'clock in the morning when Captain Wranley breezed into the homicide offices of the Portland Police Department. A white-haired veteran, he wore an immaculate uniform, and walked with a military gait. He stopped abruptly at a row of chairs fronting his glass-partitioned office and glared down at the prone body of Detective John Davis, whose long form took up the length of five chairs. Davis had bundled his suitcoat beneath his head for a pillow and was sleeping with a hat covering his eyes.

"Do you mind?" boomed the captain.

Davis lifted the hat and stared upward and backward to see Wranley's angry face.

"We don't mind showing hospitality to visiting officers, Davis," said Wranley, "but you do your sleeping in a hotel, not outside my office."

Davis got up stiffly, brushing out his coat and slipping it on.

"Don't they teach you people manners down in Frisco?"

"I've got to see you right now. I've been here waiting all night."

"I'm busy. Make an appointment with the desk sergeant." Wranley marched to his office door, opened it with a flourish, and stepped inside. Davis moved quickly, stretching out his arm so that the captain could not slam the door in his face.

"Didn't you hear me?" Wranley said as he moved behind his desk.

Davis closed the door and withdrew the reports. "We don't have time for appointments, Captain." He held up the coroner's reports. "I've read these." He shook his head. "How in the hell could you term this woman's death a suicide?"

"I know you were down in the morgue last night, Davis." Wranley smoothed back his thick white hair and blinked large watery blue eyes. "Herkimer called me at home later. You've got a long nose, fellow. I'm going to be calling your superior—what's his name—Vertali—this morning. I've never heard of such conduct!"

Davis held out the reports and tapped them with a bony index finger. "This woman was found in a trunk in her attic by her son."

"That's right," nodded the captain.

"And she was strangled to death."

Wranley shrugged.

"A coat, some cheap jewelry and a few bucks are missing from the house."

"Right again. So?"

Davis stood by the desk, angry. He was also bone-sore tired and hungry and that deepened his anger. "So you tell me, Captain. How does a woman strangle herself and then stuff herself into a trunk? Or better yet—how does Mrs. Beale get into the trunk alive—if she was alive, and then strangle herself to death in a cramped space of five feet?"

Wranley gritted his teeth and then spat: "We *don't* have your strangler in this city, damnit!"

"That woman was murdered, Captain." Davis said this almost in a whisper.

"A suicide."

"If you label this a suicide then you're guilty of gross negligence, and you know it."

"Get out of here, Davis." Wranley pointed to the door.

Taking a few steps backward Davis said: "It'll be your head. He'll kill again and soon. I've seen the pattern in California. Christ man, you can't ignore this—"

"Out!" Wranley jumped up with this shout.

Davis went out the door.

Vertali was on the phone, calling long distance from San Francisco. Davis paced the floor as the officer rasped over the wire, "Can you hear me, Davis? Can you hear me at your end?"

"Yes, Captain, loud and clear."

"I got a call from Captain Wranley up there. He's madder than a nest of hornets. Says you're prying, meddling in his procedures up there. Are you doing that, Davis?"

"Captain—" Davis stopped pacing and leaned against the wall of his hotel room. He began to pick at a flap of loose wallpaper, horrid-looking wallpaper imprinted with roses against a dark green background. "They've got a dead one—strangled—it's the work of our man."

"No, no, no, no, no—Davis. Not *our* man—you must not put it that way. He doesn't belong to San Francisco, this killer, remember that."

"He started in San Francisco."

"How do you know that? Maybe he's been killing in Texas for years or something like that. Don't call him 'our man,' pu-leese!"

Davis took a deep breath. "The woman was strangled two days ago and Wranley called it a suicide. He's going to ignore it."

"Well—" Vertali was conciliatory. "You can't tell the man what to do. We don't run that department up there, you know."

"I'm not telling him what to do. I'm telling him to open his eyes." Davis peeled a long strip of the wallpaper downward. "The man is stupid. He can't see that there will be more like this up here. Captain, believe me, I'm convinced that the strangler is in Portland." There was no response, but Davis could hear that the line was still open. "Are you there, Captain Vertali? Are you there?"

"I'm here, Davis. You're right." His voice was soft, almost meek. "He's probably in Portland all right."

"You mean that," brightened the detective.

"Yes. They—ah, Captain Wranley told me that, ah— well, they've found another woman this morning."

"What?"

"An old woman named Lee, Cora Lee, I think he said. Now don't jump to conclusions."

"Where did she live? Was she a landlady?"

"Yeah," Vertali confessed. "An old woman, about sixty, she lived a few blocks from that other one up there, Mrs. Beale. Her handyman found her early this morning behind the furnace of her boarding house."

"Strangled?"

"Wranley didn't say."

"Of course he didn't say!" Davis turned his face from the mouthpiece. "Goddamn him!" he whispered.

"I heard that, Davis. You watch what you say—and

what you do up there. Remember, you're representing the police department of San Francisco."

"Yes, sir. Was she renting rooms?"

"She had a sign in her window, but that don't prove anything. Wranley did tell me that there was some money, some jewels, and some clothes taken. I guess that ties in."

"Did you tell Wranley that, Captain?"

Vertali's voice grew firm. "I don't tell officers in other departments a thing. That's how we keep good cooperation."

"Cooperation? They've got blinders on up here. They don't want to hear anything or see anything. As far as they're concerned, Portland has never seen a strangler."

"See—you're jumping to conclusions. Wranley wants to see you, talk to you, get the benefit of your thinking, Davis. So you're wrong. Go and see the man."

Davis tore a long, long strip of wallpaper down the wall. "Fine."

"And be polite. We might need a favor from these people some day."

"Yes," said Davis, "like information on how to determine unusual suicides."

"Now, no smart-aleck stuff. Just go and see Wranley, will you? You're a polite young man. You know how to conduct yourself. Report to me on Friday."

"Yes, sir."

The line went dead.

Davis hung up and stared for a second at the phone. "I'll send you the body-count."

He used the phone to hunt for Gloria. For several

146

hours now he had been calling schools, asking for her, describing her to bewildered principals. He remembered how she had said she wanted to teach young children some day. His calls were cut short; the elderly women in the rooming house where he was staying—he had rented a two-dollar room just that morning—pestered him to give up the phone in the first-floor hallway. They peeked around the stairway and clucked and shook their heads. "We have calls to make, too, young man," one said impatiently. Finally, having no luck in his search, Nelson slammed down the receiver, then strode into the dining room, and sat down heavily at the huge table. Mrs. Lindstrom, the landlady, opened the swinging kitchen door a crack to look at him. She checked the clock on the kitchen wall and shook her head.

"I'm sorry, Mr. Victor," she called to Nelson from the kitchen door. "Dinner won't be for another half hour."

"I'll wait," he grumbled, staring ahead vacantly.

"But it's four-thirty and we haven't even set the table yet, Mr. Victor."

"I'll wait," he repeated in a low angry voice.

"Suit yourself, young man."

He thought of the dead, two dead women in two days. Handsome profits, almost one hundred dollars, plus the jewelry. And he had had them both, like the others. The young one looked funny stuffed down into the trunk, a rag doll. The old one belonged where he had dumped her body. She was old and smelled bad; she belonged back there behind the furnace with the rubbish.

I should have moved to the other side of the city, he suddenly thought. It's not safe here. You're too close, only four blocks away. Why would the police come here? They would never come here. They would look on the other side of the city, wouldn't they? And who are they looking for? No one saw you enter those houses, not a soul. If they came here, I'd laugh at them. I have money. I got a job today at the electrical plant. I start next Monday. But I won't start any stupid job next Monday. Why should I? There's profit and ease and satisfaction in this. And it's holy, isn't it? They're only harlots. The soul of a whore is dead anyway.

Mrs. Lindstrom was at the table, snapping out a fresh tablecloth, stretching it out before him. She looked up at him as she leaned over the table, smoothing the cloth, and he gave her an idiotic smile, or rather a smirk. Nervously, she averted her eyes.

"Do I remind you of anyone?" he blurted to her.

She went on with her work, placing plates in front of the twenty chairs. "I can't say that you do," she replied, without looking at him.

"Take a good look. I'm sure it will come to you."

Mrs. Lindstrom looked, and then turned to scoop up silverware from a tray, placing the utensils carefully, slipping a napkin beneath each table setting. "No," she said flatly. "No one."

The smile on Nelson's face remained as if painted. "I've been told that I look like Jesus Christ," he said.

She gave him a startled look and then said, "The Lord was bearded."

"All right, just picture me with a beard then, Mrs. Lindstrom."

She refused to return his stare as she readied the table.

"Impossible. There was only one Lord and *no one* looked as He did." Then she stood still, placing her hands on her wide hips, and wagged a matronly finger at him. "That's close to blasphemy, Mr. Victor. Don't vex the Lord with your whims."

"God created man in His image, isn't that right?"

"That's what it says in the Bible." She began placing large platters in the center of the table.

"Well, he made me identical to His own Son." Nelson shrugged. "I don't know why, maybe it was *His* whim." Nelson realized in the incredulous stare of Mrs. Lindstrom that he had overreached himself. "I only say these things because of what I have been told. Perhaps I should forget what people say."

"Yes, you should."

"I am a deeply religious man of high morals...of great ethics, Mrs. Lindstrom."

She continued to stare, paralyzed in her position at the table.

"I'm *very* hungry, Mrs. Lindstrom." His voice at that moment was that of a small child. "I don't mean any harm."

A little smile came to her thin lips, presenting tiny wrinkles about the mouth, a sight that made Nelson detest her. "I know you're a good man at heart, Mr. Victor."

"Not a day passes," he said in a hushed voice, "that I don't read my Bible."

She rubbed her careworn hands in relief, giving him an even broader smile. "You're just hungry. Let me get you some soup. You can start before the others come in—it'll be all right, just as long as we don't make a habit of it. The

149

JAY ROBERT NASH

other guests would start making demands." She walked briskly to the kitchen.

Nelson gazed after her, fixing on the kitchen door swinging after her. "Whore," he said under his breath.

When the other guests came to the table they found that Nelson had spilled soup on his shirt front; he was carelessly shredding bread with a dirty hand and tumbling this into his mouth, wholly unconcerned with the disgust registered on the faces of his fellow roomers. He was equally oblivious to their sideways glances as they picked at peas and lamb chops. Nelson ate ravenously, mouthing huge chunks of potatoes. When pieces of meat fell from his fork he quickly snatched them up with a bare hand and popped them into his mouth, chewing rapidly and loudly.

Nelson focused finally upon the elderly, thin man sitting opposite him. "What are you looking at?"

"Nothing," the old man said, and he bent his head to his dinner.

"What do you do?" Nelson asked this with a mouth full of food that almost made the elderly woman sitting next to him swoon.

"Me?" The old man sheepishly peeked up.

"You."

"I'm a streetcar conductor, or I was. I'm retired now."

Nelson thought for a moment without blinking. He chewed and swallowed and said, "I hate streetcars!"

The old man pulled back in fright at the outburst.

"They're dangerous," Nelson screamed. "They can kill people! Some conductors murder people. Some conductors are not to be trusted with other men's wives!" He shifted his gaze to encircle the table. The guests sat

150

immobile and in silence, in awe of him. He rubbed his forehead slowly. "I'm sorry," he told the old man in a voice empty of apology. "I got hurt by a streetcar when I was a kid. I don't mean anything."

"It's all right," the old man said and went half-heartedly back to his food.

"What's your name?" Nelson plied.

"Morrison," answered the old man without looking up.

"I'm sorry, Mr. Morrison. You were probably a very good streetcar conductor."

The old man nodded. As he spooned his peas his mottled hand shook.

The roomers finished their meal with haste and left the dining room wordlessly. Nelson lingered, sipping the black coffee Mrs. Lindstrom had placed in front of him. Two women, both in their late sixties, Nelson guessed, remained in whispered conversation at the far end of the table. One looked in his direction. He nodded. She quickly looked back to her friend.

"Excuse me, ladies," Nelson said, suddenly full of charm. He gave them a smile when they turned toward him. "May I speak with you?" He did not wait for an answer, but stood up abruptly, taking his coffee to the end of the table, and sitting down next to them. They wore high-necked dresses, he noticed, and their flesh sagged under their chins in wattles. Their liquid eyes were wide and were full on him. "I'm sorry to bother you two nice ladies, but I was noticing that you both wore jewelry. That's a very attractive pin, ma'am," he told the one closest to him.

"Thank you," she said.

"And those earrings," he said to the other, "are a compliment to a noble face."

"Why, thank you, young man," smiled the other woman.

"You're such nice ladies," Nelson cooed. "You remind me of my saintly aunt."

"Oh, where does she live?" asked the woman next to him.

He dipped his head, looking down at his battered shoes and tucked his feet beneath his chair. "Poor woman, she died recently, in Seattle."

"I'm so sorry," the woman said with genuine concern.

"Terrible," agreed the second woman.

Nelson emitted a great sigh. Slowly, he reached into the pocket of his suitcoat, withdrawing a handful of women's jewelry—pins, rings, brooches, necklaces. Gently, almost lovingly, he placed the trinkets in a mound before the two women. "Yes, a grand good woman. These are her things, left to me." He leaned away from the mound of jewelry and sighed again. "But what does a fellow like me do with such baubles? I ask you?"

The first woman put her long, white hand to the mound and gently pushed it after Nelson. "But they are of sentimental value, young man. She wanted to be remembered by you, I'm sure. That's why she left them to you."

Holding up his hands as if to ward off the woman's pity, Nelson said, "It's too painful, these curios, these ornaments that once adorned that wonderful woman. I simply cannot keep them any longer. They're too painful

152

to keep. I want you ladies to have these mementoes." He watched carefully for their reaction.

"Oh, we couldn't do a thing like that," the first woman said, "could we, Julia?"

"Certainly not, Harriet."

"No, no, young man. You keep your aunt's things. Perhaps you will have a wife someday to give them to."

The second woman nodded emphatically at the thought.

Nelson stood up, pretending to be offended. "I'm entering the priesthood next spring," he told them. "You must take these things."

They looked up to him, perplexed.

"Please, or I will throw them away and I would hate to do that. Then there would be nothing left of my aunt, nothing at all. Please."

The second woman looked at the pile of jewelry and separated some of the pieces with a hesitant finger. "They *are* very nice, Harriet."

"Yes," said the first woman, holding up the pin that Nelson had snatched from Mrs. Beale's dress before he assaulted her corpse.

He smiled. "She was particularly fond of that pin."

The second woman unconsciously began to divide the jewelry into two piles, pushing one toward her friend. "I don't see any harm in it," she said. Then she added, "But we *must* pay you something."

"Yes, certainly," the first woman said. "We insist, don't we, Harriet?"

The first woman cupped the pile of jewelry, weighing

it, but continuing to look at Nelson. "We must pay you, young man." She looked down at the jewelry. "Ten dollars?" she quizzed, staring upward again, hopefully.

"Ten dollars each?" Nelson said, still smiling.

"Well—ah, of course," the second woman said as she nervously glanced at her friend.

"That's very generous of you kind ladies." He gloated to see them snap open small purses, fishing inside for the cash. "I will use the money for my divinity studies."

He leaned forward to collect the neatly folded bills, his head bobbing appreciation, gratitude. "God will remember you for aiding a disciple," he told them.

The women beamed. Warm satisfaction spread with wide smiles across their pale faces.

TEN

The city of Portland was in a panic. The strangler had struck again, killing another landlady, Mrs. Mabel Landing, whose body was discovered in the attic of her boarding house. The newspapers had spread the terror and the police department was deluged with incessant wild reports concerning the killer's whereabouts. Captain Wranley could no longer deny the existence of the strangler. The third victim was found bruised and cut, a knotted scarf tied so tightly about her throat that it had cut the flesh. Wranley had turned his entire division loose to search for the killer. He ordered squads of men to canvas every boarding house in Portland. He had circulars that gave the skimpy description of the killer sent to every boarding house. And, to complete his spiritual mortifica-

155

tion, Wranley had begged for help from Davis, assigning an entire squad to do the bidding of the out-of-town cop.

The furious flurry of police activity did little to appease an apprehensive public. Hours, then days became one as the police agonized. On the morning of the third day of the massive but fruitless manhunt, Davis met with Wranley, spreading out maps of the city of Portland, Davis crossing off sections of the city that had been combed by the police hunters.

Wranley was by then a wrecked man. His lips quivered and he rubbed his large pink hands constantly on his trousers. He had no answers for the press or his superiors. Worse, he had no ambition to lie for the public good.

"I want to take men back into the original neighborhood where he first struck," Davis said to Wrangley, standing at his side and circling an area on the map where the three murders had taken place, "this murder cluster here."

"Murder cluster," murmured Wranley. "How you say things—awful."

"I want to go back in there, Captain."

Wranley waved him on. "Go in, go in—anything."

A desk man came into the office, knocking, but not waiting for a response. "There's two old biddies outside to see you, Captain."

"Tell them to give their report to the duty sergeant."

"They got the circular on the strangler," the desk man said. "They say they know him."

Davis became ramrod stiff. "Show them in," he said, then looked to Wranley for approval; the Captain nodded wearily.

They came forward meekly, holding a copy of the

circular Wranley had ordered sent to the boarding houses. Small, timid, the elderly women also held out two handfuls of cheap jewelry.

"He told us these came from his dead aunt," Julia Bennings said.

"He told us that he ... that he was entering the priesthood," said Harriet Donnelly. She was close to tears.

Davis motioned the women to nearby chairs but they shook their heads. Their hands trembled as they talked.

"We paid him ten dollars for this," Julia said. She and her friend placed the jewelry on Wranley's desk. "Your circular said he was taking jewelry from his victims. And he looks like how you describe him in your circular. Poor, sad women."

Davis waved over the desk man standing near the door. "Check this jewelry against the list of those items stolen from the strangler's victims."

The desk man looked to Wranley. The Captain nodded and the desk man scooped up the trinkets and hurried out of the office.

"How did you come to meet this man?" Davis asked.

"Oh, where we live," Harriet said. "He was staying there."

"What?" Davis fished for a pencil. "Give me the address."

"He's gone," Julia informed him. "He left yesterday."

"What time?"

"In the early afternoon, before three o'clock."

Davis turned to Wranley, who was staring at the map. "That's when he usually murders—between noon and three PM." He turned the map so that it faced the women and leaned forward. "Show me where you live, ladies."

Julia Bennings studied the map for a moment, then pointed with a bony finger to the circle on the map Davis had drawn minutes before, an area showing three large Xs."

"My God!" Wranley said.

"He sold the jewelry," Davis said, "then left, walked a few blocks down the street, and murdered Mrs. Landing."

The desk man was back, this time ignoring Wranley and telling Davis, "The jewelry matches the stolen items, down to the last pin."

"He's still in there." Davis emphasized his point by tapping the map where the circle was drawn. "I know this arrogant bastard. I want to take every available man in there right now, Captain."

Wranley only stared at the map and shook his head. "My God!"

"Give me fifty men, seventy-five if you can spare them, right now." Davis made it sound like a command. "I want a house-to-house search!"

Wranley leaned back and looked up helplessly. "Take the whole goddamn force. It don't matter to me anymore. I'm finished. There'll be someone else at this desk next week. Bank on that."

Davis brushed past the women, who stared at Wranley, perplexed.

"I knew that suicide theory wouldn't hold up," Wranley groaned as Davis left the office, closing the door quietly.

They converged on the district from several points in

the city, scores of cops in large Packard touring cars, six, sometimes eight men to a car. In some instances officers stood on the running boards, so packed were the autos. They did not use their police gongs but sailed silently into the neighborhood, a car stopping at each block, the police running in pairs to every house. They swept by startled men and women, barging into living rooms, kitchens, dashing up stairs to throw open bedroom and closet doors. They crept into attics, slowly peering about through cobwebs and dust. They went into basements and storm cellars, pulling back large, slanting wooden doors at the backs of houses. Down the alleyways they scurried, and through garages. The sound of their running footfalls was everywhere, like rain beating on tin roofs. And their revolvers were drawn, held stiff at the waist, pointing downwards, as they ran.

Davis sat in one of the Packards parked in a small square. A cop named Bundy came forward, shoving a fat little man in front of him. "I caught this fella tryin' to get through a screen door at the back of a house down the block."

The man, Bundy holding him by the collar with a hamhock hand, breathed heavily, sweated and babbled, "I didn't do nothin'." His large dark eyes begged. "I sold the lady over there some toiletries. She says—'come back when the old man leaves.' So I go back. She's no beauty, but what the hell."

Bundy shook him like a terrier might shake a rat. "You were tryin' to unhook the latch of the screen door. I saw you now."

"He's bald, fat, and old. Nothing like our man," Davis

said in a low voice. "Book him anyway," Davis told Bundy.

"For what?" yelled the little fat man.

"Mashing."

A detective sitting at the wheel leaned close to Davis and whispered, "I don't think we've got an ordinance on mashing, Sergeant. Do they have one in Frisco?"

"What ordinance can you book him on?" Davis asked this officer Bundy.

"Well, now, he wasn't inside the house, mind you, so breaking and entering is out, I guess."

"Will you let go of my collar?" whined the fat man, "you're ruining my suit."

Bundy shook him a bit, as he turned the man about to look at him. "We got an ordinance that no person who is extremely ugly—hunchbacks and the like—can walk down a public street."

"Fine," Davis nodded.

"What?" yelled the fat man. "I ain't ugly! Fat, yeah, but I ain't ugly! You guys must be crazy!"

"Book him for being overweight," Davis said in a flat voice, but exchanging smiles with the detective at the wheel.

Bundy, chuckling, dragged the man away.

"There might be trouble about that pinch," the detective at the wheel said.

"Why take chances—" Davis began, when there was a sudden shout from the end of the block. A patrolman was waving his billy frantically. "Get down there," Davis ordered the driver. The Packard jerked forward and into a roar. Other police cars pulled up to the waving policeman.

"Middle of the block—" he shouted to Davis. "Heard a woman's scream!" He pointed to a three-story building with a large fence around it. "From that old gray house—it was—upstairs."

Leaping from the car, Davis led a half dozen officers to the building; they took the front stairs two at a time, crashing through a door, sliding to a stop in an empty foyer. They remained silently petrified, sweating, panting, for a moment. Then came another scream, faintly distant, high up. They bounded up the stairs, Davis' long legs stretching over three steps at a bound to the second floor, the patrolmen following with thudding feet. Davis turned, waved the men into silence and listened. There was a dull, heavy thump on the floor above. Doors of the second-floor corridor cracked open and the faces of elderly roomers peered anxiously into the corridor now clogged with cops.

"Third floor," Davis said and made his sprint upward, the winded policemen struggling behind him. When he reached the landing, Davis tried the first door, and found it locked. "It came from in here," he said to two cops with anxious faces. "Break it down." They stepped back, took a little running start, and crashed against the door with their burly shoulders. The wood at the lock splintered and the door fell inward on one hinge, the cops falling forward with it. Davis rushed forward almost on top of them, stepping on one man's leg.

The woman was sprawled on the floor. Her apron was tied around her throat and trickles of blood came from her nose and mouth. Her eyes were open in one final stare of fright. Her long dress had been pulled above her

161

waist. In a glance Davis knew what the stains were that coated her genitals. He took in the horrid scene before him inside a moment before he saw the back of a man swinging out of a window at the end of the long attic room. "He's there!" he shouted and ran forward, drawing his revolver. As he moved, he heard loud banging and ripping sounds, metal screws being wrenched from their places from the side of the building. Once at the window he leaned out and downward to see a man leap from the drainpipe torn loose from the side of the building and scurry around the corner. There was no time for a shot. Davis signaled to the officers at the front of the building. "Get to the back—he's going out the back way!" Davis watched the officers race forward into the yard, but he knew they were too late. The hollow feeling in his stomach told him that.

Nelson made his way through the backyards, running when he could, but mostly walking fast, cutting through block after block of the city. Several times he noticed after moving across a street and into another yard that the police were right behind him, cutting off the block he had just traversed, searching that and then moving to the next block after him. But he stayed ahead of them, moving fast on thick legs, fondling the jewelry and the short beaver-skin coat he had taken from the last house.

They are too close, Nelson thought. They *did* come into the neighborhood. They saw me, or only that one man saw me slide down the drainpipe. Was he the man from the train? His voice sounded like it—that deep voice shouting after me. Why was he in Portland? Did he know Gloria? I must forget about Gloria for now. Come back

162

for her, only her, none of these old smelly whores, no. Get out now, go south. It's cold here anyway, cold, and the police are getting too close.

Better to avoid the train depot, he reminded himself. The police will be there, too. Keep walking south, then cut west to Hillsboro. Catch a train from there. No, no, not a passenger train. Those men are on the passenger trains, remember. Catch a freight going south in the Hillsboro yard, a freight will take you nicely down to San Francisco. You need to relax, Earle. Sleep. I'll find work in San Francisco. Yes, there's plenty of work to do there. Maybe I'll go over and take a look at the lumberyard. Maybe they sent Garfield to prison for that bit of arson. Gee, I hope they sent Garfield to prison. Wouldn't that be wonderful?

He laughed out loud at the thought of it and then he whistled a nameless song, one he had made up as a child. I'd love to see him there, dressed in those prison rags and behind the bars. You could see him. At San Quentin. Why not, go as a visitor. No, that's no good. You got out of that place seven years ago, over the wall and into the water, remember? Yes, but think of it—to go and see Garfield as a visitor. They would never expect that. They don't ask questions of visitors. The guards are always looking the other way, inward. You'd be coming from the outside. They never look that way. I'd love it! We'll do that some time, go and visit Garfield in San Quentin. Big, dumb bastard, that's where he belongs. Arson is a serious crime. I wonder if the saw burned. He should have let me work that big saw. I'll go back to that Oakland yard some day when Garfield's in San Quentin. They'll let me work the big saw then. You bet they will.

Now he could hear the police gongs, dozens of them,

and he envisioned the big cars soaring through the streets behind him. He walked and hummed to himself, confidently, as the sound of the gongs faded in the distance. He neared the edge of the city and began to slow his pace, walking almost leisurely. It was sundown when he approached a man carrying large bundles. Nelson whistled his lonely song.

"That's a pretty tune," the man said.

"I like it," replied Nelson. He stopped. "Is this the way to Hillsboro? Am I going in the right direction?"

"Yes. Head down this street for four blocks, then cut over to the right, to the highway. Then follow the highway west."

"Thanks."

"Wait a minute, young man."

"Yeah?"

"What have you got there?" He pointed to the woman's beaver coat draped on Nelson's shoulder.

"Oh, just an old coat a lady gave me for doing odd jobs around her place."

"It don't look too old to me." There was suspicion in the man's voice.

Nelson suddenly grew tense, but he kept smiling widely. He slipped the coat into his hand and turned it inside out. "See—the lining is all torn and worn out. Old, like I said."

The man reached out and felt the coat. He narrowed his eyes, looking directly at Nelson. "Did you steal this coat, young man?"

"Hell, no," Nelson said, growing indignant. "I told you—a nice lady gave it to me for doing some chores."

164

"Okay," nodded the man. "How much do you want for it?"

"Huh?"

"My wife could use that coat. How much?"

Nelson looked, and examined the coat himself, turning it about, pushing his lower lip out as if in serious contemplation. "I dunno—twenty dollars."

The man put his hand into his pocket and brought forth a lone bill. "I'll give you a fiver for it."

Nelson tossed the coat to the man and snatched the bill. "You're right. Your wife will look better in it than the old lady who gave it to me."

"Nice to meet you," the man said as he tucked the coat under his free arm and then walked on.

Studying the five-dollar bill, Nelson brought forth more bills from his pockets, crushing the paper money together in a fist. Hell, I'll just catch me a passenger train in Hillsboro, he told himself. If those men are on the train, and they bother me, well, I'll kill them. I'll kill them all.

They gave up the search around midnight. Davis, exhausted, sat on the running board of a police car in the Portland PD motor pool, tiredly checking off those areas searched and researched by the squads of police who shuffled forward, equally exhausted, to report. The officers moved like ghosts in the dim high lights of the giant garage, their cars idling nearby, then dying. Davis nodded grimly at each dismal report.

A lone reporter who had been loitering against the garage wall moved over slowly to Davis and sat down on the running board next to him. He looked at the detective and then down to the city map with large red Xs through almost every precinct. "Looks bad, huh?" the reporter managed in a low voice.

Davis rubbed his face, feeling the thick stubble of his dark beard. He continued studying the map with red, sleepless eyes.

"I was over to that house," the reporter persisted. "It looks like that drainpipe was pried away from the wall with a chisel."

"He went down that drainpipe like an alpine climber repelling himself on a rope, leapfrogging downward, knowing he could pull the pipe away from the building without harm as long as he moved fast enough. He moved so fast...like a chimpanzee."

"Like a gorilla," amended the reporter.

Davis only shrugged at that.

"Do you think he's left the city, Mr. Davis?"

"Are you going to put that in the paper?"

The reporter thought for a moment. "No, if you don't want me to."

"I don't. Yes, I think he's a very smart man. He knows what escape is all about. It's a way of life for him, these murders, escapes. To stay in Portland now is death for him, he knows that. He's come as close to us as humanly possible, like an angry man who bumps up against you in a crowd to see if you'll complain about it."

"That sounds like the talk of an alienist." The reporter's voice had an edge of wonder in it. "Are you saying he's challenging the police of four cities?"

"Authority, maybe. And the cities don't matter."

"But why did he pick Portland?"

166

"I don't know. Perhaps he thought we were getting too close in the Bay area."

"This guy—this gorilla murderer—can go anywhere, can't he?"

Davis put the map down, throwing his hat on top of it and ran his fingers through thick, black hair. "Right now he's as free as you and me." He turned to the reporter. "Why did you call him the gorilla murderer, is that the new tag you're going to hang on him?"

"You called him a chimpanzee," said the reporter defensively. "It fits."

Standing up, Davis smoothed down the wrinkles in his vest. "Sure it fits—into a headline." His voice remained calm as he said, "Goddamnit, you'll scare the wits out of this city with that kind of label." He looked about the now-empty garage. "And if he reads that sort of thing it will feed his raw-meat appetite, don't you know that?"

"I'm no different than you," complained the reporter, his head down. He lit a cigarette without looking at Davis. "My editor's gotta have something, just like your superiors. So I give him a new headline, a new label, something." He paused, puffing rapidly and sending up billowing clouds of smoke. "That's all I've got."

"Gorilla murderer," Davis groaned. "Oh, yes—darkest Africa, the jungle, unseen perils." Then he mocked: "And there—lurking in the tree above you as you pass in search of orchids and butterflies—is the beast with glowing red eyes, all power and all death." He watched the reporter's head slowly tilt upward to look at him as he went on. "Waiting to pounce, this kill-crazy animal, an ancient ghost of our own shabby heritage."

167

With a snicker, the reporter stood up to face the detective. "Are you telling me you believe the theories of that crazy teacher in Tennessee that Darrow defended last year, that guy Scopes? That this killer is some sort of throw-back to our ape ancestors?"

"No," Davis said, as he rubbed the back of his neck, disgusted with himself for bothering to talk to the reporter. "I was making fun of your 'gorilla murderer' headline, tomorrow's headline." He pivoted on one heel and began to walk away slowly. Over his shoulder he said: "I guess people would rather believe the idea of the beast than a human doing this to other humans."

"Well, I'll tell you what I think, Mr. Davis," the reporter's voice echoed after him. When Davis continued to walk away without responding, the reporter raised his voice so that his words reverberated throughout the cavernous garage. "I think we *are* dealing with a beast, and not my great-grandfather—something out of another age!"

Something out of another age, Davis puzzled as he walked to the garage entrance. There is a beast in the Bible, isn't there, some sort of avenging beast?

"And this loony is it!" the reporter shouted after Davis. "Yeah! Gorilla murderer it is—tomorrow's headline!"

Davis remembered the Gideon Bible in his hotel room. He intended to read it from cover to cover, starting with his trip back to San Francisco.

ELEVEN

Gloria read the papers each morning while sipping her coffee in her boarding house apartment. She stared at the headline GORILLA MURDERER STRIKES AGAIN and shook her head. Four women killed in Portland within ten days, the story told her, all landladies, sexually assaulted. What tormented heathen mind could do such a thing, she thought? As she pondered these dark horrors the image of her long-ago Roger shimmered before her, an apparition now, but a one-time reality that was always vaguely present.

Roger was disturbed, she was convinced, but he was not a homicidal maniac, never a killer. Then she thought about the newspaper report of the army messenger who

169

had been murdered in Los Angeles. But she had never fully accepted that death as Roger's doing. No, she could never have given her heart to a murderer. It was coincidence, wild imaginings on her part, nothing more. How easy it was to conjure troubled Roger as a killer after all the terrible things he had done, all he had said. You cannot reason with an injured heart, Gloria told herself. Roger existed only in the long dead past.

She had a new life now, teaching music in a private girls' school. It was a comfortable life now; she had her music and the children. Men were not part of it, although she had dated a few times. She was fond of one man, a young teacher at the school, Joseph Raines, three years her junior. He was kind, but full of liberal ideas, and adventurous minds still frightened her. Men were capable of anything, she knew from her experiences with Roger; they could, no matter how charming, how wonderful they might appear, wound the heart terribly. Never, Gloria vowed, would a man again come close to murdering her heart.

She moved from the small breakfast table, going into the bedroom where she discarded her bathrobe, and began to dress. She heard a light knocking at the door and put on the robe over her slip and stockings, almost running to the door.

"Who's there?"

"Mrs. Nathan, dear."

Gloria opened the door to her landlady, a gentle, thin old woman.

"I'm sorry to disturb you, dear," Mrs. Nathan said,

"but the police were here and asked that we distribute these circulars to all our tenants."

"Why?"

"As a matter of fact, they didn't ask—they ordered me, Gloria." Her voice was hushed as she glanced nervously down the hall. "It's about that maniac in the papers, the one who has been attacking women." Mrs. Nathan handed the circular to Gloria. "They don't know who this loathesome creature is, but they've made up some sort of sketch. One of the officers chasing him caught a glimpse of him." She leaned forward and clasped Gloria's hand for a moment. "Keep your door double bolted, dear, just in case. Apparently this man will stop at nothing. He's killed four women here after strangling five in California." She clucked her tongue, then turned to go down the hall to the next apartment, saying almost to herself: "I do wish these murderers would stay in their own state!"

Gloria closed the door slowly, stepping back from it, started again for the bedroom, then stopped and double-bolted the door. She placed the circular on the kitchen table next to the newspapers without looking at it.

Once dressed, Gloria returned to the kitchen and picked up the newspaper, turning to an advertisement for a dress sale, which she had circled in pencil. She tore this from the paper and folded it, slipping it into her purse. Then she glanced down at the police circular Mrs. Nathan had given her, studying it for a moment, an apelike face staring up at her from the crudely drawn sketch. Gloria's earlier worries were suddenly gone. She sighed with great relief—the sketch looked nothing like Roger Wilson.

That could be anyone, she thought. It could be the movie star Fatty Arbuckle if the face were heavier. He raped a girl in San Francisco some years ago, didn't he? Or was he exonerated? He must have done something terrible; they don't show his movies anymore. No, Fatty always smiled. This man isn't smiling.

Gloria lit a cigarette, a newly developed vice, and sipped some cold coffee. She flipped the circular over and jotted in pencil a hurried grocery list, putting this into her purse. A glance at the clock on the kitchen wall told her that she had a half hour to get to her classes.

"I've compared and analyzed the thumbprint you sent on to the Clearing in Chicago, John," Oscar Heinrich told Davis. "The Chicago people think they've matched the print and sent on a criminal record to me, as you requested." Heinrich paused for dramatic effect, then held up the rap card high in the light of his laboratory. "The prints on this card, or the thumbprint, is a perfect match to the print I took from the page of the Bible."

Davis snatched the card, his eyes darting to the old prison photo in the left-hand corner. It was his man! Slowly, Davis read the name printed at the top of the card: "Earle Leonard Nelson, convicted of rape, 1917, sent to state reformatory, escaped six times, sent to San Quentin, 1918, escaped within a month." Davis snapped the card with a finger as he gave Heinrich a triumphant smile. "A real escape artist—I knew it. And the thumbprint matches?"

"Down to the last whorl."

"He's the man all right," Davis said as he clutched the

card in an iron grip, bending it slightly. He read greedily on, aloud: "Orphaned at early age, sent to live with aunt in Oxnard, Mrs. John Ward. Childhood injuries caused mental disturbances." Davis looked up at Heinrich, who was methodically scratching notes on the laboratory counter. "I wonder what that might mean, Professor Heinrich?"

Heinrich did not look up. "All manner of things. You'll eventually solve that mystery, too, I'm sure."

"Petty thief, violent with authorities, rape, reformatory, prison, escape after escape, and now...murder by the carload."

"What will you do now?" Heinrich seemed disinterested as he continued making his notes.

"Now I have an identity."

"He has many of those," Heinrich said, finally putting aside his notes and looking up.

"All I want is the original. Can I use your phone, Professor Heinrich?"

"The one on the wall over there, certainly."

Davis moved quickly to the phone and called Captain Vertali. "I'm going down to Oxnard, Captain," said the detective. "Nelson is our man. I'm over here with Professor Heinrich. No, not at all—I think we owe him a great deal. He agrees with Chicago. He's matched the thumbprint with the rap card and I've just seen the photo. Yes, it's an old photo, but it's him, the same fellow at the train, and the one who went down the drainpipe in Portland. Oxnard? His aunt lives there. I want to see her. I want to know more about this man. Yes, yes, I'll make detailed expense accounts. What? I didn't hear you. Uh-huh. I sure will." Davis turned from the phone to face Heinrich.

173

"Captain Vertali says he's thankful for your work. He wants to know if there's anything you'd like?"

A faint smile formed on Oscar Heinrich's lips. "Cases ...all the impossible cases he has."

Peering through the screen door on the back porch, Davis watched a tall woman with white hair in a bun approach. "Are you the young man from San Francisco who called?"

He dug into his coat pocket and produced his badge. "I'm Detective Sergeant John Davis, yes, ma'am. I rang the front bell but no one answered. You're Mrs. Ward?"

She unlatched the door and swung it open for him. "I am. You've come about Earle?" She walked through the kitchen. "The front bell is out of order. Won't you step into the parlor?"

They sat in the parlor on small stuffed chairs. The furniture was a quarter of a century old. Religious items and pictures were everywhere. There was a crucifix over the mantlepiece. On one side there was a tinttype of a young girl, another of a young boy on the other side.

"That's Earle you're looking at, Mr. Davis," Mrs. Ward said. "He was only ten then, just before the accident."

"What accident was that?" Davis remembered the "childhood injuries" statement on the rap card.

"Poor Earle," lamented Mrs. Ward but her voice possessed no empathy. "He was playing with his ball in the street out there and a trolley car struck him...he was caught in the cowcatcher and it dragged him along the cobblestones for fifty feet before the conductor managed

174

to stop the car." She made a circle with her thumb and index finger, placing her hand to her forehead. "There was a hole in his head the size of a half dollar. Terrible."

"He lived through that?"

Mrs. Ward glanced at the portrait of the small boy on the mantlepiece, an unsmiling child with a low forehead. "Perhaps it would have been better if he hadn't," she told Davis in a deliberate voice. "At first the doctors said he would die from the concussion. But he recovered, very slowly he recovered. He was never the same after that."

"How was he?"

"Mad."

"Insane?"

Mrs. Ward took a deep breath and let it out slowly with her words. "I didn't know it, of course, at the time. It was so gradual, so . . . planned."

Davis squinted at the remark. "Who planned his change, Mrs. Ward. I don't get that."

She arched her eyebrows as if surprised at Davis' lack of perception. "The Devil, of course, the real planner of the boy's mind. Would you like some tea, Mr. Davis?"

"No thanks. Go on. About the Devil."

"After the accident Earle became an evil thing. Only weeks after I found him playing with my own two children. I overheard his talk and it was filthy." There was a flash of anger in the old woman's eyes. "Smut spewed from his mouth as raw sewage might overflow a gutter opening. I forbade him to play with my children again. I gave him a Bible, thinking to save his soul." Mrs. Ward wagged her finger at the portrait on the mantlepiece. "'You read that Bible at least two hours out of the day,

175

young man,' I would tell him. He read the Bible constantly, but it did little good. The Devil knows the scripture."

"He's still reading it," Davis put in. "I've been trying to catch up to him." Davis slipped from his pocket the copy of the Gideon Bible he had taken from his Portland hotel room, resting it on his knee.

"It was all an act with him," said Mrs. Ward. "He never really read the good book, only pretended to. He mocked me with it, taking the book into attics where he would hide for hours...or into basements. That was another habit of his—to go into basements.

"He quit school early, seventh grade, I think, but he was intelligent; cunning is a better word for an unschooled person. I suppose he learned in the streets. He wasn't home much. I didn't really want any part of him, although I was his legal guardian. When he grew older, I told him he could see us during the daytime but I didn't want him sleeping under my roof with us."

"Why was that?" Davis asked.

"He frightened me. Everything he did when he was grown was frightening." She bowed her head for a moment. "Not human. He would not wait for meals to be served, but march into the kitchen, his head always held up high, as if to heaven, as if he were sneering at God, and once in the kitchen, he would help himself to anything I was cooking, whether the food was raw or not, eating with his hands. The children thought him amusing, but they knew no better. I knew better, Mr. Davis. He never fooled me. Some of the neighbors thought he was charming at times because of the crazy things he did. He could walk on his hands for great distances. We all watched him walk on his hands down the entire block once. And he could pick up a chair with his teeth and lift the chair over his head that way. I didn't think that was charming."

"What was his profession?"

Mrs. Ward snorted. "Never had one, never wanted one. Odd jobs, first he was a carpenter, then an electrician, then a plumber. The Devil only knew. He usually had money. When he didn't, I gave him money to sleep in hotel rooms, but he usually had money. He would disappear for weeks at a time. He would go away wearing a new suit and return in rags. He dressed strangely. One day he arrived dressed all in white. Another day he appeared dressed like a college boy, knickers and a sweater and a bow tie and those brown-and-white shoes—what are they called?"

"Two-toned oxford."

"Yes." She grimaced. He made a joke about that. 'Oxfords in Oxnard,' he said, and then laughed hysterically. He was never amusing to me."

"What else did he do with his earnings?"

"Waste it."

"On what?"

"Junk." Mrs. Ward scowled. "He would buy trashy jewelry from the five-and-dime—brooches, pins, and the like. He would give these cheap things to me. I told him I didn't want anything from him. He insisted. I would take these disgusting items and later throw them away. He found a gaudy brooch he had given me in the trash can and went into a rage. Well, I tell you, I ordered him from the house and told him never to return. I was frightened but firm. He listened to me, Earle did, he always listened to me." Mrs. Ward thought for a moment. "I think he was afraid of me, yes, perhaps he was, but I was glad to be rid of him. Some nights later I caught him standing outside my daughter's window, peeping through a crack in the shade to watch her...undress. Disgusting creature! Watching a fourteen-year-old girl undress!"

"What did you do about that, Mrs. Ward?"

"What was necessary. I grabbed a rug beater in the back yark and hit him again and again, driving him away."

"And he didn't strike you?"

Mrs. Ward puffed her lips and let out the air with noisy disdain. "Him? That coward. I had cut his face with the beater and the blood ran from his cheek and all he did was back away, giggling like a small child, back away into the darkness."

Davis pulled out the rap card on Earle Nelson, reading it silently for a moment. "His criminal record states that he was convicted of raping a girl in this town."

"The animal," grunted Mrs. Ward. "Yes, the neighbor's girl, just a poor child, only seventeen. A bit over-developed, but still a child. Earle was a plumber then, or claimed he was. The neighbor, Mr. Peters, had some trouble with his pipes and Earle went into the basement— I told you, Mr. Davis, that he had the habit of going into basements. Oh, that monster loved to go into basements." She swallowed slowly, then said: "He took the Peters girl into the basement with him." Mrs. Ward tilted her head to one side. She took a lace handkerchief from beneath her long sleeve and dabbed an eye. "That poor girl...he ravished her...this creature who had lived under my own

178

roof." She put away the handkerchief, then gave Davis a stony look that told the detective she was brave enough to finish the repugnant tale. "The girl's screams brought the father to the basement. Mr. Peters almost killed Earle. He had his hands around Earle's throat and Earle, mad as Rasputin, laughed and spat at the man, challenging him to kill him. Imagine? It would have been better for all if he had killed him, instead of having him arrested and taken to jail."

"Why do you say that, Mrs. Ward?"

She was suddenly smug with great knowledge. "Your visit is no mystery to me, Mr. Davis. I know why you're here."

"All right, go ahead."

"He's the man isn't he?" Mrs. Ward's eyes narrowed, her lips pursed. "The one who's been murdering helpless women up and down the coast. Isn't that right?"

"What makes you think that?"

"I read the papers, Mr. Davis. I'm in touch with the world. A man with a Bible, stealing cheap jewelry, ravishing...killing. That's Earle's handiwork. It's in the papers."

Davis reached out, showing the photo on the police rap card to Mrs. Ward. "Is that Earle?"

The woman nodded solemnly. "I *knew* it was him."

"Then why didn't you come forward, Mrs. Ward?"

"It was not my place. That's the duty of the police, your duty." She got up abruptly, her long dress rustling as she moved to the mantlepiece and withdrew the tintype of the young boy, handing this to Davis. "Take this last memory of that awful creature with you." Mrs. Ward returned to the mantlepiece and caressed the cross. "Only in this sign will you conquer." Turning around she presented a lean, hard face, unflinching and resolute. "The man you are seeking," she spat out derisively, "is the product of this Godless age—flappers and gin, fast cars and speakeasies, women half naked on our beaches and half naked on our theater stages, it corrupts all. Even Sister Aimee Semple McPherson has succumbed to a tawdry affair with an employee!"

"I can't arrest them all," Davis said dully as he stood up, pocketing the Gideon Bible and the rap card. He withdrew a police circular and put this on a small table. "If you see him, call me—I've written my phone number on the circular."

Mrs. Ward walked briskly to the table and picked up the circular. "This phone number is in San Francisco. That would be a long distance call. Besides, I haven't seen Earle since his arrest."

"You can call collect." Davis edged toward the front door.

Mrs. Ward walked to the front door, saying into space: "It was all foreseen, all predicted in the depravity of my sister and her husband." Turning the handle of the door, opening it for Davis, who stepped forward, the tall woman announced, "It was really the sins of my sister and her degenerate husband that brought this evil into the world."

"How's that, Mrs. Ward?"

"She died only a few weeks after giving birth to Earle. She was twenty. That was in 1897, just before God abandoned America for its sins. Her husband died six months later."

"Were they ill?"

"Diseased! Both of them perished of their own perversity." She sneered and said, "Do you know what syphilis is, Mr. Davis?"

"Yes, I do, Mrs. Ward." Davis stared out to the street, wanting to leave as soon as possible.

"That is what killed them both, their carnal perversity, and produced that syphilitic monster you are seeking. It drove them insane before death; Earle was born insane. The accident only brought out the insanity sooner.... He always had headaches, violent headaches. He will die like his parents!" She began to cry, tears coursing over her wrinkled, hollow cheeks. Her hand went to her bosom in a fist gently beating against her breast. "Perhaps, young man...there is sin in me, too,...or God would not have plagued me...with such agony."

Davis had no comfort for her; he had known religious fanatics as a child, neighbors and friends of his father's. They were a cold, self-serving, sanctimonious lot, he believed, who thrived on the fear of an avenging God. Their loving hands always gripped sticks. And in their last moments, their prayers were murmurs of terrible fear. No, Davis could not console this severe old woman. He stepped straight ahead without looking back at her, saying in a low voice: "Thank you...please call me if you have any information." He knew that he would again never see or talk with Mrs. John Ward.

It was mid-November before Earle Nelson killed again in San Francisco, strangling and raping Mrs. Edmund Williamson. Her body was found in the base-

ment of her boarding house; she clutched her ROOM FOR
RENT sign in a dead hand. Again there was jewelry and a
small amount of cash taken. Davis led squads of police in a
house-to-house search throughout the victim's neighborhood, but he knew it was now a routine that would yield
nothing. The killer, following his successful habits, had
already fled again to another city. North or south, that was
the nagging question in Davis' mind. He, along with the
entire coastal population, had to wait. He used his one
weapon, Nelson's true identity, releasing this to desperate
newspapers. The killer's old prison photo was published
repeatedly, but he had changed since the photo had been
taken. He was heavier, fuller-of-face now. Davis also
knew that Nelson's real name meant nothing to the killer.
He had all sorts of names, all sorts of identities, as he
anonymously mixed with an ever-mobile itinerant population, tens of thousands of men, jobless, veterans of the
Great War, farmers whose land had dried up, been
foreclosed, homeless men in rags silently drifting from
town to town, an expanding hobo society, impenetrable to
the police. Davis felt that Nelson walked secure and safe
in his own mind. He could go on forever, year after year,
decade after decade. There was little Davis could do, or
police science produce, that would bring about this man's
apprehension. Davis could only wait until Nelson's mistakes trapped him, until the idea of his own security
proved false—follow whatever trails opened and wait.

Four days following the murder of Mrs. Williamson,
Davis received a call from a Dr. Hussland at St. Mary's
Hospital. The physician's voice seemed unsure, the caller
embarrassed.

"Captain Vertali said I should talk to you, Sergeant,"

the doctor said in a hesitant voice. "We had a strange theft some weeks back."

Davis sat back in his chair, bored. "Go ahead."

"I don't know if it means anything, but your department has contacted all the hospitals, asking if anyone from the Portland area was ever treated for mental disorders."

Davis remembered asking Vertali to send out just such a request when he had been in Portland but that was before he knew Nelson was a native Californian. "So?"

"Let me explain. We don't treat mental disorders."

"You called to tell me that?" Davis was about to hang up.

"No. We're missing a patient's card in our file room. The lock on this room was broken some weeks back and the files tampered with."

"Did you report the break-in?" Davis said without interest.

"Yes, but—"

"Did you question staff members on duty?"

"We did that, too, but none of our people—"

"Look, Doctor Hussland, this is the homicide division. You want robbery."

"I'm not so sure. I think it's got something to do with that gorilla strangler you're looking for."

Davis straightened in his chair. "How's that?"

"Some years back I was an intern here and a woman, a patient, was attacked by her husband. I remember having to subdue the man. He seemed to be raving mad. His wife finally left him."

"There are a lot of husbands who attack their wives," Davis said, skeptical.

"Just a minute. We've checked our files with dupli-

cates in storage. Only one file is missing since the break-in.
It's the file of that woman. She moved to Portland to
escape her nut of a husband, a man I've seen since—on the
front pages of newspapers. The strangler, this fellow
Nelson, only he used the name of Roger Wilson then, he's
the man, I'm sure of it. I'd never forget that face. I didn't
place it until we started checking those files. When they
told me it was Mrs. Wilson's file that was missing, that face
came back to me, and I saw that same face in the newspaper a couple of days ago."

"What's the woman's name?" Davis asked excitedly.
"Her address in Portland?"

"Her name is Gloria Stearn Wilson. I don't know if she
uses the name Wilson anymore. According to our records
she entered St. Mary's using her maiden name. She's a
music teacher, the record says. But, I'm sorry, we have no
current address. I hope this helps."

"Doctor," Davis told the physician slowly, "you deserve a medal. In fact, the city of Portland has posted a
five-thousand-dollar reward for the apprehension of
Nelson—"

"I don't want any money," Dr. Hussland put in.

"I'd like to see that duplicate file," Davis said.

"All right. I'll have one of our orderlies deliver it to
you this afternoon, Sergeant."

"I want to thank you, Doctor."

"It's my hope that you get this fellow, that's all."

Davis hung up, pushing away from his desk. He
thought for a moment. "So that's why four women died in
Portland," he said to himself.

TWELVE

The bitter wind swept through Nelson's threadbare jacket and blew fresh snow up his billowing, baggy trousers. He wore no socks or underwear and that made his discomfort fierce. As he hurriedly walked the Seattle streets he warmed himself at sidewalk drums where knots of unemployed men had built meager fires. He spoke little to anyone; they were all strangers like himself and, in his dark fantasies, he imagined these ragged fellow-wanderers to be competitors in his gruesome trade, all takers-of-life for survival.

He studied their weathery faces, their gnarled hands, dull eyes, and saw them performing his own deeds, methodically slaying as he did, appeasing their lust as he did, rummaging through small jewelry boxes on bedroom bureaus as he did. In Nelson's mind, they all belonged to a profession, or rather a secret society, its members wordlessly, without compunction or compassion, dispatching the gem-hoarding crones of the land.

The thought edified and nurtured him. He was not alone in this fantasy; they were all in it with him, striking back at miserable fate, a human river engulfing the land, swallowing those witches who had cursed their lives. They survived on vengeance as did Nelson, he was convinced.

At one corner Nelson leaned over a barrel fire and studied the small circle of tattered men who silently stretched out their hands to the fire's warmth. A tall wizened man next to him peered into the fire, then, sensing the stocky man's gaze, looked sideways and down at Nelson who smiled back at him.

"You know me?" the tall, gaunt man said to him.

"I know all of you...and what you do," Nelson replied with respect.

The tall man turned back to the fire. "You don't know me. Never met you before."

"We all know each other," Nelson insisted. "We're all friends."

"To hell you say. I ain't got no friends...and don't want none."

Nelson moved a few inches closer to the man, saying slowly, "I'm your friend."

The other men around the barrel exchanged nervous glances. One of them said in a whisper, "Maybe a sneak for the cops." They withdrew from the fire, moving down the block.

The tall man did not budge. "I built this fire," he told Nelson in a determined voice. "Those are my scraps in there burning. I'm gonna stand here till it goes out. You can keep warm, too, but I don't want no nonsense."

"Oh, no nonsense from me, friend."

"I *told* you, fella, I ain't got no friends. Shaddup and leave me be."

Nelson thought for a moment, accepting the human scarecrow at his side as a brother in wrath, then blurted, "What do you do with the women?"

"Women?" the tall man said, dumbfounded.

"You know—what do you do with them after."

The tall man snorted. "There ain't no after with me. Women!" His voice went limp. "I ain't had no woman in three, maybe four years. I don't like thinking about that." He faced Nelson, angry. "Get outa here!"

Nelson became indignant. "It's a public street. I got a right—"

"Not at my fire! Beat it! I don't want no lunkheads askin' me about women—not at my age. Get out!"

Backing away a foot, Nelson glowered at the tall man. "Okay, mister. You won't tell me. I won't tell you."

"You ain't got nothin' to tell me. I don't think you're right in the head."

"Smarter than you, " snarled Nelson. "You're just trying to get my goat." He began to move away. "My head's all right, it's fine." He tapped the side of his head slowly. "I like everything I've got up here. You're just trying to get me to tell you so you won't have to tell me about your women." He shrugged. "Fine with me. I know that old dodge. Hah, it won't work. Keep your goddamned fire." Suddenly, when several feet distant from the tall man, Nelson dug for some currency and waved it violently. "I can buy all the fire I want!" He spun around, showing his back, and walked briskly down the block, swinging powerful arms high, whistling.

The tall man stood transfixed by the sight, mouth ajar, eyes bulging, watching Nelson intently until he turned the corner.

Moments after he had relieved himself, Nelson sat down on the floor next to the body of Mrs. Florence Almmons, a heavy-set woman in her sixties. She was lying on her back in the room she had shown him only minutes earlier. Nelson reached forward and plucked a stickpin from her dress. He held it toward the light, startled for a moment to realize that the pin was encrusted with small diamonds. "You're a rich one, huh?" he said with a glance at the corpse, unconcerned with the woman's thin shawl knotted around her throat, so that the flesh of her neck was bunched heavily beneath her chin. "How nice for me. Real money this time." He braced himself, placing his arms behind him, his large hands flat against the floor, and planted his powerful legs against the side of the body. Grunting, he drove the body with his legs across the floor and under the bed. He stood up and pulled the bedspread down low so that it hid the corpse. He was silent, listening for any movement in the large house. When he felt secure he moved quickly into the hallway, crossing into another room where the door was open—Mrs. Almmons' room; she had stopped there to get the key to the room she was renting. He looked up and down the hallway, then closed the door.

Inside the landlady's room, Nelson went to her large bureau. Expensive, he guessed, teakwood. The woman and her house looked and smelled rich. He began to open drawers, carefully moving aside articles of clothing.

Look for the handkerchiefs, he told himself. They always keep it there, under the handkerchiefs. Think they're so clever. Stupid whores. At one side of the bottom drawer he found a mound of neatly ironed handkerchiefs. Beneath this was the jewelry box, large, with several drawers lined with green velvet. He grinned at the treasures that met his wide eyes. He fondled the gems, scrutinizing rings and pins and brooches.

"They're real," he gasped. He began to pocket them carefully. "No costume junk. Real! Rubies, emeralds, sapphires, diamonds, I'm sure they're diamonds. Wait." He looked up to see his own shabby image reflected in the bureau mirror. He held up a ring, which appeared to have a large diamond, and placed this against the mirror, pressing hard and streaking downward with the stone against the mirror's surface. A narrow crevice in the mirror appeared in the wake of his downward slash. Nelson stared back at his own image, spliced by the scratched mirror, his grin severed. "You've been blessed with riches," he said happily. He moved to the closet and, after inspecting the hangered clothes, selected a short fur coat, turning this inside out, so that when he bundled it beneath his arm only the brown satin lining showed.

As he was about to leave the room, Nelson's eyes were caught by a copy of *Liberty Magazine* on a table near the door. Smiling up from its cover was a benign face. Nelson picked up the magazine, admiring the man who was dressed in full evening wear, a high silk top hat

189

adorning his white-haired head. "Otto Kahn," he read
from the cover caption, "millionaire playboy." He rolled
up the magazine and slid it into the bundled coat, then
stepped quietly from the room.

"I won them in a crap game," Nelson told the
pawnbroker in a flat voice.

The pawnbroker held the jewelry in an upturned
hand. Fixed in the squint of one eye was a jeweler's
eyeglass. "You can win such stones in a crap game?"

"I did."

The pawnbroker quickly examined each item of
jewelry, tenderly placing the pieces onto a blue felt mat.
Then he examined each item again as Nelson waited
patiently at the counter, resting his head on the palm of his
hand and staring vacantly at the man inside the cage. The
pawnbroker finally looked up. He removed the eyeglass.
There was a look of anticipation on his face. "So what do
you expect for these?"

"I know what they're worth, old man, so don't try to
Jew me."

"Are you a Jew?" asked the pawnbroker with a trace
of anger.

"No."

"Then how can I 'Jew' you?"

"Just give me the fair price. Right now, or I'll go
somewhere and get a fair price."

The pawnbroker ran a thin hand briefly over the
dozen pieces of jewelry. The fingers of his other hand
tapped nervously on the counter. He took a long time to
say, "Four thousand."

"They're worth ten thousand, aren't they?" Nelson did not move from his lazy position.

"Go somewhere else and get ten," the pawnbroker said defiantly. He began to take the gems from the blue felt pad, sliding them slowly toward Nelson.

With a yawn, Nelson said, "I could probably get twenty somewhere else."

"Ridiculous," said the pawnbroker.

"But I don't have the time. I got a sick mother to take care of. I need the money for the goddamned doctors and the hospital."

"Mister, with four thousand you can buy the hospital."

"Go get it then," Nelson ordered him.

The pawnbroker reached beneath the counter, and brought forth a large ledger, opening this with a flourish. "I must write you a check for that sum."

Nelson straightened, reaching through the small opening in the cage and closing the ledger. "Cash only, or I go somewhere else."

"You think I keep that kind of money here?"

Nelson placed both hands against the cage so that his fingers curled through the wire. "I ain't pawning this stuff, I'm selling it. Outright. Understand me?"

"That kind of money I keep in the bank, mister."

Nelson was matter-of-fact. "You got it in that safe behind you there. You people don't believe in banks, I know."

The bell on the front door of the shop rang, and another customer walked inside, examining the tables of luggage. The pawnbroker paused, looking toward the front of his shop. He rubbed a balding head nervously,

191

then shouted to the customer, "I'm sorry, we're closed!"

"I wanna get one of these valises."

"We're closed."

"Then why the hell is your door open?"

"It's after five. We're closed. Thank you."

The man pulled the brim of his fedora downward, peeved. "For what? I didn't buy a thing." He marched to the door, opened it, and shouted, "Whyncha lock your door, then?" He slammed outside.

"How about it?" Nelson was calm, his eyes on the safe.

The pawnbroker moved sideways, his hand dropping to the handle on the cage door. He tugged at it to make sure it was locked.

"C'mon, c'mon," Nelson reassured him, "I'm not going to rob you."

Without responding, the pawnbroker took the jewels on the mat and squatted before the small safe against the cage wall. He fiddled with the combination, and, with his back blocking Nelson's view, swung open the safe door, withdrew the cash, and then placed the jewels inside, and closed the safe.

Bundles of money were placed in a neat row on the counter. The pawnbroker deftly removed the rubber bands encircling each bundle, and methodically counted aloud the small bills. As he finished counting each bundle, the pawnbroker again put the rubber band about the bundle, and shoved it through the cage opening to Nelson, who slipped the bundles into his coat pocket. When the pawnbroker finished, he watched Nelson pocket the last bundle of bills and said, "You ain't gonna count it, mister?"

"Why should I? You counted it all—I watched you good."

"You should count it," the pawnbroker said. He appeared tense and placed his hands on the counter, both balled into fists.

"It's here. *You* don't *ever* want to see me again. You made sure it's all there, all four thousand."

"I gotta have a receipt," the pawnbroker said lamely.

With a snort, Nelson moved away from the cage, heading for the door. "You got the jewelry. You don't need a receipt." He stopped in front of a rack of men's suits, running his hand through them, checking the sizes. The pawnbroker watched in silence as Nelson removed a suit from the rack. He said nothing when Nelson picked out a shirt, tie, socks, and underwear, and also scooped up a pair of shoes. At the door, Nelson threw the woman's coat he had been carrying onto a table. "I'm taking these things."

"Go ahead," the pawnbroker said timidly.

"I'm leaving this coat in payment."

"Sure," mumbled the pawnbroker.

Nelson put the copy of *Liberty Magazine* into the pocket of the suit he had taken. Before he went out the door, Nelson said, sneering, "I know you'll get twenty thousand for those jewels."

"A million," shrugged the pawnbroker.

As Nelson stepped into the raw wind outside the shop, he saw himself reflected in the window of the pawnshop, and felt elated at the sight of the money bulging his pockets. "What does a playboy do?" he asked his reflection and moved on with a laugh.

It was wonderful, grand, the way Nelson felt as he traveled south on the train, wearing his new clothes. His shoes were almost new, a size too large and squeaky when he walked, but the sound exhilarated him. He took a compartment and dined alone, ordering his meal from the porter. He tipped lavishly, crazily giving the porter a fifty-dollar tip before arriving in Portland. The porter brought him cigars and he puffed madly, biting on a cigar, and clouding the compartment, as he feverishly counted the money again and again. On the couch next to him, was the magazine with Otto Kahn's picture. Nelson repeatedly cocked his head in the manner of Kahn, and tried to imitate the man's smile.

A snowstorm swept along with the train, and when Nelson alighted at the Portland depot the snow swirled about him. He lifted his face to the flakes and enjoyed the melting snow fresh on his cheeks. He walked to a waiting cab.

At first he was confused and sat immobile when the driver asked his destination. Glancing anxiously out the cab window, he spotted a billboard advertising THE HOTEL EXCELSIOR, PORTLAND'S FINEST. He told the driver to go to the Excelsior.

Nelson had stayed in hotels before, but the grandeur of the Excelsior overwhelmed him as he entered the lobby and sheepishly approached the desk.

"May I help you, sir?" The clerk behind the desk, wearing a spotless black and gold uniform, displayed a haughty air.

"I want a room, the best," Nelson said.

"A single? A double? A suite? Which do you prefer, sir?"

194

"A suite? What's that? More than one room, right?"

The clerk nodded. "They begin at twenty-five dollars a night."

"What do they end at?"

"Well," the clerk said, drawing out the word, his tone rising upward to the effeminate, "our suite supreme is fifty dollars a night." He critically surveyed Nelson in his second-hand suit. "But perhaps that might be prohibitive, sir."

"You mean can I pay for it?" Nelson dug into his suitcoat pocket and withdrew a bundle of money, removing a rubberband. He carefully counted out some bills. "Two hundred dollars," he said, and shoved the bills toward the clerk.

The clerk nodded again, this time with a faint smile. "Four nights, the suite supreme, yes, sir." He hit the bell to summon a bellhop.

Nelson signed a register card as "Edward Fuller, salesman." He watched the clerk write something on the register card. "Let me see that," Nelson demanded, and turned the card around, reading the clerk's notation: "No luggage." He glared at the clerk and said: "My bags were lost on the train. I need some things."

"We'd be glad to provide you with any service you require, Mr. Fuller." The clerk turned away and filed the registration card.

Nelson put fifty dollars on the counter. "I want some things right away," he said.

With a patronizing smile, the clerk took the money and pocketed the bills. "Anything."

Nelson withdrew the copy of *Liberty Magazine*, showing the clerk the cover. "See this fellow's suit? I want

195

you to get me someone to make me a suit like this."

"A tuxedo? Yes, sir, we have a tailor we can send to your room. Of course, it will take a few days."

"I want it today, this kind of suit. I'll pay for it—double, triple. And that high hat, too. One of those. Get the guy up to my room right away."

The clerk only stared in silence at him.

Taking more money from his pocket, Nelson threw the bills at the startled clerk. "Right away, and I want some other clothes, too, and a nice bag to replace the one that got stolen."

"I thought you said your bags were lost, sir?" the clerk said.

"Stolen! Are you gonna get what I want?"

"Yes, sir." The clerk took the bills.

"Good." Nelson was satisfied for the moment; he had gotten his way. He looked sideways to take in the cigar stand, his glance traversing the contents of the glass case. "I want some good cigars—two, three boxes of them," he told the clerk, who nodded. "And some cigarettes... and candy, some candy without nuts in it." He stopped for a moment, delighted with his own orders, delighted with the clerk's now slavish obedience. "That reminds me—I'm hungry."

The clerk's nod had changed to a short bow. "There's a menu in your suite, sir. Room service will send up anything you order."

"You do it." Nelson suddenly hated the man for deviating from his orders. "You pick out the food—the best food you have. Send it up right away, understand?"

"But sir—" The clerk was apologetic, perplexed.

"Fish...fowl...meat? I'm sure you'd want to make your own selection."

An eager bellhop stood waiting at Nelson's side. Nelson kept his eyes glued to the clerk. "You pick it out, the best food you got. Give me...ten dollars worth of food."

"Ten dollars worth of food?"

"Make it fifteen," Nelson said, and turned to go with the bellhop. "Make it the best food you have." He moved off with the bellhop toward the elevator and shouted, "And have that guy come up and make that suit right away."

Another clerk moved down the counter to the man who had waited on Nelson, saying, "That bird doesn't sound right to me."

"He's eccentric, that's all," the head clerk replied, then peeked into his pocket to check the money Nelson had given him.

He had experienced nothing like it in his life. All day long Nelson was waited on. The tailor came and left with a fistful of money, promising the tuxedo, patent-leather shoes, top hat, and an evening coat by that night. Room service sent up two tables laden with steak, salmon, turkey, myriad dishes of vegetables and fruit, and Champagne. Bellhops swooped into his room carrying cigars, candy, even flowers, the latter a personal touch of the head clerk.

Nelson roamed the three-room suite, all in delicate Louis XVI decor, moving from window to window, parting the heavy drapes and peering down six floors to

JAY ROBERT NASH

the snowswept street. He sprawled fully dressed on the
bed, making marks on the white satin spread with his dirty
shoes. He sauntered into the large white-tiled bathroom
and whimsically spun the shower handles, letting the hot
water run until steam gushed from the room, never
intending to bathe. Minutes later, he was back on the
phone, calling the desk, talking to the head clerk. "I'm
trying to find a cousin who lives in Portland," he said. "She
teaches music in some school here. I don't know the name
of the school, but her name is Gloria Wilson." In that
second he remembered asking for Gloria under that name
before, his last time in Portland, and having no luck. She
wouldn't use the name Wilson, he reasoned, that was *my*
name and she ran away from *me.* "No, her name will be
Gloria Stearn. Yes, that's it. Gloria Stearn...Just make the
calls and find her for me, and don't tell anyone my
name....I want it to be a surprise."

He gloated over his own cleverness. It would be a
surprise for Gloria. He would greet her as a rich man. How
would she like that? She had escaped him once but she
would never escape the rich man he had become. No, he
would trap her finally, and have his way as he had with the
others.

A half hour after the exhausted tailor delivered
Nelson full evening wear, the purchaser, in childish glee,
dressed for the night. When completely clothed, Nelson
sauntered into the bathroom and washed his filthy hands.
He looked into the mirror to see a face smudged with the
food he had gorged. He washed by throwing cold water
on his face, then rubbed away the dirt with towels, which
he indifferently dropped on the floor. He combed his hair

198

flat to his head, parting it in the middle. Donning the silk top hat, he smiled back at his reflection, revealing jagged and blackened teeth.

Nelson went to the phone in the sitting room and called the head clerk, only to be told that the man had gone off duty. The head clerk, Nelson was told, would continue his search for "the cousin" tomorrow. Nelson slammed down the receiver. He sank into a chair, leaned an elbow on his knee, and rested his head on the out-stretched palm of his hand, the top hat perched at a crazy angle.

Now what are you going to do, he asked himself. You got all dressed up to see Gloria and that bastard at the desk goes home. You see, that's the way people are, no man-ners. Take the money, make the promises, leave. He made the habitual vow that gave him strength: If that man doesn't find Gloria tomorrow for me I'll kill him. It would be simple to kill a man like that; offer him money to meet me somewhere alone and kill him as he's counting the money.

The thought of the money brought Nelson to his feet. He walked quickly to the closet in the bedroom and pulled the bundles of bills from his second-hand suitcoat. He sat on the bed and counted the money slowly. Only four hundred dollars gone, plenty left. He looked about at the expensive suite. But I must not go so high as this for too long. A little while, a little fun, I deserve it. I have worked hard for it, taken all the risks.

He stuffed the money into the large, inside pockets of his new black overcoat. From the inside pocket of the old suitcoat he withdrew his Bible. He wedged the book into the large pocket with the money. I take no risks with the good book next to my heart, he reminded himself.

Nelson heard a noise and rushed into the sitting room. A black maid stood at the open door. "I came to turn down the bed," she informed him.

"Go ahead," he replied, not knowing what she meant, and passed her, going down the wide, brightly lit hallway.

The hotel lobby was busy, a throng of handsomely dressed people chattering as they moved about or sat in overstuffed chairs, sipping what appeared to be coffee from small cups. As he wended his way through the crowd, Nelson peered into a coffee cup a woman held, and noticed the liquid was clear.

"That's gin, isn't it?" he said accusingly, pointing to the cup.

The woman, unruffled, looked up at him, interrupting her conversation with a distinguished-looking man. "Of course it is."

"It's illegal," Nelson said.

"Of course it is." The woman laughed and ignored him.

"I had Champagne in my suite this afternoon," he told her, but she did not respond. "That was illegal, too. The hotel is illegal."

"Run along, that's a good gentleman," the woman's escort told Nelson in a soft voice.

Nelson began to walk toward the entrance, hearing the woman exclaim, "I'd say he had too much Champagne in his suite this afternoon."

Snow swirled in heavy gusts outside the revolving

door of the hotel. The doorman stepped up to Nelson as he watched the storm. "Cab, sir?"

"I have nowhere to go," Nelson told him. Mechanically, he took a large bill from his inside pocket, and placed it in the doorman's hand.

The doorman nodded and showed Nelson to a cab waiting at the curb. "Pink Slipper," the doorman told the driver, then turned to Nelson, who slowly got into the cab. "A hot club, sir. You'll enjoy it."

The jazz band was loud and tinny, muted coronets and saxophones wailing in Nelson's ears as he sat like a stone at a small table, sipping Champagne and gawking at the well-dressed revelers. The Pink Slipper was a terraced nightclub designed in a large circle; on each level small tables, each with a white tablecloth and lamp, were jammed together, and crushed against the tables were customers in evening wear, men and women, drunk-loud, attempting to yell above the sound of the blaring jazz.

"Liven up, bud," a man at the next table said to Nelson.

"Who are you?" Nelson looked at the rail-thin customer, who held up a large glass, drinking quickly. He wore a tuxedo and shirt with a winged collar. Nelson looked down to the streamer-laden floor to see the man's patent-leather shoes move rapidly up and down with the beat of the band. A woman all in blue sat next to the man, peeking at Nelson from beneath a cloche hat. She chewed sensuously on an olive she had plucked from her martini.

"Me?" The thin man exclaimed as he put down his

glass. "I'm Jack Gilbert, the movie star." He laughed raucously. He pointed in an exaggerated manner to his pencil-thin mustache. "Can't you tell from this, bud?" Leaning forth, he slapped the shoulder of the woman in blue. "Lois likes the movie stars, don't you, kiddo?"

"I don't go to movies," Nelson told him, and turned away to look at the dancers crowding the small dance platform next to the bandstand. "It's not real in the movies." He heard a dull crash and saw that the thin man had passed out on the table, his glass rolling to the floor and breaking. He watched with interest as the woman tugged a blue satin purse from beneath the man's head, picked up her martini, and carefully stepped around the broken glass to sit down at his table.

"What do you want?" he asked her.

She had to sit sideways at the table for lack of room and crossed her long legs so that her short dress, shingled at top and bottom, shot upwards to reveal healthy thighs. Nelson grew excited at the sight of her silk-stockinged legs and, especially, the deep U shape of the back of her powdery blue dress, which revealed an expanse of creamy flesh. "I don't want anything, buster," she said in a husky voice. Suddenly she drained her martini and held up the empty glass. "Except another drink."

"I got Champagne here," he told her and took the bottle from the holder, dripping, pouring the Champagne into her martini glass.

"It's all the same to me," she said. "I'm Lois."

"I'm Mr. Fuller."

"Mister—how come so formal, buster? Don't you have a first name?"

"Richard," he lied.

"Oh, like Barthelmess." She looked into space, her head swaying with the sound of the jazz. "I love that boy!" She drank some Champagne. "Did you see him in the *Tol'able David*?"

"What's that—a movie? I don't see movies. Those are actors, not real people. Life isn't like that."

"Life should be like the movies," Lois said dreamily, and held out her glass for more Champagne.

He poured again with a slight sneer. "Actors don't work—and the people who go to movies don't work."

"Hah!" She gulped down the drink. "I work, buster— you better believe it!"

"What do you do?"

She gave him a wink of a dark eye and laughed again, from deep in her throat. "I'm doing it, buster."

"You mean you work here?"

"I'm one of the hostesses," she said. "I'm here to make sure you're happy." Her arm reached forward; her hand rubbed his knee slowly as she puckered her blood-red lips. "Are you happy, Mr. Fuller?"

"You can get into a lot of trouble in these places." Nelson's voice was firm, his large jaw set and jutting.

Her hand went higher on his leg. "I love the trouble," Lois purred.

He pulled back slightly. "I think I'll go back to my hotel."

"What hotel is that, honey-bun?"

Nelson thought for a second, deciding. He stared downward at her legs. "Excelsior. It's a suite. The number is six-oh-four." He threw down a twenty-dollar bill. "Pay for this stuff, Lois." With her hand concealed by the long tablecloth, the woman for a moment reached high on Nelson's thigh and then placed her hand on his groin, a wide smile on her lips. He froze, then returned a weak smile before standing up and heading for the door.

"See you later, honey-bun," Lois said after him.

"Look at you—you look like a man with your hair cut short like that!" He slapped her again, striking her chin with the ball of his hand.

She moaned as she lay beneath his naked body, her own body bruised and welted from his repeated assaults. He slid forward on to her breasts, holding down her arms with his thick legs bent at the knees, his knees pinioning her.

"I said you could do anything," Lois said imploringly, "but not this hitting. You've got to stop hitting me! Please!"

He struck her again, hitting her nose in the eye socket, a closed fist striking her. "You danced for Herod, whore!" Nelson gritted.

"Oh, God, please!"

He began to slide forward toward her face, which she attempted to twist to one side. He chanted rapidly, "And when a convenient day was come, that Herod on his birthday made a supper to his lords, high captains, and chief estates of Galilee..." His words began to rush together in a wild mumble. "And when the daughter of the said Herodias came in, and danced, and pleased Herod and them that sat with him..." He forced himself against her.

"Please—I don't like it that way! Please!"

He ignored her, banging her head with both fists from the sides until she obeyed. In a moment he shrieked in pain and ecstacy: "Mark, six, twenty-one—twenty-two!" He slid to the side of the bed, pushing her from him in disgust. Nelson stared at her throat, but he cautioned himself. You are in the hotel, on the sixth floor. Difficult to escape. He watched smugly as the woman struggled to sit up. "Go on, get out, your dance is over, Salome."

Lois turned to look at him, a look of hate.

"Not like the movies much, is it?" His voice was light and airy. He stayed on the bed as she dressed, stumbling about in her beaten condition. He watched her, delighted at her weakness, her helplessness, as she struggled with her torn dress, and wobbly legged slipped her naked legs into pumps. She caught his stare and defiantly yanked a compact from her purse, quickly applying heavy make-up to her bruised cheeks. She snapped the compact shut and spat, "It's men like you, degenerates like you, who bring all the hate into the world!"

He jumped from the bed and ran to her, lifting her from the chair by her short black hair. He marched her into the sitting room of the suite, holding on to her hair.

"Let go, you bastard!"

He laughed and freed her. She snatched up her coat and hat and, without looking at him, said, "I want to be paid."

"Money?" He raised his voice quizzically, childishly.

She faced him squarely as he stood before her, naked. "You're gonna pay me plenty for what you did, buster."

"Going to the police?" He grinned.

"Pay me!"

Nelson shrugged and leaned over a chair to pick up his overcoat. He took out some bills. "How much for your dance, little Salome?"

Lois' head began to bob in anger; her lips quavered. "I don't want your money—you—you slime!"

Nelson shot out a powerful hand and held her by the jaw. "Open your mouth, whore!"

She clenched her teeth.

He began to squeeze her jaw. "I'll break your face," he promised.

Her mouth opened slowly and Nelson jammed the bills between her lips, forcing the cash into her mouth with two fingers. He spun her about, shoving her to the door, opened it, and pushed her into the hallway. He closed the door slowly as she stood petrified in the hallway, a terrified look on her face, the money protruding from her lips.

"See you at the movies, Lois," he laughed.

THIRTEEN

"Are you Gloria Stearn Wilson?"

Gloria stopped, a bit breathless, near the top of the stairs, where a tall man leaned on the railing next to her apartment.

"Yes, but I don't use the name Wilson anymore, just Gloria Stearn."

"I don't blame you," said Detective John Davis. He showed her his credentials. "I'm from the San Francisco Police Department and I'd like to have a few words with you."

She nodded solemnly as she climbed the last few stairs to the second-floor landing. "It's about Roger, isn't it?"

207

"That's one of his names."

Gloria walked around Davis to the door of her apartment, unlocking it. "I saw the picture in today's newspaper." She held out the paper that she had been carrying. She was in that moment exhausted, and, as Davis took the newspaper her arm went limp to her side. She moved slowly to the small kitchen, Davis following her, and sat down. "I can make some coffee," she said.

"Maybe later," Davis said. "I want you to tell me—"

"I haven't seen or heard from Roger in five years," Gloria blurted. "I don't know why he's doing these awful things...I don't want to think about it...I get sick to my stomach thinking about it."

"If you don't mind," Davis said gently, going to the stove and picking up the coffee pot, "I'll make some coffee for us both."

Gloria sat immobile at the kitchen table. The bright sunlight poured through the nearby window and glared on her face, and she shielded her eyes with her hand. "I knew someone would come to see me about Roger. I knew it would happen."

Davis busied himself with the coffee, speaking softly. "I don't want to talk to you, Miss Stearn, about what Roger did to you. I know all that."

"How could you know all that?" She looked at him intently, the blood drained from her cheeks.

"I spoke with the hospital officials at St. Mary's. I know what he was then, and I know what Nelson is now. I'm not here for that."

"Then what good is it to talk to me?"

Davis put the pot on the stove and turned on the gas.

He sat down opposite Gloria. "I don't want you to worry, but you must understand something about this man."

"I won't think about him," she said, determined, brushing the newspaper with Nelson's photo on the front page onto the chair next to her.

"I'm afraid you'll have to think about him for a little while longer. You see—he's been in Portland on and off these last few months. Well...he's been looking for you."

"Me?" Gloria shrank back in her chair. "God, not again."

"He stole your hospital record to find out where you are."

"And he's killed all those women here while looking for me?" Her face contorted into a startled, painful expression. "Me?"

Davis took a deep breath. "He's been killing you over and over again, not only here in Portland, but all over California."

Gloria held up her hand, palm outward, as if to stop the thought.

"I don't know all the reasons why," Davis went on, "but it's you he's after and he won't stop until he's found you."

"What can I do?" She was frightened; her hands trembled.

"Keep your nerve. You're protected right now, and we'll go on protecting you until we have Nelson."

"That's not enough," she said in a quavering voice. "Last time he almost—"

"I know," Davis said and reached out to pat her hand. "But you're safe. We're going to watch you. We'll be close

209

by all the time. I've got three squads of police and detectives working with me, in three shifts, all around the clock."

Gloria pulled her hand away, realizing the meaning behind his words. "You *want* him to come after me, don't you?"

Davis turned his head toward the stove as the coffee began to perk.

"That's it. You're going to use me to trap him. Isn't that it?"

"You're the only fixed point in his travels," Davis finally said.

"A decoy, isn't that what you police call it? No, no!"

Davis got up and walked to her side. He patted her shoulder. "Stand up, please." Gloria stood up, and Davis led her gently to the window. "You see that man out there on the sidewalk?"

"Yes." Her eyes darted as she scanned the street, then focused on the large man pacing the sidewalk.

"There's another man in the back of the house. There's a man in the parlor downstairs, and another plainsclothesman in the kitchen. And I will be as close to you as your own skin."

She turned to face the detective, still full of fear. "You don't know him. Five men. He's not afraid of men...or God." She began to plead. "He doesn't think like us, any of us." Gloria broke away, walking quickly through the small living room and into the bedroom. Davis followed her, watching as she pulled a large valise from beneath the bed. He watched her hurriedly begin to clean out the drawers of a small bureau. "I've got to get away," she said, and began to sob. "I'll go to another city, anywhere, away."

Davis leaned on the bedroom door. "He'll only follow," the detective said tiredly. "Any city, and he'll follow. Time, distance, none of that matters with Nelson. He's driven by a host of devils." He walked to the bed, clasping the beveled wooden railing, desperate. "You can't escape that man any more than the poor women he's killed. But you can put an end to this by staying where you are, and let him come to us."

Gloria stopped packing for a moment, looking at Davis through great tears. "I can't do that, don't you understand? I'm not—I'm not a courageous person."

"It's not a matter of courage," the detective said, his voice strong, his hand slapping the bed rail. "It's common sense, Miss Stearn. Look, if you run, we can't protect you. If you stay put, we can surround you—and get him. That's common sense."

"To you." She went back to her packing.

"And to a lot of women who might be dead in the months to come."

"What do you mean?" Gloria pushed down the top of the valise and snapped it shut.

"If you don't allow him to get a little close to you, well, he'll go on strangling other women, that's all." Davis looked away when he said this.

"You're trying to make me feel guilty—responsible for what Roger—for what that man does!"

"Yes, you're right," Davis said with a sigh. "I'm sorry." He faced her, gripping the bed rail, and now he was pleading. "We've been after this man for months. You're

our only chance, our only real opportunity to apprehend
Nelson. He operates alone, so no confederate can turn him
in. He won't surrender because he does not feel guilty, and
catching him by accident, by luck—that could take
years...and God knows how many more lives."

Gloria sank down on the bed next to the valise. She
bowed her head. Her lips began to move but Davis could
not hear her words.

"What's the matter?" he asked.

She paused and said softly, "I'm praying."

The limousine hummed at the curb, waiting for
Nelson, who emerged from the hotel in the early afternoon, stinking of cheap cologne. It was easier than bathing, he had reasoned, and had merely coated his body
with the cologne he had ordered sent to his suite. The
doorman stood far back from him as he opened the door
to the limousine that Nelson had rented for the day.
Nelson sat back comfortably in the deep-cushioned seat.

Sliding back the glass panel separating the driver's
section from the rear of the long auto, the chauffeur
tapped the bill of his cap in a friendly salute to his patron
and politely asked, "And what is your destination, sir?"

Nelson unfolded his cupped hand to reveal a sheet
from a hotel memo pad. On it the head clerk had written:
"Gloria Stearn, music teacher, Aspinal School for Girls."
Nelson read aloud the address the clerk had jotted down.
He had given the snobbish clerk another fifty-dollar bill
for the information, but it was worth it, well worth it, he
felt.

The chauffeur put the car in gear and it soared off

down the street. Nelson adjusted his bow tie, pushed aside the flaps of his overcoat, and brushed off his tuxedo. He removed his top hat and placed it next to him on the seat. His own image, which he viewed with pride in the large panel mirror on the back of the driver's seat, and the surging movement of the huge auto gave Nelson a sense of power he had never before experienced. He was beyond men and laws now. The big Buick Special limousine sailed down the street, passing horse-drawn wagons, buggies, and small cars, mostly Model Ts, little black boxes on wheels that chugged and rattled and quaked. Nelson took it all in and beamed at his own new opulence.

He lurched forward and slid the glass panel back. "Go faster," he instructed the driver.

"I'm going twenty now, sir. That's the limit."

"Won't it go faster?"

"Why, yes," the driver informed him, "she'll do fifty-five miles an hour, but that's only for the open road."

"Go as fast as you can." Nelson shut the panel and sat back.

The limousine's speed increased slightly, sending the slush in the street flying onto pavements and showering angry passersby. Nelson doffed his top hat at them and waved in glee.

They moved northeast through the city, the pavements fading into dirt roads, which were frozen. Here Nelson viewed row after row of trim family cottages with displeasure, for inside him welled a hatred for those who lived in those small homes—families herded together for warmth and strength. "A gutless people," he whispered to himself. "Don't know what it means to be on your own in a world of—of expensive hotels and dirty whores!"

With a free hand, the driver inched the panel back. "Did you say something, sir?"

"Mind your own business!"

"Yes, sir." The driver closed the panel and sat stiff at the wheel.

Nelson stared angrily at the driver in his immaculate tan livery, neatly trimmed white hair escaping from beneath his chauffeur's cap. "Probably live in one of those goddamned houses yourself, you sneak," he said softly.

The driver suddenly slowed the limousine to a crawl. He slid back the panel. "That's the Aspinal School on the corner, sir."

"Stop here," ordered Nelson. As the car idled, Nelson thought about seeing Gloria, savoring the idea. "Okay, go around the block and drive slowly, but don't stop," Nelson finally told the driver. They drove by the school, a large old-fashioned limestone structure three stories high. Nelson saw two men sitting in a car parked in front of the school. He thought he recognized one of the men and turned to look out the small back window of the limousine.

That man! It was the same man as before—at the train, and at the last rooming house where he had escaped down the drainpipe. Yes, he was sure of it, that was the same man with the long face and nose and dark eyes, the one who followed. What would he be doing with Gloria? He doesn't know Gloria. How could he know her?

At the end of the block Nelson ordered the chauffeur to drive through an alleyway. As the Buick pulled down the alley, Nelson spotted two more men sitting inside a car parked behind the school. They glanced briefly in the

214

direction of the limousine, which went on to the next street.

Nelson began to feel panic. They were surrounding her, the police. He could not get near her. She knew, the bitch *knew* he was coming and surrounded herself with police. I'll kill her for that! I was going to kill her anyway, but now I have a better reason. What was the reason before? No, I wasn't going to kill Gloria. No, why should I? Gloria loves me. I'm the only one Gloria loves. You can't kill someone because she loves you, can you?

"Should I drive around the block again, sir?"

"Stop by the side of the road right here." I've got to think hard now, Nelson thought to himself. He studied the large school with open areas on three sides. The limousine was parked across the street from the side of the school. From this vantage point Nelson could barely see the back of the police car parked in front of the school. The police car at the rear was out of sight. His wide-set, bulging eyes scanned the side of the school, a blind spot to the waiting detectives. A row of windows, half above ground level, could be seen, and, at the side of the building, what appeared to be a walk-down staircase and a door. Nelson smiled. "Keep the motor running," he told the driver, and got out of the Buick, walking in such a way as not to be seen by the detectives parked in front of the school.

Hurriedly Nelson went up a walkway and scurried down the short stairs to a door marked JANITOR. He reached for the door handle and turned it. The door sprang open. "Nothing can stop a rich man," he snorted and eased into the underground area. He made his way through the shadows of the cavernous basement, going into the main

215

hallway only after being sure no one was around. He crept down the hall, listening to noises above. In one area he heard running feet, thudding sounds, and concluded that above him was a gym. He moved further and heard the sound of a sweet chorus. He walked quietly to the point directly beneath the sound of the singers. "What's that song?" he smiled, his head tilted, ear cocked. "I *know* that song, a spiritual, yes... 'Deep River,' yes." He hummed along with the singers for a minute then looked about desperately for a staircase.

The Portland detective smoked one cigarette after another. Davis sat quietly next to the driver, looking at the school. If I know this man, he thought, he'll come to the school. She's easier to find at the school. He'd have a helluva time trying to get her home address and her phone's not listed under her name, but under the landlord's. If he comes for her, it will be the school. He'll have a sweet surprise.

"I don't like stakeouts," the Portland detective said, "they bore the pants off me."

"Keeps your blood pressure down," Davis told him.

"I've never been on a stake-out where anything happened. Not once in my life. Just sat around like a frog on a lily pad. Want a cigarette?"

"No, are you watching the cross street up there?"

"I know every bare bush on that corner." The Portland detective lit another cigarette, using the butt of the one he had been smoking to light the next one. "I don't get this, Sergeant. If this nut only goes after landladies then it's for sure he won't go stalking some music teacher, don't you think?"

"He'll go after her," Davis said with confidence. "How about starting the car and getting that heater going again?"

Annoyed, the Portland detective fiddled with the ignition key. "Do we have to do that again? It gets hot in here, then we turn off the heater and I'm all sweated up, so I roll down the window and I get cold. That's how you get pneumonia, Sergeant, that's how you croak at an early age."

"Turn on the heat for a while."

The driver pushed the key in the ignition forward, complaining, "I wish to hell I was driving around in that limo."

"What limo?" Davis gave him a curious look.

"The one that went around the block about ten minutes ago."

"I didn't see any limo."

"You were watching the school. It sailed past and turned at the corner, going slow. Probably some rich bastard picking up his kid."

Davis fished out his watch from his pocket. It was 2 PM. "School's not out for another hour."

"Your kid can leave any time if you got the bucks, Sergeant. Maybe that's not the way it is in San Francisco, but that's how it is in Portland." The driver shrugged. "Maybe the kid's sick and going home early. Happens all the time."

Moving his eyes slowly across the face of the building

from left to right, Davis thought of the rich, particularly Joshua Simmons and Anne. He missed her. He thought of her bright face and clear, deep-set blue eyes, her full lips, her body. He remembered the smell of her body nestling next to his.

The driver went on carping, "The rich can go south in the winter. Get on the damned train and go south. They can follow the sun—they've got the money for the sun. Me? I'll probably die in Portland." He turned slightly to face Davis, who did not look at him. "I'll probably never even get south to San Francisco, you know that?"

Davis was too busy to answer the man; he watched the building and remembered Anne.

Nelson made his way down the first-floor hallway, pressing against the wall. At the far end of the long hallway he could see a man sitting in a chair. He was facing the street, his back to Nelson. He crept forward, hardly breathing, as he approached the music room. He stopped and peeked through the clear glass window of the door. Gloria! She stood directing a large group of girls, her arms crooked and wrists playing in the air, keeping time. With a quick rush, Nelson opened the door and stepped inside.

Gloria turned and froze as she looked at Nelson. The song in the mouths of the young girls died. Nelson approached quickly, smiling. He was at her side in an instant, saying, so that only she could hear, "It's me, beloved, your Roger—come for you."

"You're not anyone named Roger Wilson," Gloria said firmly, somehow finding valor. "You're a man named

Nelson, Earle Leonard Nelson. I know all about you."

He grabbed her arm. "You're coming with me, dear," he hissed.

She pulled away. "I'm not going anywhere."

"Oh, you've gotten stubborn," Nelson whispered. The hand in his coat pocket nudged her side. "So have I, Gloria, darling. There's a revolver in my pocket. Either you come with me, or I'll shoot six of these beautiful little girls."

Gloria's eyes quickly, anxiously scanned the faces of the children, all looking back at her in puzzlement. She knew she dared not hesitate. "I'll have to leave for a little while, children. You sit at the tables in the back and study the songs for our concert." She turned to him, no trace of fear on her face. "Well?"

He placed his free arm around her waist, pulling her toward the door. When he noticed the group of girls curiously watching him, he said to them with exaggerated sweetness, "Be good little girls and mind your teacher." The children began to walk to the tables at the back of the room. Nelson squeezed Gloria tight to him, looked up to see her coat hanging from a peg, and then pulled it down, handing it to her, keeping his other hand in his pocket, balled into a fist in an imitation of a hidden revolver. "You do as I say or I'll shoot you," he whispered in her ear, a smile still glued to his lips. "If you don't, I shoot you and then run back in here and shoot as many kids as I can. Understand?"

Gloria nodded, as if this fate had long been ordained, accepting as if in a ghastly dream the breathing terror at her side. Following her initial outburst, she had lost the will to resist. She had used it all in that one little act of defiance. She had told Detective Davis the truth, there was no courage in her; or, perhaps, it was sorrow that made her cower at Nelson's grotesque demands, a deep unrelenting melancholy for having loved a monster. She meekly went with him as he shoved her into the hallway and led her down the dark passage toward a side staircase. Once in the basement, Nelson held her firmly at the back of the neck and stiff-armed her down another hallway and to a side exit, out into the cold and up the stairs, where he suddenly held her by the waist again, smiling happily, guiding her toward a waiting limousine.

A large man in a brown suit, his thick overcoat flapping in the strong winter wind, came down the steps of the school two-at-a-time, and ran to Davis' car. Davis rolled down the window and the man leaned inside.

"I don't know if it means anything, Sergeant, but there was a limousine that came down the alley some ten minutes ago."

"Did it stop?"

"No."

"Aww, it was probably some rich guy picking up his kid," repeated Davis' driver.

"No, it wasn't," said the large man to Davis. "That limousine was rented. It had rental plates on it. I know this school, Sergeant. The only one who picks up her kid in a limo is old Mrs. Ludwest. She's the richest dame in the area, and she *never* shows up here until three-thirty."

Davis was already opening the car door. "Where did that limo go?"

The large man jerked his head in the direction of the street facing the side of the school. "It went up that way."

Davis was running up the front steps of the school, shouting to the man in the brown suit, "Check that janitor's door!" He raced through the front entrance. The startled guard stood up, kicking back his chair. "Were you facing the street?"

"Well, I—"

"I told you to face the hallway."

"It's dark down that hallway—it hurt my eyes."

"You dumb son of a bitch!"

"Say, I don't have to take that from you!"

Davis raced down the hallway, threw open the door to the music room and looked vainly for Gloria Stearn. "Children! Where's your teacher?" His outburst startled the giggling girls into silence. "Miss Stearn—someone tell me where's she's gone to."

A small girl with dark brown hair in bangs edged toward him. "She went with a man all dressed in black," the girl said timidly.

Davis knelt before the girl and brought forth a small photo. He spoke softly, "Did he look like this, honey?"

"That's him," the little girl said as she touched the photo lightly. She blushed and added, "He liked Miss Stearn."

"How could you tell?"

"He hugged her," the girl said in a tiny voice.

Davis went to the hallway. The detective in the brown suit was rushing up the stairs, the school's janitor in tow.

"I checked the janitor's entrance," the detective told Davis, panting. "Wide open. This jerk left the damned door open!"

"I told you to keep that door locked, didn't I?" Davis confronted the frightened little man, who cringed inside his baggy overalls. "Didn't I?"

"I only left it open for a few minutes, officer, honest. I had to get rid of the garbage from lunch. I had to take it out, you know. It smells awful bad in this kinda weather if you leave it inside too long, and it brings rodents. Honest, officer, it was only for a few minutes."

Davis slumped against the wall for a minute, his body drained of energy. "Sweet Christ, I promised that woman —I promised her."

"What's that, Sergeant?" The large man in the brown suit came forward.

"Check that limo—did you get the number?"

The large man gave him a determined smile. "I sure did."

"Good man, trace it, trace it right away."

Davis' driver came walking fast down the hallway toward him. "Went around the block, nothing. Got the other car going block by block, and I called in more cars— downtown is sending out ten more cars." He shook his head. "This fella's on the side of the angels, ain't he?"

Davis began walking toward the school entrance, the other detectives following. "They *were* angels once," Davis said, through gritted teeth, "before they fell!"

"You quotin' scripture, Sergeant?" the driver quizzed.

"I guess so," Davis said in a tired voice, not quite sure of his next move.

Gloria stood dumbly, as if in a trance, before the railing of the enormous dance floor. Nelson, grinning at her side and slightly behind her, anxiously watched the scores of dancers glide and bounce and skip over the floorboards. At the end of the long dancehall blared a band, its members dressed in tight-fitting tuxedoes.

It was night. Gloria could not remember how many hours she had spent in the back of the large car as it rolled through the streets of Portland before Nelson ordered the driver to stop in the downtown district, where he paid the man off and then forced her to begin walking. They had walked until she thought her ankles would break. Then Nelson spotted the two-story dance-hall sign glaring. He pushed Gloria into the place before him, humming, and grunting words she could not understand.

Dancers streamed past them, hopping to the "Black Bottom," then gyrating into the knock-kneed "Charleston," frantic bodies swaying, swinging, elbows flaring, legs kicking. The fleshy panorama of the dance hall was only a distant vision to Gloria; she considered herself dead. Nelson would kill her this night, like the other women, she was sure. Now he was toying with her in a bizarre cat-and-mouse game invented by his tortured mind.

"This isn't dancing," he finally said close to her ear.

"Why don't you get it over with?" she asked, resigned.

"Later," he promised. "I want you to have fun first." He shoved her forward onto the dance floor. Gloria moved woodenly backward as he pressed next to her, holding her about the waist with one arm, his other hand still in his coat pocket. Her eyes glazed with dread, she

223

barely moved her feet. Her arms dangled lifelessly at her sides.

"You're not dancing, my darling," Nelson said with mock endearment.

She looked down at his scuffed and cracked patent-leather shoes. "Neither are you. Look at your feet—you can't dance. You're stumbling."

"It's my own dance," he laughed. His features twisted into a mask of grotesque humor. "The dance of death, sweet Gloria."

Gloria decided that she preferred death instantly, death inside of this scene of flashing life. She would goad him into shooting her. Then there would be no more waiting, no more anxious nights. She would make an end to gloom and despair. She would force him to kill her now, in the middle of the dance floor. She would die but he would be caught. They would swarm in on him, trap him and take him away, and he would die, too, on the scaffold, for his hate and his murders.

Raising her hands to his chest, Gloria pushed away slightly. "You might as well do it now." She returned his seething stare. "You're an animal, without any virtue, thoroughly repulsive. Decay—that's what you are, as rotten a piece of life that ever walked the earth. You justify what you do with that Bible in your pocket."

"Trying to make me mad, huh?" He pulled her to him again.

"You smell," she said, "you stink of the dead, the smell of your own dead victims is on you—in you!"

"Insulting me will only make it worse for you later." He thought for a moment, scanning the crowds flying past

224

them. "You keep that up and I'll make it slow for you, Gloria...a *lot* of pain!"

"You don't frighten me anymore." Resolve was in her voice. "You can't frighten anyone who doesn't care.... You killed all that in me long ago."

Nelson's eyes darted about, a flash of panic streaked his face, his jaw muscles twitched. "You'll frighten!"

"You need a bath," Gloria told him and spat in his face.

He stopped dead still.

Gloria laughed loudly. "It looks good on you—they should all spit on you."

"Wipe it off," he growled, standing away from her.

She spat at him again, the spittle dashing against the front of his tuxedo and part of his open coat. Gloria laughed again, loudly.

Nelson moved his head rapidly back and forth as he nervously glanced at the dancers who began to stare at the scene.

A couple nearby stopped dancing, the man asking Gloria, "Anything wrong, miss?"

"Yes," she said in a cool voice. "My escort is a murderer! He's the man—"

Nelson jumped forward, grabbing her, and whisking her away, almost lifting her bodily from the dance floor. He smiled and laughed at the dumbfounded couple, telling them, "She's right—I've been murdering her feet all night!"

Gloria raised her voice, imploring those about her, "He's the killer! He's Nelson, the strangler!"

The dancers looked briefly at her, curious, without

alarm, as Nelson rammed his way from the dance floor, propelling Gloria before him, all the while shouting and laughing, "Aw, poor girl, that bootleg hootch has got her." He turned to one group that had stopped to gawk at them and snickered, "The lady's drunk and it's not even ten o'clock!" With his arm tight about her waist, holding her from behind, Nelson aimed for an exit and, when reaching the door, suddenly turned sideways and used his massive shoulder to ram the twin doors, which flew open into the alleyway. They stumbled down the alley, slipping on ice, brushing against the snow drifts as they went deeper into the dark alley.

"Get it over with," she begged Nelson in a tired voice.

"Oh no, little wife. Not here, not yet," he snarled. "First, you must perform your wifely duties." He was breathing hard as he forced her into a slippery trot. "Home—your home—my home—wife and husband— may we make—a family tonight—little wife—move into —a bungalow—sure—that's it—that's it!"

Gloria closed her eyes and let his powerful hands guide her. As they progressed into the dark alley, she could only feel that she was descending into hell.

Davis sat in the dark, miserable, thinking of his errors, damning himself. You've killed that girl, he said, you've consigned her to her own murder, as surely as if you were Nelson yourself. It was your own arrogance, your own conceited belief that you could control that man, predict his actions. He's too damned clever. You've been thinking of him as a criminal, a professional man, when all the while he's something else, like the beasts you found in the

Bible. He operates on instinct, on whim, and you played him as a man with patterns. He's a ghost, drifting over the land.

God, what tortures must that woman be going through? Davis envisioned finding Gloria Stearn's corpse, as he sat in the darkness, a single shaft of dim light filtering through the lace curtains covering the window. She would be strangled, a strip of cloth about her throat, knotted at the back of the neck, her genitals exposed, left like carrion as the others had been. It's your fault, mister detective, your responsibility, the death of this brave girl. Detective? Huh! You're no detective, just another dumb cop, groping in the shadows, counting the bodies. And think of it! They pay you for that; the taxpayers shell out money so that you can set women up for monsters like Nelson.

It's stupid to blame anyone now, he consoled himself with flabby self-assurance. There was the janitor, the cop facing the wrong way, all of it. You did what you could, so did the others. You traced the limousine, you found the driver at home, eating dinner. He told you what he could, and you followed up on that, too.

It was just like Nelson to get out of the car with the girl that way, throw money at the driver, and disappear down the street. And you can forget the hotel where the limo picked him up. He's too cunning to go back to the Excelsior. "Mr. Fuller" would never go back to his suite. He has money to go anywhere, take that girl anywhere. His Seattle killing delivered a motherlode, real jewels.

Davis got up from the chair in the small bedroom and moved to the window, feeling useless, and wondering why he had chosen to return alone to this room and wait.

There was nothing else to do, he reminded himself. Send out the night shift squads to search the city, also a useless gesture, and wait for the landlady to call you to the phone and a voice from headquarters to tell you that Gloria Stearn's body had been found.

Give it a chance, will you? No, you're not operating on police procedure now, hotshot. It's only a chance, a hunch, luck, all the elements of fiction you disbelieve. He'd never come here. How do you know? You just admitted you don't know the man at all, only what he is, or what he becomes.

A noise startled him, the sound of a door closing downstairs at the back of the building. It could be anybody, one of twenty boarders coming in late. Davis went to the open bedroom door, looking into the silent, dark sitting room of Gloria Stearn's apartment. He walked to the front door and listened. He heard footsteps on the stairs.

Davis pressed back into a small alcove behind the door, waiting and hoping. He was positive now that the footsteps belonged to more than one person. He unbuttoned his suitcoat and placed his hand around the revolver nestled in a shoulder holster tucked beneath his arm. Ever so slowly, as the footsteps approached, he eased the revolver out, holding it downward and toward the back of the door.

Then someone was on the second-floor landing, walking toward the door, pausing in front of it. Davis heard a man's voice demand, "Give me the key!" He pressed hard against the wall and took a deep breath.

A key went into the lock, turning first one way, then

the other, its user unfamiliar with its mechanism, Davis guessed. The lock suddenly sprang back with a click, thunder in the ears of the detective. The door opened inward slowly and the soft yellow glow of the hallway light filtered into the apartment. Through the crack of the door, Davis saw Gloria Stearn, her mouth bleeding, her eyes blank, sagging against the chest of Earle Leonard Nelson, who stood behind her, a wide smile on his face.

Nelson looked over Gloria's shoulder cautiously, craning his neck to look into the darkened apartment. He glanced up and down the hallway. Then he said, "We're home, dear." With that he gave Gloria a violent push that sent her flying into the apartment. She toppled to the floor where she sprawled in silence. Nelson surged forward confidently. He clutched the edge of the door and swung it shut.

Davis did not move. He heard Nelson take a step toward the prone woman in the darkness. The detective was trying desperately to remember how close the light switch was to the other side of the door.

"Don't pretend to be asleep, Gloria, dear," Nelson cooed. "It's time we got ready for the bedroom, sweetheart."

Davis heard him take another step forward and the sound of what he thought to be Nelson's coat dropping to the floor. He inched out of the alcove, pressing against the door, slipping behind Nelson, one hand holding the revolver in the direction of the killer, the other groping for the light switch.

When Nelson began to walk toward Gloria on the floor, Davis reached out and found the switch, thumbing it upward. As the overhead light came on, Nelson wheeled about, his eyes popping.

"You're under arrest," Davis told him, leveling the revolver at Nelson, aiming it at the man's heart. "Put your hands in the air!"

Gloria twisted her head to see the detective. She lifted herself by her arms to a sitting position and began to crawl away from Nelson, who had his back to her. "He'll kill you, Sergeant," she moaned. "He has a gun in his coat pocket."

"His coat's on the floor," Davis told her. "Get over by that window, Gloria, out of the way." Then he told Nelson, who stood smirking, his arms stiff at his sides, "I told you to put up your hands."

"I'm not afraid of you," Nelson replied softly. "I know who you are—the man at the train, aren't you?"

"That's right." Davis took one step forward, then pressed Nelson's coat with his foot, trying to locate a weapon.

"You can't hurt me," Nelson's voice diminished in volume, the tone going higher, becoming a child's voice. "You tried to hurt me before—I saw you lean out that window before."

"I'll shoot you," Davis warned, "unless you do exactly what I say."

"Don't kick my coat!" Nelson shrieked, a piercing outburst that startled the detective for a moment.

With his free hand, Davis slipped handcuffs from his pocket. "Walk toward me very slowly," he ordered Nelson.

Nelson took short steps forward, paused, then back-stepped rapidly, going toward the window where Gloria had positioned herself.

"I said get over here, Nelson, this way, toward me!"

"I know what you want here," Nelson said.

"This way!"

"You want to rape my wife, don't you?" He turned slightly to look at Gloria who was staring ahead at Davis.

"I'll take you in alive or dead, Nelson, it doesn't matter to me, but no more talking. If you don't step over here, I'll send a bullet into that black heart of yours, I swear!"

"I get it now. You and Gloria have been sleeping together." Nelson's words began to tumble together. "Dirty sex creatures—invading a man's home! Raping his wife! Shooting innocent workingmen!"

Davis cocked the revolver and with the sound, Nelson became instantly submissive.

"You wouldn't want to shoot a kid, just a kid," Nelson said in a pleading voice. "I'm coming, I'm coming." He bowed his head, shuffling forward slowly.

The revolver in Davis' outstretched hand grew heavy. The detective's hand twitched slightly as he lowered the weapon, and dangled the handcuffs in Nelson's direction.

Nelson gave Gloria a furtive look, then glanced out the window, looking downward for a moment. The next second he wheeled about and dove for the window.

Davis instinctively raised his revolver and fired, just as Nelson's thick body struck the glass, crashing outward, his arms crooked at the elbows, protecting his head. The bullet cut across Nelson's right shoulder, tearing the fabric of his tuxedo as he dove outward into black space.

231

Nelson landed heavily on the low garage roof close to the building, sliding down to the gutter and leaping onto a high snowbank. As he moved he clutched his shoulder and shrieked upward, "You hurt me! You hurt me!"

Davis, leaning from the window, saw his black form running down the snowbank toward the back of the building. He fired the remaining five shots in his revolver, the bullets smacking after Nelson. Then the man was out of sight.

"Goddamn you," Davis swore.

FOURTEEN

Reassignment came toward the end of May, 1927. Davis was ordered back to the pool of homicide detectives after being officially removed from the Nelson case. Nelson himself had disappeared. No new strangulations with his brutish trademarks presented themselves. There wasn't a whisper of the killer. He had vanished, in the early part of the year. Following his miraculous escape from Gloria Stearn's apartment, though known to be wounded, he left no trace, which pleased the much-vexed Captain Vertali.

Davis, however, continued to believe that there was a trace, a weedy path that could be followed. He was off the case, so he spoke to no one about it, not even his trusted Oscar Heinrich, who occasionally called to ask if Nelson had surfaced elsewhere. Davis told Heinrich nothing. He brooded and kept his opinions to himself, working half-heartedly on routine investigations—a wife-killer who surrendered meekly, bloody carving knife in his hand, sobbing with remorse; a son of an Italian fisherman who pushed his father into the Bay one sun-filled morning as they headed their little boat to the fishing waters and confessed two days later that his father's death was no accident, he was merely tired of waiting to inherit the business; a sing-song girl in Chinatown who shot her lover to death because he kissed a waitress. All the while Davis thought of Earle Leonard Nelson, spending his spare time in his small house, sitting at the dining room table and working on the maps and reports that dealt with the strangler, reports that he had secretly taken from department files.

He saw Anne less and less, sick of the memory of his boast to her father and the idea of his own failure to catch Nelson which, he was convinced, made him a failure in her eyes. He hated to fail.

Another failed cop, that's what he thought himself to be, fondling archives growing yellow and dust-laden in his own hands. As each month slipped by he lost more and more belief in himself. Perhaps, at his weakest moments, he mused grimly, I should go hat-in-hand to old man Simmons. Beg him for his nepotistic job, marry Anne, and live on the third floor of the mansion. Oh, yes, I'd do well at their parties, her afternoon teas. Her socialite friends would find me quaint—I believe that's the word they'd pin to my back. What did *you* do, Mr. Davis? Me? I'm a live-in son-in-law, Mr. Simmons' ward. I used to be a cop, which, of course, was worse. I'm reformed now. I don't put my finger into the public sewer and scoop up scum. It was a bad habit, trying to enforce the law, like drinking. I'm over that now. Yes, I'm very happy being a toady to Mr. Simmons, counting the boxes of silk that sail in from China. Counting the spiders that crawl out of the boxes, Chinese spiders. I'm *so* happy, ladies. Not a care in the world. Not a bone in my body.

Davis had these thoughts mostly late at night, off duty, sitting at the dining room table and scanning the Nelson files, a bottle of whiskey and a shot glass never empty and always close by. He poured, drank the illicit booze, and endlessly thought about Nelson, always about apprehending Nelson.

The killer was more than Davis' nemesis, more than a haunting challenge. He was the reason Davis had become a policeman—an uncaring but scheming henchman of hell who did what he pleased with the innocent and who could retreat into comfortable insanity whenever retribution loomed.

It was late on one such guilt-glutted night that Davis heard a knock at his screen door. He got up slowly from the dining room table and walked unsteadily to the entranceway. A small, balding man wearing large glasses stood on the other side of the door.

"May I come in, my boy?" Edward Oscar Heinrich said.

Davis flipped the hook lock upward. "Sure. Come in." He went back to the dining room, plopping back into the chair. "Want a drink, Professor?"

Heinrich sat down at the end of the table. The overhead lamp made long shadows on his dark face. He nodded at the whiskey bottle. "Is that what you do with your time now, John?"

Davis filled a shot glass to the brim. He held this up in a salute to Heinrich, "To the man who solves his cases." He drank the whiskey in one gulp. He quickly poured another shot. "And to his shabby imitator—me." Again he threw the drink into his open mouth. Staring at Heinrich, he added, "A man who never solves his cases...or the important ones."

"You mean Nelson."

"Yes, that bastard Nelson!"

"I understand they've written him off on the Coast."

"He's gone inland," Davis said with a slight slurring of words. "He killed eleven women from Santa Barbara to Seattle and...after I loused it up in Portland...he went inland."

"How do you know that?"

Davis grimaced, then picked up a map, sliding this down the table to Heinrich. "Look at that, Professor." Heinrich bent to study the map. "See those red circles on the map of the good old United States? Hmm? I put them there, Professor. I been putting them there since last December. See that circle on Council Bluffs, Iowa?"

Heinrich moved his finger to the red circle, then looked up quizzically at Davis.

"That represents Mrs. Bernard Cuthright, landlady. Strangled with her own stocking, then violated on December twenty-third, last year, just before Christmas. Cheap jewelry, some clothes, a few dollars taken. That's Nelson."

236

Davis pushed his face forward. "That's him, all right."

Running his finger around the red circle on the map, Heinrich said, "There were no reports in the papers of this killing?"

"I wrote to every department personally after that maniac got away from me in Portland, weeks of writing, asking the cops to look for his handiwork. They write to me, here, at my home." Davis leaned back in his chair, tired, reaching out to pour another drink. "They find a body, like the bodies we've had, and they write to me. It's all on the map there. Run your finger down the Kansas-Missouri border, Professor, to Kansas City. See another circle there?"

"Yes," Heinrich answered dutifully. "Who died there?"

"Number thirteen, Mrs. Linda Lawrence, and number fourteen, her eight-month-old child. He strangled and raped her, this landlady, and took, his mementoes." Davis gulped down another drink. "But before he left the poor woman's home, he strangled the child. No good reason to do that. The kid could never identify him. But he killed the child anyway. I can see this devil playing with the kid, the mother dead on the floor, and I can see the red lights going on in his eyes and those big hands going around the child's throat. *That* killing was special for Nelson."

Heinrich looked up. "Why the child, do you think, John?"

"You're asking me, a man like you?"

"I'm a scientist, not an alienist."

"I'm a cop, not Sigmund Freud. I can't explain this man, except that when he killed that child, a useless

murder in his way of things, he wanted only to take life—
he hates life." Davis closed his eyes briefly. "Sometimes,
sitting here alone, I can crawl into his head, walk around in
that mind of his, stumble over all the rocks up there.... It's
a terrible geography, Professor, full of nightmares."

"And these other circles on the map?" Heinrich tilted
the map, pulling it to his left, his unblinking eyes traversing the country from west to east. "Here, at Philadelphia?"

"Mrs. Katy McDonald, strangled and raped on April
twenty-seventh."

"And here," Heinrich said, moving his finger upward
on the map, "at Buffalo, New York?"

"Mrs. Joan Scott, murdered, raped, jewelry and
clothes missing, a man with a Bible wanting to rent a room
in her home, just like the others. Everything the same.
Nelson...killing his way across the country."

"Astounding." Heinrich sighed and put down the
map. "Is there a pattern in his movement, in this time
element?"

"I don't know. Want a drink?"

"Not now."

"Maybe some sort of pattern, but God only knows
what it is. If he comes back west, if he kills in a
midwestern city that will mean he's returning home, to the
Coast. Maybe. Right now he has sixteen deaths to his
credit." Then Davis said to himself, "I wonder if he keeps
track?"

"There seems to be a long period of time, according
to your calculations, from December of last year to April
of this, where he hasn't murdered."

"I wouldn't even try to figure what that means," Davis

sighed. "He started last year in February, killed again in March, then laid off until June, then stopped until August, then went hell-for-leather through October, November, and December."

"And after a four-month hiatus," intoned Heinrich, "he started again this spring." He tapped the map. "If your calculations here are correct, and I assume this is the same man...."

"No pattern to it, Professor, not one that I can see. You tell me—what is it—the full moon, change of season?"

Heinrich stood up and walked the length of the table, dragging the map back to Davis. "It's beyond the test tube and my laboratory, John." He flicked his finger against the whiskey bottle so that it rang. "It's beyond this, too, my boy."

Davis leaned so far back in his chair to look upward at Heinrich that he almost toppled. "No lectures, Professor."

"John," Heinrich said in a patient voice, "to the police departments across the country, these deaths indicated on the map are random murders, to you they are the work of one man. It's your trail. But it's also your obsession." He spread his hands out to encompass the reports and maps littering the table. "All of this is part of it. He is taking up too much of your mind, plaguing you, persecuting you."

Davis let the words sink in, then eased his chair forward. He placed his long hands flat on the table. "You don't understand—I've failed. I missed this fellow three times." He doubled his hands into fists and slammed them against the table. "Three times!"

"That shouldn't astound you, John. You yourself told me that this Nelson is an escape artist. He learned the arts

239

of the yegg in prison. Didn't he pick his way through nine different locks in San Quentin? Didn't he scale walls no ordinary human could get over?"

"Yeah," Davis said disgustedly, "my little gorilla murderer."

"And other jails and other prisons—he's escaped from some of the best of them. Why shouldn't he elude you, one man? You're fortunate in that you got that close to him."

"Aww, let's face it, Professor—we don't have the wherewithal to track down a man who has spent his whole life evading the law. He's clever and experienced. We're not. We're exactly like those Keystone Kops the public laughs at in the movies. You're right—Nelson learned the art of getting in and out of anywhere. The same hardened criminals who taught him that art in prison schooled him in how to evade the police, or maybe he learned *that* technique on his own. He knows how to get through any dragnet because he knows how we conduct our searches —like pedantic idiots—how we section off a block systematically, so he works his way not through alleys but across lots, running low along the shrubbery or behind garages. He's like a panther that way. *He* can predict our moves. To him we're stupid and old-fashioned . . . and he's right. Our procedures are crude in this country. Why, only a few cities have officers patrolling in cars, most cops are out there pounding a beat, walking the neighborhood sidewalks, and this man's an expert on the sidewalks— that's where he lives.

"Do you know that in Paris they've installed radios in cars, real communication between headquarters and their street men. The only radio we've got in this country is a crystal set in a precinct office so the desk sergeant can listen to Rudy Vallee or some other honky-tonk crooner. Our cops don't even talk to each other; they don't even study the circulars or the photos we give them. They hand them out but they don't look at them. They think it's a waste of time.

"The cop in America today understands shooting it out with a robber running from a bank or a store with the loot in his hand, or running in a drunken husband who throws a punch, or breaking up a gang of kids on the corner. *That* he understands. Everything else is unreal, useless 'newfangled' procedures devised to upset a system they've lived comfortably with for fifty years. We are flatfoots, goddamnit! Unless some informer provides us with information or we stumble upon an actual crime being committed, we're as about effective as a drunk trying to find his way home in an earthquake. No, a lone killer like Nelson has it all his way. He's the sophisticated one—we're the hicks!"

Davis thought in silence for some moments, then let loose his razor-sharp anger: "The next time I'll kill him. I won't talk it away as I did in Portland. I'll just shoot the son of a bitch!"

Heinrich took a few steps toward the front door. "I'll be running along, John. I hope there is a next time for you with Nelson...only so that you can be free of him."

Captain Vertali stared out of the window of his office, purposely keeping his back to Davis. The map Davis had marked was spread out on Vertali's desk. "I'm sick of this," Vertali finally said in a low voice. "You were removed from the strangler case months ago. Now you come to me and say you've been working on it—and on the sly. I hate that kind of stuff, Sergeant."

"Take another look at the map, Captain. Three more dead women. Three more landladies, two in a Detroit rooming house, another in Chicago. All strangled, all raped afterwards. Jewelry and clothes missing. All in the span of four days."

"I don't want to talk about it anymore, Davis. So take your maps and files and go back to your regular duties."

Davis studied Vertali's broad neck, then snatched up the map, rolling it angrily. "Nineteen murders, Captain, *nineteen*, all landladies, except for a child."

"He's out of our jurisdiction."

"He's our responsibility!"

Vertali swung about. "You're doing fine where you are, Sergeant. Why not let this strangler thing die? The board's been talking about giving you a promotion. That's a lieutenant's badge, Davis, and more money."

"I want to go back on the strangler case." Davis waved the map at Vertali.

"Why?" From the tone of Vertali's voice it was clear that he was not interested in knowing Davis' reasons.

"Because I think I now know his direction. He's murdered as far east as Philadelphia, Captain. Then, just in the last ten days he's cut back from Buffalo to Detroit and Chicago. He's staying close to the Canadian border in case it gets too hot for him. If it does he'll slip into Canada."

Vertali put his hands on his hips. "Then let the Canadians worry about him."

"That's just it—those people up there have no idea what he's all about. More than that—he'll be our problem again soon."

"How's that?"

"He's heading back to the Coast...now."

"No," Vertali said with a small groan. He sat down, his head bent, pondering the thought.

"Look, Captain—I've talked to the Chicago police. In the boarding house of their victim, Mary Loomis, they found a travel folder, under her body, a Canadian travel brochure."

"Canada's a big place." Vertali knew what was coming.

"The brochure was folded to the description of Winnipeg."

"Maybe the victim was thinking of vacationing in Winnipeg."

"Not a chance," Davis said. "The Chicago cops checked her background. No relatives in Canada, and she hadn't taken a vacation in twenty years. Nelson got careless, that's all. He's on his way to Winnipeg, I know it."

"How do you know it?" Vertali reached out for the map in Davis' hand, taking it, and spreading it out once more.

Davis leaned across the desk, pointing. "Here, in Winnipeg, is where the Canadian Pacific has a main line that runs straight through the four western provinces, all the way to Vancouver." Davis ran his finger along the Canadian border. "Once in Vancouver, Nelson can hike it down to Seattle, then it's Portland again where he thinks his ex-wife is living."

"Is that where she is?"

"No, she's over in Richmond. I helped get her a job over there in a music school."

"Richmond! Chrissakes—that's just across the Bay! What are you trying to do—put him back in our lap again?"

"No, she's safer here than in Portland. Besides, I think I can nail him in Winnipeg."

"Jesus Christ! I don't want that bastard back in San Francisco!"

Davis met Vertali's look and said in a determined voice, "Let me go to Winnipeg, Captain."

Vertali shook his head. "He moves too fast. By the time you took a train up there, he'd probably be out of the city—*if* he's in Winnipeg."

"I'll fly."

"Fly? Are you crazy? How?"

"With the mail service. If I leave now I can be there by tomorrow morning."

Rubbing his head, Vertali shoved the map away. "You must be crazy, Davis. You gonna get into an open cockpit in one of those beat-up World War One Jennies? Those damned crates are cracking up all the time. Death-traps."

"Hell, Captain, Lindbergh flew the Atlantic less than two weeks ago."

"You going with Lindbergh?"

"Claire Vance will take me; I've arranged it with him—"

"You're too damed sure of yourself. Who's this fellow Vance?"

244

"He flew the first west-east load of mail from San Francisco to New York two years ago. He'll take me right into Winnipeg."

"Without stopping?"

"We'll set down every couple hundred miles. From here to Elko, Nevada, then to Cheyenne, Wyoming, then—"

Vertali waved his hand. "I don't want to hear it. What's it gonna cost the department?"

"About a hundred."

"That's a lot of money for a joy ride."

"He'll be in Winnipeg, Captain." Davis sensed the reason for Vertali's willingness to continue the discussion; it was fear. "If he isn't stopped in Canada, Captain, he'll be back here, on our doorstep."

"I dunno."

"He'll be outside your door."

Vertali opened a desk drawer and pulled forth a pad of paper with printing on it. He began to scribble. "I know I must seem like a lousy bastard to you, Davis, like I don't care what's been happening to these women. I do—but I never had any idea how to handle it—this kind of killer. Every time he murdered I thought about my wife, my little girls—everybody's wife and little girls, and when it was happening to them I had to go to my superiors and admit that I didn't have a thing...that I didn't *know* *anything*, except that I was helpless...so I dumped it on you. That kind of feeling—helpless—it don't make a man like me be anything but angry all the time, so a man like me turns his back on it, forgets it if he can. But you didn't forget. I'm—I'm grateful for that. Here—go ahead." He tore off a sheet from the pad and handed it to Davis. "It's your expense voucher—two hundred."

Davis grinned at him as he took the voucher and swept up the map. "Thanks."

"That bastard better be in Canada!"

"I'm leaving in an hour." Davis walked toward the door with an enthusiastic stride.

"You'd better wear one of them things—parachutes."

"They don't use them. Too much weight."

"Make sure the pilot doesn't drink," Vertali warned.

"I'm the one who'll need the drink."

Anne Simmons saw Davis off, taking the Oakland Ferry, then driving to the airfield, where she watched mechanics roll the single motor bi-plane onto the dirt runway. A small truck bounced over the ruts of the field to the plane and bags of mail were unloaded and put into the front cockpit.

Davis held a small leather cap in his hand. He slipped it on. "I guess I look pretty silly in this?"

"Rather dashing." She placed her hands up to the leather helmet and pulled gently at the straps so that his head tilted down to hers, meeting in a kiss. "Call me from Winnipeg, darling."

"Sure. Even if I have no news, I'll call."

Anne suddenly gripped Davis' arm, pulling close to him as she shuddered.

"What's the matter, darling?"

"None of this is very real, is it? Flying to Canada to look for a madman killer."

"I thought you understood my work, Anne." He stared at her. "It's my *work*."

She rested her head on his shoulder. "This is beyond your work, darling. . . . This is an obsession."

"Of course it is, I realize it is. But I'm dealing with an unusual creature who is also obsessed. To get him I must be like him."

"But he's deranged."

Davis kissed the top of her golden-haired head. "My mind's all right, Anne, believe me."

"I worry. I'm sorry, I didn't want to say that, but I worry about this and what it's doing to you all the time now."

Davis pulled her to him in a full embrace. "I need your worry." He kissed her. "It's part of your love, but I'm all right—do you believe that?"

She looked at him and then nodded slowly.

"Good. Besides, your father thinks you're going to marry a crazy cop anyway."

She let out a little laugh.

"I'd like to put that lovely smile of yours in my pocket." He kissed her again.

A husky youth approached, wearing a leather jacket, jodhpurs, and riding boots.

"He's got everything but the spurs," Anne whispered.

"Vance? He's a great pilot."

"We've got good weather all the way, Sergeant." Vance handed him a blanket he had been carrying. "Better put this around you. It gets cold up there."

Anne squeezed Davis' arm. "Take good care of him," she told Vance, who nodded and gave her a reassuring smile.

Davis and Vance began walking toward the waiting plane. The pilot buttoned his jacket. "Ever been up?"

247

"Never."

"Frightened?"

"Plenty."

"That'll go away in a few minutes after we're up there. There's nothing like it." Vance signaled the mechanic to stand by the propeller. He guided Davis onto the wing of the plane and helped him wedge himself downward into the front cockpit, moving aside mailbags to make room. Vance strapped the detective to the seat, saying, "It's just like a car, only the road is wider." He patted the side of the plane, affectionately. "She's a good one, never failed me." He moved backward and got into the rear cockpit. "Okay!" he shouted to the mechanic at the propeller. "Contact!"

Davis looked at Anne standing across the field and waved. She waved back, and he wondered if he was not as mad as Earle Nelson. The propeller wound into motion until it was a blur and Davis suddenly felt a surge of power as the plane moved forward down the runway. He closed his eyes. He felt the forward motion of the plane running through his body and the blast of wind from the propeller in his face. Then he was in the air, climbing.

The plane made one low circle about the runway and Davis opened his eyes to look down on patchwork fields, sucking his breath at the wonder of the scene. He scanned the runway and saw Anne still waving. He waved back.

"It's something, isn't it?" Vance shouted to Davis above the whine of the motor. "I never get over it!"

"Neither will I!" Davis shouted back. He kept watching Anne until her diminishing form became a dot on the landscape.

248

FIFTEEN

The money was getting low. Nelson walked the streets of Winnipeg bitterly recalling how he had lost most of his fortune in Gloria's apartment long months ago, leaving the bulky cash in his discarded overcoat, just after being surprised by that man, that cop. But he had his Bible which, as a premonition or not, he had moved to his suitcoat pocket just before entering Gloria's rooms. The book comforted him as he eased down the streets, stopping to browse through books on wooden tables outside shops, peering into windows at women's clothes.

Nelson had arrived in Winnipeg only two hours earlier, having hitched rides from Chicago through Wisconsin and Minnesota, listening to the chatter of salesmen

249

and farmers, his sullen manner unchanged. He had hated them all, but their company, their happy identities were necessary to cover his movements, for the police were everywhere in the States searching for him. Canada offered relief, a fresh field of endeavors.

Spotting a pawnshop, Nelson went inside and quickly bartered a new set of clothes, exchanging a red sweater, tan pants and slippers, and a light cap for a blue coat, dark trousers, and some old boots. It was a poor transaction; the coat was missing buttons on one side, but Nelson was in a hurry and was in no mood to haggle with the pawnbroker.

After buying a newspaper, Nelson climbed aboard a trolley car and went to the rear of the vehicle, sitting far away from other passengers. He methodically turned the pages of the paper, hunting for the ads offering cheap rooms.

Scanning the paper, Nelson was suddenly jolted upright in his seat at the sight of a printed photograph of Garfield, the foreman in the Oakland lumberyard. The interview appeared in the back columns of the paper, but to Nelson it might as well have been on the front page. The foreman told the story of how the lumberyard had been set ablaze and how he had first been accused of the arson when his jacket had been found at the lumberyard entrance. He was quoted as saying: "But the authorities quickly realized that this strangler, Nelson, using another name—he called himself Harris at the time—was the maniac who set the fire. If I ever get my hands on that jerk I'll throttle him." Nelson, scowling, looked up to the top of the newspaper column to see Garfield staring into the camera, fists poised like that of a boxer.

THE DARK FOUNTAIN

I'll be back to see you, Mr. Garfield, Nelson promised, as he glared at the newspaper photo. You're not
going to throttle me or anyone else when I get finished
with you. Maniac, calling me a *maniac*. *You* set that fire,
Mr. Garfield! Why aren't you in San Quentin? Paid them
off, that's what you did, paid off the police and the
newspapers to make you look good—you heroes from the
war are all the same. Sickening, the way you get away
with things. I'll be back to see you, sir. Yes, I will. As soon
as I get a little money, enough for the Canadian Pacific
fare, I'm on my way, yes, sir. On my way.

A man with a long beard and smelling of lye soap
dressed in black sat down next to Nelson. He wore a large
black hat with a wide brim and stared straight ahead.

Nelson folded the paper and dropped it on his knees.
"It's a beautiful day to be in the city," he told the man.

The man glanced at him, then straight ahead. "God's
own miracle," he said softly.

Nodding at that, Nelson withdrew his Bible, placing it
on his knee over the newspaper so that the gold cross,
embossed on the cover, clearly showed. "You seem like a
religious man," Nelson said.

"I am a Hutterite," the man said, after looking down
to see Nelson's Bible.

"What's that?"

"A religious body."

"A sect?"

"Some call it that. We abide by the word of God,
young man." He gave Nelson a long look. "Our commu-
nity is centered in Pigeon Lake, not far from this city."

"Are you a minister?"

"No."

"But you have a clean face," Nelson told him. "I can always tell a religious person."

"How's that?"

Nelson twisted in the seat to look at the man, smiling knowingly. "Because I am the champion of the world at telling faces. And I am a religious man myself, deeply religious, a practicing Catholic every day of my life."

"That's commendable," the man said, a nervous edge to his voice.

With a sigh, Nelson blurted out, "Even in God's grace, I've sinned. I guess it's the cities I've been to and the people I've been with—the cities are evil." Nelson bowed his head for a moment as if looking at his Bible. "I sometimes drink too much."

"You should stop that," the man warned.

"Yes, I know, I must stop it." Nelson ran his thick fingers over the Bible. "Satan has too much power over educated men."

The man nodded in agreement and looked about briefly as the car rattled forward, appearing to look for his stop. He grasped the handgrip on the seat in front and pulled himself forward. He looked down at Nelson and intoned, "Strive for purity, my boy, and God will reward you."

"I know, I know," Nelson said in a submissive voice, and watched as the man went to the door of the trolley car and got off at the next stop. He went back to his newspaper, tearing out the Garfield interview and putting this flat into his Bible. He quickly looked over the ads for rooms and circled several.

252

It took Nelson two hours to find the large boarding house of Helen Spaulding. He impressed the woman as being very religious and rented a room for five dollars a week, giving the landlady a one-dollar deposit. He went to his room immediately and took a nap. Some time later Mrs. Spaulding heard him in the upstairs bathroom, whistling an odd tune as he shaved.

Inspector Albert Bergson of the Winnipeg Police was unlike any law enforcement officer John Davis had ever met. He was not only polite but deeply interested in the story of the strangler and expressed his awe at the fact that Davis had hazardously flown to Winnipeg to apprehend Nelson. They sat in Bergson's office drinking coffee as Davis outlined the history of Earle Leonard Nelson.

"You must want this fellow badly," Bergson finally said, "to have flown all that distance from San Francisco. Lord! I could never imagine myself inside one of those machines. And you think this Nelson is in Winnipeg, Sergeant?"

"Yes, so do the Chicago police. He left a travel brochure advertising Winnipeg at the site of his last killing."

"Why would he come all the way up here, I wonder?" Bergson got up slowly and walked to two large, arched windows that offered an excellent view of the old city.

"It's the Canadian Pacific, I think," said Davis. "He'd risk too much by traveling in the States back to the West Coast—the entire nation is looking for him. I believe it's his idea to take the Canadian Pacific to Vancouver, then cut back down to the American west coast. He has an ex-wife in California he's drawn to—like a nail to a magnet."

"Fascinating," Bergson said, then wheeled about, his large red face wearing a frown. "Where do we start?"

"Send some squads to all the boarding houses, interview all the landladies. I've brought photos to be shown, a picture of Nelson."

Bergson enthusiastically slapped the back of his high leather chair. "Good. If he's in Winnipeg, we'll find him."

John Davis sighed with relief and gratitude.

When Nelson spotted the golden-haired girl selling flowers on the corner his head almost exploded. He had to lean against a building and press his fists against his temples in an effort to push back the pain that gripped him. He stumbled away from her, not daring to look in her direction. He went down an alley and sank between two garbage cans, waiting for night.

He tried every which way to blot out the vision of the flower girl, her small baskets of bright iris, tulips, roses, and lilacs before her on the pavement, the timid way in which she held out small bunches of flowers and the sweet voice asking, "Buy some posies, sir?" Nelson tried to force other visions into his head but the image of the girl returned, reminding him of his young cousin in Oxnard and how he had stood one night outside her bedroom window, clutching the window sill with sweating hands, gaping at her lithesome body as she undressed for bed. And how his aunt had found him there in the shadows and beat him until he bled and how, to cover his fear and embarrassment, he had laughed at her.

Now, at this painful moment in a Winnipeg alley, the flower girl down the street and his cousin were the same person inside the boiling brain of Earle Nelson. He knew he would not be driven away this time, his face running blood, unsatisfied lust burning in his loins. No, he had waited years and years for the girl and would have her.

Some hours later, at twilight, Nelson slowly pushed himself up the wall of the building in the alley, brushing off his clothes. He reached into his pocket and examined his money. He selected a silver dollar, and held this in a fist, thrusting bills back into his pocket. He pulled the brim of his hat low on his forehead and walked from the alley, turned, and went straight to the girl who was bent over her baskets, covering her flowers.

"I'd like to have some tulips " Nelson told the girl in a weak voice.

"Yes, sir," she said, and quickly wrapped a bunch. "It's ten cents, sir."

Nelson looked up and down the dimly lit street. "All I've got is this dollar." He held it out to her.

A pained expression came over her pretty face. "I haven't change, sir, business has been poor."

Nelson knelt suddenly, hooking his arms through the hoops of baskets, smiling at her. "Come with me, I'll get the change for you."

"It's little Lola Bendetti," the officer told Inspector Bergson. "She's the flower girl at Sixth and Spring—I check on her each evening. And she's not there. And she's not gotten home. I found her baskets of flowers in the alleyway down the block. And this—" He held up a strip of bright cloth. "From the bottom of her dress—her mother identified it a half hour ago."

Davis had been working in Bergson's office, planning the house-to-house search for Nelson with the inspector when the officer appeared, responding to the alert Bergson had issued hours earlier, that reports of all missing females were to be delivered to him personally.

"Could she have wandered off, a boyfriend or something?" Bergson asked the cop.

The burly officer shook his head. "Nothing like that. She worked hard, Lola did, and went home to her parents, bringing back the pennies for her flowers."

Bergson looked at Davis. The sergeant bit his lip and said: "I don't know—it doesn't fit Nelson's *modus operandi*." He hunched his shoulders. "But then—" He turned to the officer. "How old is this girl?"

"Only fourteen."

"His cousin's age," Davis said, thinking aloud, "in California."

"Is it the madman, sir?" the officer asked Bergson.

"It could be," Davis answered for the inspector.

"We won't waste time waiting for possibilities to become reality," Bergson said to Davis. "Not here in Winnipeg. I'll put every available man in that district right now. I know all about what happened in Portland."

Davis was suddenly struck by the idea that he might be wrong, that Nelson might not be in the city. A missing child did not prove the strangler's presence. If he were wrong, if he threw the city into a panic over what he all along realized was thin evidence—he couldn't think of that now, only swallow doubt and plunge forward.

Nelson held the lifeless girl in his arms, waiting for the last lights on the second floor of his boarding house to go out, hiding in the dark, wedged between high bushes close to the house. He had taken the girl into the alley and strangled her, and then, for reasons unclear to him, carried her limp body as one might carry a large doll. He had torn the hem of her dress on an ashcan in the alley, he remembered, but it would appear to be nothing more than a rag to any passerby.

Then he recalled the flowers in the baskets. Fool! You should have dumped them into the ashcans and covered them with garbage. You left a trace, you told them about the girl when you left the flowers. Why didn't I remember the flowers? Why? You were too busy thinking of her, you remember how you felt when you did it, the feeling that came to you when you jumped into the alley and got her by the throat? That was all you could remember. Fool!

When Nelson looked up from his leafy hiding place he saw that the house was now dark. He pulled at the small body, grunting. As he staggered forward he thought she had gotten heavier, like a great weight trying to pull him down a long hill. He let himself in through the unlocked back door of the building, going silently, slowly up the back stairs, the girl's head bent backward over one arm, her long blonde hair flowing as he inched forward, sensitive to every creak in the staircase.

Once on the second floor, Nelson got into his room

quickly, putting the body of Lola Bendetti on his bed. He turned on the lamp at the bedside and sat looking down at his victim, oddly at peace for the moment.

"I'm not a savage," he said, softly to the corpse. "I know you think I'm a savage...a monster...but I have feelings, good and bad feelings like everyone else. I really meant to pay you the whole dollar for the flowers. I don't hate you for making me do what I did to you. I know you know that."

He placed a large hand gently on her forehead. He petted her. Then he stretched an uncontrollable hand to the bottom of her dress.

The Winnipeg police were not alone in their search for the strangler and Lola Bendetti. Scores of Provincial Police joined their ranks, along with dozens of Mounties and detectives from the Canadian Pacific. Their dragnet enclosed the entire city of Winnipeg. Squads of men worked through the night, going from door to door, inspecting every alley, every open lot and abandoned building.

It was early the following morning when Nelson was awakened by a loud banging on his door. He sat up groggily on the bed. "Who's there?" he said with a voice still full of sleep.

"It's Mrs. Spaulding, young man," came the landlady's pleasant voice.

"Sleeping," Nelson responded.

"You must open the door, young man," Mrs. Spaulding said firmly. "Two men are here to see you."

He paused for a moment, remembering. Nelson stood

up, turned to face the bed, and pulled down the coverlet so that it went to the floor. He opened the door, letting it swing wide as he moved back to the bed and lay down.

Two men wearing homespun suits and wide slouch hats entered the room partway, looking down at him.

"Who are you?" Nelson's voice was calm, his demeanor unperturbed.

"Police. Sit up, fella."

Nelson sat up.

"You come in yesterday?"

"Yes," answered Mrs. Spaulding matter-of-factly, still in the hallway. "He rented the room yesterday. But, officers, he's a nice young man."

One of the men pointed to Nelson's dust-covered boots. "What's that on your shoes?"

Nelson was prepared. "Lime—from the pits over in St. Boniface. I've been working the night shift there for a couple of months...." He rubbed his eyes sleepily. "Moved over here for a better room when I got a raise."

"What's your name?" the other detective asked.

"Pearson, Judd Pearson."

"Judd," said the detective, writing on the small pad, "does that mean Judson?"

"Yeah."

"We can check on that pretty quick. What's the name of your boss in St. Boniface?"

"McElroy, at the Toomey works." Nelson closed his eyes and lazily put his arms behind his head, slipping them beneath the pillow. He felt secure in his alibi; he had called the Toomey Company and had gotten the name of the night foreman, information he might have required for just this emergency. "Can I get some shut-eye, now, please?"

"He's a working stiff," Nelson heard one of the detectives whisper to the other. "Let's go."

"All right," whispered back the other detective. "But I want to check one of the other squads that have the photo of this gorilla man."

"We might want to talk to you later, Pearson," one of the detectives said loudly, "so don't go anywhere."

"I'll be here," Nelson said dreamily. With his eyes still shut, he heard them close the door to his room and go down the hallway. He opened his eyes and jumped from the bed, slipping on his shoes and grabbing his coat. Ever so slowly, Nelson turned the doorknob and cracked the door so he could see the landlady and detectives go down the hallway toward the front of the building, knock on another roomer's door, and go inside. He moved into the hallway and crept to the back stairs, easing himself to the first landing, then taking two steps at a time until he was out of the back door and walking quickly down the alley.

He sweated heavily as he walked, the hot sun beating down on his bare head. Sweat ran down his cheeks and chin, dripping on to his soiled shirt. He was weak in the legs and there was a hollow feeling in his stomach. He had had nothing to eat. You must eat if you're going to get away, he told himself. He looked about desperately into back yards as he moved. Nelson spied an apple tree next to the alley, a branch hanging over a fence, the weight of green apples pulling it down. He rushed forward and filled his pockets with the unripened fruit, then raced on, gnawing on a bright green apple. You'll get sick from these, he cautioned, but you need the energy. Eat now, get sick later. Keep moving. Move faster! Faster! No, don't break into a run. They'll be looking for a running man. Walk quickly, that's all, like you're late for work.

Nelson had gone about nine twisting blocks when he stopped to catch his breath and chew on another apple. He stood next to some high bushes on an empty lot, shrouded in their shade. He stared blankly at a trim white house surrounded by a picket fence next to the lot. The back door of the house suddenly flew open and a man emerged carrying a lunch pail. He was followed by an attractive dark-haired woman, and, toddling after her, two small children. Nelson stepped deep into the bushes, chewing on the apple, watching.

The man reached the fence gate, opened it, and stepped through. He closed the gate and turned to the woman who had followed him, kissing her briefly on the cheek.

"Right home from work now, Bill. It's stew tonight, your favorite."

"Bye-bye, kids," the man said, looking down at the two small children. "Be good for your mommy." He nodded to his wife and went down the street away from Nelson. The woman watched him go for a minute or two, then turned, and walked back to the rear of the house.

Perfect, Nelson concluded, and no time to waste. He ran through the bushes of the lot alongside the house, then cut over to the waist-high fence and leaped over in a single bound. He glanced back to see the small children playing on the front lawn before rushing into the house just behind the woman.

She turned around, wide dark eyes blinking. "What do you want?" she gasped.

"Money," Nelson said.

The woman looked about the kitchen frantically.

"Stay away from those kitchen knives on the counter over there," he warned her.

"We don't have money. We're poor."

"I'm poorer." Nelson side-stepped to the counter and picked up a large butcher knife. "You better get some money, lady, right now!"

"Please."

"Right now!" He stepped backward until he reached the screen door, which he locked. The two small children came to the door at that moment and Nelson said sweetly to them, "Go ahead and play, kids, play outside." He closed the inside door, smiling and saying: "I'm going to play inside with mommy!"

"Over there—next to the icebox," the woman pointed, terrified. "In the can marked FLOUR."

Nelson went to the counter, unsealed the cannister, and dumped the contents on the counter; a large cellophane bag followed the flour. He inspected it carefully, still pointing the knife in the woman's direction. "Good, looks like about fifty bucks."

"Twenty-three dollars," the woman corrected in a quavering voice. "It took us eight months to save that."

Nelson pocketed the bag and was about to leave, then shook his head, as he looked at the woman standing before him.

"You look pretty good, lady," Nelson appraised her.

She spoke quickly: "I'm old, really, thirty-six, and I

can't have children any more.. I'd—I'd be no good to you."

He advanced on her. "You're okay." He held the knife to her stomach, curling his fingers about the neck of her dress and yanking downward. He took no notice of her tears, as he stared with cretinous fascination at her large, naked breasts. He began to back her out of the kitchen, down a short hall and into a small bedroom, telling her, "You do the rest of it, lady."

"Please," she begged, "I'm a married woman with two small children. Don't make me—"

"You talk too much," Nelson said, and began pulling away the rest of her clothes.

The two detectives who had been to Mrs. Spaulding's rooming house early that morning returned inside of a half hour after seeing photos of the suspect. They bounded up the stairs and dashed into Nelson's room, half expecting to find it empty.

One held the small photocopy in his hand, showing it to the other. "That was the man, wasn't it?"

"Older than that photo, but it was him, absolutely."

"Lime-pit worker!" The detective went to the bureau, pulling out drawers in anger. All of them were empty.

The other detective moved to a small closet and, after opening the door, ran his hand down a single rail, gathering empty hangers. He then walked to the bed and pulled the coverlet, then the sheets from the mattress, hurling these to the far end of the room. He knelt down and peered beneath the bed. "C'mere," he said in a half-moan to the other detective. "It's little Lola Bendetti—good

Lord, look what he did to her!"

The other detective leaned down hesitantly and looked. He turned his head away. "That lousy bastard!"

"I got a girl about that age," the first detective said, transfixed by the sight of the mutilated corpse.

"He'll hang for it," promised the other detective, reaching beneath the bed for a lifeless arm.

"I wanna be there. Jesus—I wanna be there!"

William Epps returned home from work early that afternoon, along with hundreds of other frantic working-men in Winnipeg. News of the strangler's presence in the city and the discovery of Lola Bendetti's corpse had been bleated by newsboys carrying extras. The frenzied movements of police and militia canvassing the city in hordes, bursting into homes, offices, and plants, roughhousing any and all suspicious-looking males, had added to the panic.

Epps had heard that the Bendetti girl had been found in a boarding house less than a mile from his own home. He had run most of the way back to his house, crashing through the fence gate and up the walk where he found his small children playing peacefully.

"Where's your mother, children?" he asked them.

The little boy pointed to the house.

Epps trotted to the rear of the house and went inside. "Martha, where are you?" he called, fear in his voice. He saw that the flour can on the counter had been dumped and the family savings taken. He stood petrified for the moment, sifting the flour with his fingers. Epps shuddered, then walked stoically across the kitchen and down the hall, stopping at each doorway, looking into each small room. He stepped into the children's small bedroom, feeling helpless.

Epps stared at a cross affixed to the wall and suddenly sank to his knees, folding his hands and resting his elbows on the small child's bed, looking up at the crucifix. "Dear God," he began to pray, "please let Martha be all right, please let her be at the store, or a neighbor's, please let her walk through our back door—"

He felt his trousers at the knees suddenly wet and glanced down. He was kneeling in a pool of blood that had seeped from beneath the bed. He bent down, looking closer, lips parting in a scream that never came as he saw his wife's naked dead body.

SIXTEEN

All about Nelson waved endless fields of wheat, oats, rye, and flax in a gently rolling countryside, a farmland sea undulating beneath soft prairie winds. The dirt road on which he trod was narrow, rutted by the iron wheels of heavy tractors, a road straight as an arrow. He looked upward every now and then to measure the course of the sun in the afternoon sky and take his bearings. He was headed due south toward North Dakota, figuring that the United States border was only a few miles ahead. There would be no checkpoint there, no guards and no questions. He would simply stroll back into his native land, hike into the Dakotas and get a job on a farm for a while. He would save his money, then return to the Coast. He

267

would find Gloria and when he did all would be right.

What a fuss these Canadians make, he thought as he walked, wrapping a bandana around his large head to keep off the heat of the sun. You'd think they'd be grateful, ridding their old city of Winnipeg of whores the way I've done. Nobody can help these stupid people, Godless Canadians. They almost got me back there, in Winnipeg, all those police and soldiers running around, but they missed me on every street. Hah! They thought I'd go to the train station. Never figured that I'd walk out, that I'd have the courage to walk dozens of miles, hundreds if I had to go that far.

How far have you come? What was that little town back there—Killarney? And that town has got to be one hundred miles, no, one hundred and fifty miles from Winnipeg. Good going, Earle, that's real walking, that's real traveling, boy! Proud of you, Earle, my boy—you've shown these bumpkins up here what a real man can do if he sets his mind to it, yes, sir. How could they catch me anyway. *Nobody* ever catches me. God knows they've tried. It's been years since anyone had their hands on old Earle Nelson, and they'll never do it again. I've proved that, I have a record, like an athlete.

"They ought to send you to the Olympics, Earle, old boy," he laughed to himself and, in his strange joy, he suddenly dove forward on his hands and began walking, hand over hand, down the dusty road, laughing and reveling in his bizarre prowess, his thick upside-down body swaying back and forth, his large head twisted upward to see his course.

I could show them something—I could walk for miles

like this and never get winded. That's what a real man can do! How do you like it, Canada? Huh? Ingrates!

He stopped, letting himself downward to a kneeling position in the road, remembering how they had described him in the newspapers as "the gorilla murderer." He stood up, sneering at the thought. I'm no ape out of the zoo! But they might see you, someone might see you out here doing that and think about what the papers said. Better stay off your hands, Earle.

Nelson looked down at his huge hands and clapped them together so that the dust from the road flew off in a cloud. He wiped them on his torn trousers, then slipped his hands into his pockets and continued walking, whistling that old familiar, nameless tune.

From far off in the distance, behind him, Nelson heard a faint noise and turned to see a speck on the horizon in the middle of the road. Another one of those stupid farmers, he thought, coming along in a tractor. They won't give a fellow a ride. Always got an excuse— I'm only going up the road a piece, that sort of thing, goddamn farmers. Well, why not just take the tractor, huh? Why not? Stop the fellow for some reason, climb up on his tractor and brain him. Then drive the tractor right down into North Dakota. You could sell it, that's all farming down there in the Dakotas, they'd be glad to have a tractor. And you'd have enough money to go back to the Coast in style. You could buy Gloria some clothes, buy a house, settle down, forget about the evil ones. Nobody appreciates what you do for them anyway. That's a good idea, Earle. Kill the farmer.

He stopped in the road, stepping to its edge, waiting

and looking back to see the speck enlarge, grinning at his inventiveness, waiting for the farmer. He'd be riding into the Dakotas soon.

Shimmering into view was not a tractor but a car, an old box Ford, and Nelson could see that two men were in it. He shrugged and turned his back on the approaching car, continuing to walk south.

The car slowed as it approached Nelson, clouds of dust billowing behind it, its motor coughing. Nelson kept his eyes glued to the horizon in front, walking steadily, almost leisurely. The car passed him, then stopped.

As Nelson came abreast of the car, a man with a heavy jaw and piercing eyes leaned from the window. "Hey, fella, come over here," the man said, a sharp command in his voice.

Nelson took a few steps toward the car and stopped. "Yes?"

"Closer," ordered the man.

Nelson stepped up to the car window. "What's the matter?"

"Oh, nothing," the man said, pushing back a soft felt slouch hat from his forehead where bands of sweat had accumulated. "It just strange to see someone walking on this road, this time of day. Where you headed?"

Nelson tensed, but said calmly, "That's my business, mister."

"Mine, too," replied the man as he pushed back his suitcoat to reveal a badge pinned to his vest. "Now where you going?"

"Down the road for about another mile. Someone told me they were hiring hands at a big farm down there."

"You sure you ain't headed for the States?"

Nelson snorted. "Hell, no—there's no work down there."

"Where have you been working?"

Boldly, Nelson leaned on the car, saying with a smile, "Have you got a cigarette, Sheriff?"

"I'm not a sheriff. I am W. B. Gray, Royal Canadian Mounties." He jerked his head slightly in the direction of the driver, a heavy-set man eyeing Nelson. "This man is William Dunn, constable for the town of Killarney." Nelson's expression did not change. Gray reached into his vest pocket and withdrew a package of Camels, working one out for Nelson to take.

"I've been farming around Morden but the jobs petered out." Nelson rolled the cigarette playfully between his thick lips.

Gray looked briefly at Dunn. The driver whispered, "He looks okay."

The Mountie worked his large jaw back and forth for a moment as he looked Nelson over. Then he said, "All right, go on. Good luck in finding a job." He turned to Dunn. "Turn around, let's go back." Dunn began to grind the gears of the car as he shifted. Nelson gave them a short wave and began heading south.

Gray inexplicably held up his hand over Dunn's, which was on the gear shift. "Wait." He leaned out the window again. "Hey, fella, one more minute." As Nelson began to return to the car, Gray told Dunn, "I want to try something direct." He turned to Nelson and, with an affable expression, said bluntly, "I'll put it on the line to you, fella. We're looking for a man who's murdered more

271

than twenty women, mostly in the States, but he's just killed two females up in Winnipeg." Gray let out his words slowly, studying Nelson's reaction. "He's a strangler, this fellow we're looking for."

Nelson gave Gray a wide grin. "Honestly, fellows—I only do my lady-killing on Saturday nights."

Dunn laughed but Gray did not. "This fellow we're looking for is a disarming type," Gray told Nelson. "A regular working fellow, average looking." He paused. "Maybe like you."

"I always thought everybody looked different," Nelson managed.

"I think...you had better get in the car," Gray said slowly.

"Going to take me for a joy-ride, fellows?" said Nelson, laughing.

Gray stepped out, opening the back door to the Ford. "Get in—what did you say your name was?"

"Loomis," Nelson told him, quietly getting into the back seat of the car. "George Loomis."

Gray slammed shut the front door to the passenger seat and then got in after Nelson, sitting next to him, smiling pleasantly. "I'm sure we can clear all this up in Killarney." He leaned forward slightly. "Okay, Bill, let's go back."

Dunn turned the Ford about and drove north.

Gray reached across Nelson's chest and rolled down the car window. "Have some air, Mr. Loomis. Go ahead, smoke your cigarette. Relax. This won't take long."

Nelson pulled the cigarette from his mouth and threw it out the window, staring after it.

272

"Born in Canada?" quizzed Gray.

Nelson did not answer for a moment. Then, while staring out the open window, he replied, "I really don't know, officer. I was born an orphan, my earliest memories are of New Orleans."

"Really? Never been down there. What's it like?"

"Hot, muggy, rains a lot."

"Not California, huh?"

Nelson glanced at him. "What makes you say that?"

"I dunno—you strike me as a man from that part of the world."

"I've been there. I've been all over the States, a wonderful country, but jobs are hard to find."

"Been to our beautiful city of Winnipeg?" Gray pressed.

"Only to Regina. I'd like to go to Winnipeg some day, officer."

"Maybe you will."

Within an hour the Ford chugged into the small town of Killarney, a town of some five hundred stone buildings and brick houses clustered north of a cold, clear lake, inhabited by nine hundred hearty souls who mostly worked the soil. The buildings, Nelson noted, were centered about the train depot. He nodded smugly as the Ford bounced over the train tracks, knowing this to be his escape route.

The Ford ground to a stop in front of a single-story stone building. "What's this?" Nelson asked Gray.

The Mountie opened the car door leading Nelson behind him. "Our local jail. It's not much."

"Looks like a garage," snorted Nelson.

Dunn was out of the car, unlocking the front door to the jail. He and Gray ushered Nelson inside.

"I'm sorry for the inconvenience, Loomis," Gray said apologetically, as he gently guided Nelson by the arm to the building's single cell. "It's only a routine check. We have to make a few calls." Dunn unlocked the cell and Nelson stepped inside, going to a nearby cot and sitting down casually. Through the bars Gray told him, "You ought to be on your way in an hour or so. A few phone calls and then you can go—Bill will drive you back down to that farm where you were headed, won't you, Bill?"

Dunn was standing at a desk inside the jail's small waiting area, slipping the keys to the cell into a drawer. He nodded, "Be happy to drive him."

Nelson lay back on the cot, unruffled, looking at the stone ceiling. The place reminded him of an ancient blockhouse, like the old towers of San Quentin. Nothing to this place, he thought happily. I can get through that lock with my belt buckle. Hick cops. Think they've got old Earle!

An old man entered the jail, walking in a half-shuffle, his back bent. Dunn and Gray were standing by the door talking softly. "Sit behind the desk, Harry," Dunn told the old man. Harry sat down and looked disinterestedly at the man in the cell. He picked up a mail-order catalog on the desk and began to turn the pages slowly.

Gray stepped to the street. Dunn, about to follow him, turned to the old man, saying, "We're going over to Maude's to call Winnipeg, Harry. Keep an eye on our guest here." Harry nodded as Dunn went outside.

Nelson bolted upright, going immediately to the door of his cell. He spoke clearly through the bars to Harry,

"Do you think a man can get some food around here? I haven't eaten in two days."

"In two days?"

"I've been out of work and I'm hungry. I'd be grateful for a piece of bread and butter and a cup of coffee."

The old man put down the catalog. "What did they bring you in for, young man?"

"Loitering, over at the depot. I was waiting for a train to go to Winnipeg, maybe get a job up that way."

Harry scratched his head nervously. He glanced around the small jail.

Nelson nodded in the direction of the window. "Look, there's a cafe across the street." He dug into his pocket. "Here's some change. Won't you be a good fellow and get me something to eat—anything, a sandwich, some chili maybe?"

Harry looked out the window to the cafe. He again scratched his head.

"I'm really starving."

The old man stood up, heading for the door. "Keep your money. We got a prisoner's fund here in Killarney. This town ain't cheap, mister."

"Appreciate it," Nelson said, and watched as the old man went out, closing the door behind him. Quickly, Nelson unbuckled his belt, whipping it from the loopholes of his trousers. He thrust the belt through the bars, bringing the buckle to the other side of the old door lock of the cell, inserting the prong of the buckle into the keyhole. "Hick cops," he laughed, staring at the door and rapidly working the lock.

Inspector Bergson received the long-distance phone call from Killarney in his office. He looked up at John Davis. "It's a Royal Mountie named Gray calling from Killarney."

"Where's that?" Davis went to a large wall map.

"Near the Dakota border, see it?"

Davis put his index finger on the name of the town, kept it there, and craned his neck back to Bergson. "He'd head that way, sure. He'd know enough to stay off the railways now." Davis nodded at the map. "He tried to walk out... if it's him.

"Describe the man to me, Gray," Bergson said into the phone, then added: "No, hold on. I'm putting a detective named Davis on the phone, tell him. He knows Nelson better than anyone."

Davis took the phone. "This is Sergeant Davis. San Francisco police."

"Sergeant W. B. Gray," came a deep voice over the line. "We have a man in our jail now. We picked him up about five miles from the U.S. border. Says his name is George Loomis, a migrant farm worker."

"What's he look like, Gray?"

"Thin brown hair, blue eyes, pudgy face, very power-fully built, but most of these farm workers are husky fellows. He seems innocent enough... but we didn't want to take any chances after getting the Winnipeg alarm about watching the borders for this strangler."

Davis' palms began to sweat. "He answers Nelson's description."

"You mean we've got *the man?*"

"Did he do anything peculiar when you picked him up?"

276

"No...oh, yes, perhaps. We were quite a ways off up the road, going towards him, and I could be mistaken, but, well, perhaps he was amusing himself, but it seemed as if he was walking on his hands down the road."

"That's him!" Davis shouted so loud that Inspector Bergson actually reeled away from the wall map he had been studying, coming to the phone. "Hold on to that man, Sergeant, watch him night and day until we get down there!" Davis handed the phone back to Bergson.

"Sergeant, where is the man now?"

"In the old jail, it's a one-room affair but it's solid."

"Is someone with him?"

"The caretaker. I had to send Dunn to the depot to wire Regina."

"Get back to the jail immediately—that man can escape from any lockup Detective Davis tells me. And when you're there, keep a weapon trained on him at all times."

"Yes, sir—I'm going now."

"We'll be there on the next through train."

"That's not until tomorrow morning," advised Gray.

"You can handle him until then, Sergeant, I'm sure. But hurry now." Bergson hung up. "It appears that your manhunt is almost at an end, Sergeant."

Davis was slipping his suitcoat over his vest. "Not yet, Inspector, not until that man is taken."

"I'll make arrangements for two squads of men to accompany us," Bergson told him.

Sergeant Gray ran down the street to the jail and burst through the door to see Harry, the old jail caretaker standing before the open cell door, his mouth agape, his eyes popped wide. He was holding a sandwich on a plate in one hand and a cup of steaming coffee in the other.

"What happened here?" Gray demanded.

Harry turned toward him slowly, unable to speak. Gray took the food and coffee from the old man, placing it on the desk. "It's all right, Harry. Calm down now and tell me what happened."

"He said he was starving, hadn't eaten in two days. I couldn't let the young man go hungry like that. You wouldn't do a thing like that. . . . I went across the street for some food—I was only gone a few minutes, yes, I'm sure, only two minutes, that's all. And I come in here and there it is, the cell door open like you see it now. And him gone. Out that side door there. That's open, too. Gone." Harry pointed to the floor in the cell. "And he left those—Gray looked down to see Nelson's shoes next to the cell door. "Ain't that the strangest thing you've ever seen?" asked the old man.

Gray went to the desk, withdrew a piece of paper and wrote hurriedly. "Here," he said to the old man, "take this message down to the depot and wire Inspector Bergson at Winnipeg."

The old man took the paper and read aloud: "Nelson escaped, still in vicinity. Send 100 men. Hurry." The caretaker blinked at the sergeant. "Sergeant, that's a lot of men to ask to look for a vagrant. My God, a hundred men!"

"He's probably a mass killer, Harry, the gorilla strangler from San Francisco. Go on—send off the wire. And tell Constable Dunn to get his deputies from the town and hurry back here."

The caretaker lurched toward the door. Gray turned to a high wall cabinet, inserting a small key from his chain into the lock. He opened the cabinet and began to remove rifles, placing them neatly on the desk.

Inside of two hours, Dunn had gathered ten deputies, all citizens of Killarney, men dressed in business suits and overalls. They stood solemnly before Sergeant Gray, holding rifles, their pockets bulging with bullets. In the dim light from a gas lamp sitting on the desk in the jail, Gray leaned forward. "This man we're looking for is not rational. He appears sane and logical at times, I know, but he's mad, and he's in our town now as we stand here, hiding somewhere."

"I hear this fellow only kills women?" one man said from the shadows.

"Yes, all his victims have been women."

"Then we better see to our women," voiced a shopkeeper.

"I was going to get to that." He turned to Constable Dunn. "Bill, you take some of these men, four will do, and gather all the women and children in town. Take them into the town hall. Lock the doors and post guards at every exit, on all sides of the building."

"Has this man killed kids, too?" a man asked.

"Yes, a baby in the States and a fourteen-year-old flower girl in Winnipeg."

"Why, the son of a bitch!"

"I ain't saving a man like that for them detectives from Winnipeg," shouted one man. "If I get this killer, I'll blow his head off."

"Bump him for sure!" snarled another citizen.

Gray held up his hands. "Now you men listen here! If we catch him—and we will catch him—we're going to hold him for the law. The law will make sure he never kills again...if this is the strangler.

"The law!" sneered a deputy. "That's why this here fellow has been able to kill all them people. I read about it. He's gotten away again and again."

"You listen to me, Jim Cummings," Gray barked, wagging his finger at the farmer. "You or *anyone else* kills that man and you'll hang in his place! I mean it." He bowed his head. "It's almost dark. I've got men on the roads leading from town, so he can't get out that way. After you lock up the women and children, Bill, and post your guards, I want every available man—everyone eighteen or over—to assemble outside this jail—"

"You're talking about five hundred men! We ain't got that many guns."

"They're to bring knives, pitchforks, anything we can put together from our homes and the general store. Have you got that?"

"What are you gonna do?"

"We're going to search every corner of this town, Bill, I want torches, a lot of them. We're going to sweep the fields around the town inch by inch, section by section."

Bill Dunn nodded. "We'll do it all right—we'll do it and catch him and hold him for the Winnipeg people. They're sending two carloads of detectives down here armed to the teeth."

"Cummings," Gray ordered, "you stand outside the jail and line up the men in town when they show up—I want groups of thirty, and no boys, no young kids—you check to make sure they're over eighteen—men!"

"My son is seventeen," piped a storeowner. "Can he go?"

"No. Tell him to stand guard with the women inside the town hall."

"He'll hate that, he'll just hate that to hell!"

Nelson watched it all go on without terror; curiosity kept him peeking from the roof of the stable where he had taken refuge after breaking out of the small jail. He had raced for three blocks behind buildings to reach the empty horse stable, and had climbed into the loft, falling asleep. Some time during the early night the commotion in the main street of Killarney woke him. He had pushed through a small roof opening of the stable and clambered onto the high, slanting roof, lying flat, as he watched hundreds of women and children, many wearing night-gowns and pajamas, herded to the town hall by scores of armed men.

He watched as the tall windows of the hall filled with light and the guards outside the two-story stone building took positions next to the doors and windows. "Fools," he whispered to himself. "Idiots! Who are they afraid of— me? I don't hurt innocent people, don't they know that?" Soon he heard the voices of the women and children lifted in unison, singing one hymn after another. "Oh, good," he said when the voices began one hymn, "I know that one— 'Rock of Ages.' "

From his high perch, Nelson could see down the street. Three short blocks away was the train depot. He would wait until dawn for that, he decided. That's when the freight would go through, straight south to the border.

Beyond the small town, Nelson could see open wheat fields, and through these by moonlight and scores of dancing torches he watched lines of men cross and recross the fields, moving ever-outward from the town. He listened long hours to their shouts and the barking of the dogs until he wearied of the spectacle and slid carefully down the side of the roof, to the opening, letting himself back into the loft. He bunched up some hay and snuggled into it, falling into a deep and peaceful sleep.

The tumult of the panicked town had subsided by dawn. The once-alert sentries outside the town hall had released taut fingers curled about the triggers of shotguns. Men slept in the stone buildings. They dozed against the walls and doors of the streets, leaning on the handles of scythes. Women and children were stretched out uncomfortably on tables and benches inside the town hall. And the manhunters who had scoured the fields in a radius of ten miles of Killarney had long since gone home to bed. The town had survived the night of terror, gone unmolested by the dreaded strangler.

Inside the stable, Nelson was busy. He took an old pair of overalls and a worn checkered shirt from a peg on the wall, shedding his own clothes for these. He found a large straw hat on a shelf. It was tight but he pulled it down hard so that it hurt his temples. He was still barefoot after having left his shoes in the jail and he groped about the stable for footwear. Sunlight slanted through the loosely fitted boards of the building and he was able to spot an old green trunk in a corner. Throwing this open, he tore away at its contents, old linen and blankets. At the bottom he found a pair of ancient skates.

Nelson looked about frantically for some minutes before he found a screwdriver and with this he removed the blades from the skates. That, however, left two short steel posts bolted to the bottom of each shoe. "They will have to do," he said and jammed his feet into the skates, hurriedly tying the long shoestrings about his legs and feet to hold the makeshift shoes to his feet. He tried walking but the steel posts caused his ankles to give way so that he walked on the insides of his feet. "It will have to do," he said again. Going to the back door of the stable, Nelson peered down the alley. Nothing stirred. He stepped cautiously into the bright sunlight.

More than one hundred men—city police from Winnipeg, Mounties, special deputies—were jammed into two coaches of the train speeding toward Killarney. Davis sat by the window, checking his automatic. Inspector Bergson sat next to him, thoughtful, silently smoking a long pipe.

A conductor came through the door and, jostled, made his way to Bergson, leaning down and whispering something in his ear. Bergson turned into the aisle, stood up and shouted, "We're coming into Killarney, men!"

The men in the coach straightened and placed shotguns and submachineguns upward—grim men all.

"Sergeant Gray wired at the last stop to tell us they

haven't gotten Nelson yet. It'll be our job to root him out of his hiding place. We'll stay in Killarney until he's taken. Can you men in the other car hear me?"

An officer at the rear of the second car waved through the open doors of both cars. "We hear you, sir!"

"Good—I want you to know that he should be taken alive, but if he offers resistance—shoot him! Shoot to kill!" Bergson looked down to see that Davis had already left his seat. The Inspector turned to see the detective standing at the head of the first car. Davis gripped a handrail. At the end of his other arm, swinging free, was his revolver.

The train began to slow. Bergson jerked up his arm. "Half of you men get off this way, the other half at the end of the car—same for you men in the second car! Go immediately to the town hall and assemble there!"

With a rush of steam and the noise of iron wheels grinding backward, the train came to a jerking stop in front of the old stone depot. The police swarmed from the train. Sergeant Gray was waiting, walking forward to greet Davis and Bergson.

"Looks like you brought an army, Inspector." Gray said, admiring the stream of heavily armed men pouring from the first two coaches.

"Enough to catch this fellow. This is detective Davis from San Francisco," Bergson said.

Gray and Davis only nodded. Both were holding revolvers.

"We'd better get on to the town hall," Bergson said, and the trio began to follow the officers from the train. They turned the corner of the train depot, stepping from the platform and onto the main street.

Davis' attention was distracted for a second by a movement inside the waiting room of the depot, a scrambling form he glimpsed through the depot window. He stopped, wheeled, and jumped back on the platform to see a man awkwardly climbing the train stairs into the first coach, a man wearing a floppy straw hat, overalls, a checkered shirt, and strange-looking shoes.

Davis dashed for the train, Gray and Bergson following. The detective stepped into the coach. He saw only one person, a man with a large straw hat pulled low over his face, sitting toward the back of the car. He pointed his revolver at the man, approaching steadily up the aisle.

"You!" Davis shouted. "Let me see your face!"

The man sat immobile.

"Pull that hat away from your face!"

The man appeared to be sleeping, oblivious to Davis' commands.

"You heard me, take off your hat!" Cautiously, Davis walked up to the man, standing on the other side of the aisle, looking down. He could see that the man's large hands were folded about a black book, a Bible, Davis knew. His feet were tucked beneath the seat and Davis could see that he wore what appeared to be skates with the blades removed.

Bergson and Gray had boarded the coach and were approaching, guns drawn, from the far end of the car.

Davis brought his revolver close to the man's head and with his free hand reached forward, trembling. He snatched the straw hat away and in that awful instant, the face of Earle Nelson jerked violently in his direction. The detective drew back. Nelson's eyes were so wide that the lids were pushed far up into the sockets and the maniacal grin he wore froze Davis' heart.

"Devil!" screamed Nelson.

Davis jammed the revolver square against Nelson's wide forehead. "You're going to die, Earle," Davis said in a quiet voice. "I promised myself I'd kill you."

"Devil!" Nelson spat out again. "Go ahead—you can't kill me—nobody can kill me!"

The detective pulled back the hammer of his revolver with a sure thumb. He began to squeeze the trigger.

"That's exactly what the madman wants," came Bergson's soothing voice. "Don't, John." He stood close by with Gray.

Nelson looked at them and then back to Davis. "Go ahead, devil! I'm ready, devil!" He held up his Bible. "I am one with the Lord!"

"Look at this hopeless thing, John." Bergson continued. The coach was beginning to fill up with detectives. Townspeople milled outside the car, attempting to look through the windows.

Davis was like granite as he held the revolver to Nelson's head. "I'm going to blow away that grin, Inspector."

Bergson reached out slowly, resting the flat of his hand on the barrel of the revolver. "Let the hangman do it, Sergeant. If you pull the trigger, you're exactly like him then. That's what he wants, that's what he proves, that we're all like him." Bergson's fingers slowly curled around the barrel of Davis' revolver. "You see that, don't you, John?"

Slowly Davis relaxed the hammer of the revolver,

allowing Bergson to push the weapon away from Nelson's face. All of the exhaustion, the anxiety, and the hate Davis had felt in his long pursuit of Earle Nelson ran out of him. He sank, empty of wrath, into a seat across from Nelson, who was being handcuffed, still wearing his wide smile. Davis slid his revolver into his holster and put his head against the window of the coach. Outside small boys were jumping and shouting, "The gorilla man! They got the gorilla man!" Davis closed his eyes. He wanted to weep.

SEVENTEEN

Davis squinted in the dimly lit corridor to watch Nelson pace the length of his large cell. The killer held a rosary in his hands, fingering the beads and mumbling as he moved. The death cell was open to view on three sides. Opposite Davis was a long bench where Gloria Stearn and Mrs. Ward, Nelson's aunt, sat tensely. Standing in the shadows next to Davis was an alienist, Dr. B. P. Elliot.

"Fascinating, isn't he?" the alienist said in a low voice to Davis. "He hasn't stopped pacing and praying in six months. He was like that before the trial, during his trial, and since, all the while claiming his innocence."

"He's going to hang in about a half hour," Davis whispered back, "and for killing twenty-two people. He may have murdered six or seven more, according to reports. I don't consider those innocent acts."

Dr. Elliot held out his hand, offering Davis a book. "Have you seen this?"

"What's that? His Bible? Yes, I've seen it before—he was always carrying it."

"I mean, have you looked through it?"

"No."

"All the passages dealing with the great Biblical harlots are underscored; the pages are worn out with constant reading, constant handling." Dr. Elliot fanned the pages for Davis. "Go ahead, take a look—Jezebel, Salome, Bathsheba, these are characters who riveted his religious attention all the years of—"

Davis grabbed the Bible, holding it firmly. "Yes—that might explain the necrophilia.... These women—he fell in love with these long dead women, women he could never possess—only through the dead bodies of other women, his victims, could he have found his love goddesses. Isn't that how they put it in your profession, Doctor?"

"Very good, Sergeant, and very close."

"Lieutenant," Davis corrected the alienist as he continued to stare at the pacing Nelson. "I was promoted last year...promoted and married."

"Congratulations."

Nelson halted before the bars, facing the two women on the bench. "What do you want here?" he asked them softly.

"You asked that we come, Earle," answered Mrs. Ward in a cold voice. "Remember?"

"Why? I've got nothing to say to you." He looked at Gloria. "Either of you."

Mrs. Ward leaned forward so that her thin, angular face showed beneath a corridor light. "Don't you think it's time, Earle, that you spoke with the priest."

Nelson held up the rosary which was wrapped around a large fist. "The Lord is my shepherd, I don't need a priest. For what?"

"Your confession."

"I've got nothing to confess." Nelson looked about the cell, glancing briefly back at Davis and the alienist. "I told that man over there everything he needs to know about me." Then he sneered at Mrs. Ward. "And you, how you made me—I'm innocent! Why should I tell you a lie? I'm going to hang this morning. There is absolutely no hope of saving my body, and I am not going to do anything to hurt my soul." With an imploring expression he gripped the bars. "I swear to you that I am telling the truth! I have never committed murder! Never, never, never!"

"And there sits the woman," Davis said in a hushed voice to the alienist, "who put the Bible into his hands."

"The aunt?"

Davis nodded. "When Nelson was young, she took in boarders—a landlady, *the* landlady he murdered over and over again—I thought it was the wife, at first, the object of the murders, but—" He gazed at Mrs. Ward. "It's her, that great moral woman over there—the leading citizen of Oxnard, California. She's the one."

"If you won't confess to a priest, then confess to us, boy," Mrs. Ward nagged in a strong voice. "Go ahead, say that you're guilty and God will do what he can for you. Go ahead, Earle, it's not difficult, now, is it?"

"Leave him be," Gloria Stearn said to the old woman.

"You see!" Nelson gloated. "Gloria knows I'm innocent! She knows! Gloria, dearest one, darling girl—go and tell the warden that I'm innocent."

Gloria stood up and walked close to the cell. She placed a delicate hand over his fist. "Goodbye, Earle. I pray that you'll find peace." She stepped into the corridor. Nelson moved to the corner of the cell to watch her walk away.

"Gloria—my dearest child, go to the warden, that's it, girl. He'll believe you when you tell him I'm innocent." He continued to stare at her until she disappeared through a door at the end of the corridor.

"Earle, you stop that nonsense!" commanded Mrs. Ward. "You have been tried in court. You were found guilty and sentenced to die. Are you going to go to your death playacting?"

Nelson sagged against the bars.

"You tell those men over there right now that you did those killings!"

Nelson turned his head to look at Davis and the alienist. He spoke from a curled mouth: "I have been most unfortunate since the day of my birth and have been sadly handicapped by the sins of both my parents, who left a taint in my blood which has caused me agony of mind and body."

"Disgusting!" shouted Mrs. Ward as she bolted upright from the bench. "You're reciting from something you wrote down years ago—I know. I found that wretched little speech. Have you no shame, no remorse, no guilt?"

"You're like my mother," Nelson moaned as he turned toward her. "Both whores!"

The muscles of Mrs. Ward's face twitched. She bowed her head for a moment, then walked around the cell, going silently past Davis and Dr. Elliot, going out of the large holding room.

Nelson eased himself along the bars, still clutching the rosary, moving toward the two men. "You know I'm right about that bitch, don't you?" He strained to see their faces in the shadows. "How come they're going to hang a crazy man?" His voice was suddenly full of amazement. "I thought they never hanged crazy people?"

The alienist stepped into the light. "You're not insane, Earle, by the standards of the court."

"You testified at my trial, I know you. You called me a con——a constitutional psychopath."

"Yes," Dr. Elliot told him matter-of-factly, "a man on the borderline, a person who has mental storms."

"That means I'm crazy."

"No—you have a homicidal mania, but you're sane, Earle."

Nelson stepped backward in the cell and flung himself on the cot. He pressed his face into a pillow and said, "You just want to kill me." With his head turned sideways he shouted, "I have no confession to make—I did not do those deeds!"

The alienist pointed to a tray of food on a table next to the cot. "Why don't you try to eat your breakfast, Earle?

It's everything you ordered—ham and eggs, home-fried potatoes, coffee, milk and peaches. Why don't you try to eat?"

The killer sat up abruptly, folding his arms across his chest. "Could you eat if you knew that you'd be dead in ten minutes?"

Davis moved next to the alienist so that Nelson could see him. "Go ahead, eat. It'll get your mind off of it."

Nelson reached out a pawlike hand, grabbed a handful of potatoes, and jammed the food into his mouth. "I'm not hungry," he said through a mouthful. The sound of a door opening at the end of the corridor startled him. He spat out the food and jumped up. "Christ—they're coming for me."

"Calm down, Earle," Dr. Elliot said.

"Calm down?" Nelson went to the bars of his cell, pressing his florid face against the metal, staring at the approaching warden and the two guards walking behind him. His fingers drummed rapidly against the bars. He glanced back to Davis and said angrily, "You did this to me—you're the one who brought me to this!"

"You were captured by a Royal Canadian Mountie named Gray."

"It was you—it was you all along," Nelson grumbled. As the warden came closer to the cell, Nelson fell back, running to the table and sitting down, his back to the cell door. He began to eat the food on the tray slowly.

"Come along now, Nelson," the warden ordered him.

"I haven't finished my breakfast," replied the killer. "You got to let a man finish his breakfast before you take him out to the hangman. That's the law, isn't it?"

The warden motioned one of the guards forward to unlock the cell door. As it swung open, the warden and the guards entered the cell. They stood hesitantly for a moment, looking down at Nelson, who pretended to be wholly interested in the cold breakfast.

"You've got to be a man about this, Nelson," the warden finally said. "But you can have it either way. You can walk out to the yard like a man or you can be dragged out there. Either way it's got to happen...now."

Nelson pushed the tray of food away and stood up. His face was pale but his words were steady. "Innocent men don't get dragged to the gallows." He brushed past the warden to pick up his suitcoat. Nelson slipped on the coat and pulled out the lapels with his thumbs. "Nice, huh?" he said to Davis. "The Province of Alberta bought me a new suit to get hanged in." He spun around, modeling the suit for Davis and Dr. Elliot. "How does it look, fellows?" Then he turned abruptly toward the warden, wrinkling his massive brow. "Say, these duds aren't stolen, are they?"

A guard stepped to Nelson's side, placing a long strap around one arm, running it behind the killer's back and tightening the end of the strap to Nelson's other arm. The warden guided him toward the cell door.

"These clothes smell of mothballs, warden," Nelson joked, a wide, ludicrous grin on his face. "Who else has worn this suit—the last guy you hanged?"

"You want a priest?" the warden asked.

"What for—you're murdering an innocent lamb this morning. God already knows about it." He was walking down the corridor now, following the warden, a guard on

295

either side of him, Davis and Dr. Elliot trailing. Nelson craned his neck to look back at Davis. "Hey cop—you believe in luck?"

"Never," Davis replied.

"Well—how's this then? A guard told me yesterday that I'm the thirteenth fellow to die on this gallows. There are thirteen steps going up to the scaffold."

"Coincidence, Earle."

"Keep moving, Nelson," the warden said as he walked ahead.

Nelson ignored the warden's remark, slowing, still twisting about as he shuffled forward to look at Davis. "Yeah? Here's the best part—today is January 13, 1928, Friday. Now what do you think, cop?"

"You might have a point, Nelson," soothed Dr. Elliot.

The killer increased his pace, walking straight ahead. "You bet I do!"

The door at the end of the long corridor swung inward, opened by another guard standing in the yard. As Nelson approached the open door he threw out his chest. He felt a chill wind blowing in from the yard and said to no one, "It's an awful cold morning to be hanged."

Towering in the small stone yard behind the provincial jail was the scaffold, its large heavy beams crossed in an H, the center beam tied with a heavy rope. Nelson stopped for a moment. His blue eyes took in the rope around the center beam, then its length, to see at the rope's end a bald, heavy-set man holding the noose.

"I don't mind saying goodbye to any of you," Nelson told the knot of men standing next to him.

Davis rested against the wall of the building, glancing

to his right to scan the makeshift stand holding fifty-some witnesses. Mrs. Ward sat in the front row, a stern look on her face that promised she would keep her vigil to the end.

Nelson plunged forward, mounting the stairs quickly, almost stumbling before reaching the platform but quickly regaining his balance. He walked to the trap door and the heavy-set man holding the rope came forward.

"You got anything to say, Mr. Nelson?" inquired the executioner.

Nelson, facing the spectators in the stand, jerked his head backward and looked upward at the lead-gray sky for a moment. A guard quickly strapped his legs together, then backed off the trapdoor.

The killer stiffened and said in a clear voice aimed at the spectators, "I declare my innocence before God and man!" He peered at Mrs. Ward. "I forgive those who have injured me...and I ask pardon from those I have injured.... May the Lord have mercy on my soul!"

The executioner slipped a long black hood over Nelson's head, then the noose, which he tightened about the killer's neck.

"That could be anyone under that hood," Dr. Elliot said to Davis in a low voice.

"I know who it is.... A man with a face I shall never forget. I promised myself long ago that I'd stand here and watch him hang...but there's no joy in it...pathetic creature...going out with a lie on his lips."

"To his mind he spoke an instant truth," replied Dr. Elliot.

At that moment Nelson's brain began to pound and the old images returned, rushing from the past in all their

gawdy costumes and sparkling jewelry, fleshy arms flail-
ing, breasts heaving, bellies undulating, the quivering
thighs and twisting ankles, his old adored ones dancing
wildly, pleasuring him.

The executioner stepped off the trapdoor and placed
his hand on the wooden lever that would spring the trap.
He pulled hard.

As he fell through space, beneath the black hood,
Earle Leonard Nelson was grinning.